Kathryn Walter

DENMARK'S BEST STORIES

AN INTRODUCTION TO DANISH FICTION

SCANDINAVIAN CLASSICS

VOLUME XXXI

JENS PETER JACOBSEN

DENMARK'S BEST STORIES

AN INTRODUCTION TO DANISH FICTION

A Selection of Short Stories by

ANDERSEN · BLICHER · GOLDSCHMIDT
JACOBSEN · SCHANDORPH · DRACHMANN
BANG · PONTOPPIDAN · WIED
KARL LARSEN · SKJOLDBORG · NEXÖ
JENSEN · SÖIBERG · GUNNARSSON

EDITED BY HANNA ASTRUP LARSEN

NEW YORK
THE AMERICAN-SCANDINAVIAN FOUNDATION
W · W · NORTON & COMPANY, INC.
Publishers

CONTENTS

[V]

Contents

INTRODUCTION

DENMARK has in the modern era often been the channel through which fresh currents of international thought have reached the Scandinavian North. Geographic nearness to the great cultural centers of Europe has been an important factor; the smallness of the country and the intellectual dominance of the capital city have favored discussion; and there has always been a school of criticism which has not only defined literary standards but disseminated new ideas.

The critic has held a paramount place in the Danish world of letters. For a full century Denmark was under the sway of two critics of widely different temperament and principles. Johan Ludvig Heiberg ruled from 1826 to 1871, when Georg Brandes began the course of lectures which initiated a new intellectual dynasty. The literature that reached its peak in the seventies and eighties stood largely in the service of the ideas Brandes had promulgated. Toward the end of the nineteenth century other influences arose, and in the present century younger critics have questioned the authority of the autocrat. At the same time, men from the provinces have rebelled against the cultural dominance of Copenhagen, and have given Denmark a literature deeply rooted in Danish soil.

When Hans Christian Andersen began to write, Heiberg, as critic, editor, and director of the Royal Theater in Copenhagen, was omnipotent. Unlike Brandes, whose criticism always concerned itself chiefly with the message of the writer he had under discussion, Heiberg regarded it as the function of the critic to pass judgment on the form, not the substance, of literature. He approved or condemned solely on the basis of whether the author followed faithfully the established formula for drama, poetry, or whatever he essayed to write.

Formless and erratic, Andersen laid himself open to a gruelling criticism which his morbid sensitiveness rendered torture. Not until he was an old man, with a world audience, did he receive the official sanction of Danish criticism, when Brandes, then just beginning his life-work, praised him warmly for his courage to be himself and to write in the manner natural to him. In the fairy tales Andersen evolved a style which has stood the test of time and the ordeal of translation into a score of languages. For his similes and allusions he drew, not on classic or mythological lore, but on his own minute observations from the parlors and kitchens, the market-places and gutters of

Introduction

Copenhagen. His language—transcribed just as he used to relate his stories to his young listeners, with all his naïve asides—was so oral in its quality that the Copenhageners said, "Of course you can *talk* like that, but good heavens! you can't *write* like that." Nevertheless, Andersen's style with its quaint inversions, its repetitions and staccatos, was the inspiration of the greatest stylist in the next generation, Jens Peter Jacobsen, and through him became the model for countless imitators.

Another writer who was at variance with the esthetic theories of his day, but is now recognized as one of the great names in Danish letters, is Steen Steensen Blicher. Somewhat older than Andersen, he belonged in point of time to the Golden Age of Danish literature, but while this age stood in the sign of romanticism, Blicher became the forerunner of modern realistic prose. Living as a country pastor on the mainland—then separated from Copenhagen by many days of sea travel—he became the literary discoverer of the Jutland heath. He wrote of peasants and gypsies, ministers and country squires, with less and less of romantic admixture, with more and more of sober realism, and with an ever deepening insight into the complexities of human nature.

If Blicher was an isolated figure, the same may be said of the novelist Meïr Goldschmidt, a writer of lesser caliber, but possessed of wit and

charm. Literary criticism in his day had hardly
begun to reckon with the novel except as a picture of some peculiarly interesting time or place,
and Goldschmidt was fortunate in finding a unique
background among his own people, the Jews,
who still formed separate communities apart from
the Gentiles.

The novel simply as a picture of contemporary
life came into its own with the Realists who received their impulse from Brandes. Jacobsen,
Drachmann, and Schandorph were young when
Brandes made his first appearance in Copenhagen.
Bang, Gjellerup, and Pontoppidan were added to
the group later. Though in several of them
there was afterwards a more or less serious defec-
tion from Brandes, they all owe something to him.
To each one of them the new movement brought
some impulse that shaped his genius and led it
into its appointed ways.

All had in common certain elements both of
strength and of weakness. Their strength lay in
freeing themselves from preconceived theories
and standardized literary formulas. They approached life with a determination to see it afresh
as if it had never been described before, and to
define it in their own words. Their weakness was
the obverse side of their strength, and lay in the
absence of any positive faith.

Curiously enough, the first commandment in

the Brandes code, that literature should "take up problems for debate," was less eagerly obeyed in Denmark than in Norway, but the Danes followed all the more assiduously its second commandment, that literature should be "a cross section of life." Inasmuch as they relied entirely upon observation, brushing aside all accepted modes in character and incident, it followed that they usually took their subjects near at hand. An exception is Jens Peter Jacobsen's *Marie Grubbe,* but the development of its wayward heroine as the product of heredity and environment is conceived entirely in the spirit of Jacobsen's own time, though the background is archaic.

Jacobsen's outlook on life was colored by the fact that he was a scientist as well as a poet. Indeed, he was for a time uncertain whether to choose botany or literature as his life-work. His love of nature is that of the scientist who sees so much in the forces actually present that he can dispense with all the nature-sprites, the elves and necks and mermaids, that had filled the poetry of the preceding era. In *Mogens,* his first story, the romantic young girl, Thora, asks the hero how he can find any pleasure in nature if he does not imagine the hill and lake and trees to be inhabited by tiny invisible creatures who have their own joys and sorrows. Mogens protests that he enjoys "the form and color, the sap rising in the

Introduction

trees and flowers, the sun and rain that make
things grow." This is exactly Jacobsen's own attitude. No one before or since has enriched
Danish literature with such nature descriptions,
so ethereal and delicate and yet glowing with
color like jewels; but it is always nature leading
its own life according to its own laws. He never
allows nature to respond to human emotions as
does Selma Lagerlöf, or makes us feel the pulses
of man and nature beating in unison as does Knut
Hamsun.

The habit of close scientific observation is present also in Jacobsen's delineation of character,
especially in his women. Earlier writers had
largely accepted a certain formula for the charms
and virtues of "the sex," based chiefly on the absence of marked and decisive qualities. Jacobsen
studied individuals and found that women like
men were of mixed clay. His women protest
against the "traditional bloodless ideal" that is
held up before them. They chafe under the dis-
guised tyranny that forces into rankest growth
the qualities once for all accepted as feminine,
while the qualities they actually possess are elimi-
nated by systematically ignoring them. To a
realist of Jacobsen's caliber the more complex
personality is, of course, the more interesting.
He feels in women certain deep primeval instincts
reaching down through the layers of convention,

as in Marie Grubbe who is a woman looking for
her master. His modern women, whether highly
cultured society ladies or gentle maidens growing
up in sheltered homes, are sisters of Marie
Grubbe, though with instincts so subtly blended
and refined that we scarcely dare to call them by
name as they gleam through the dignified reserve
of the author.

The colorful beauty and rich splendor of
Jacobsen's prose almost blind us to his sober realism and the negative quality of his message. We
have seen him so concerned for absolute truth
that he even refuses to project his human consciousness into the realm of nature. In the same
spirit he tries to eradicate the "fair vice of
dreams" by which people make themselves believe
that they are better and greater than they are,
"forgetting that the fairest dreams, and the deepest longings do not add an inch to the stature of a
human soul." And not only that, but he would
eliminate every supernatural element from spiritual experience. Strength and uprightness, he
said, were to be achieved only by rooting out the
delusion that some supernatural power would
somehow juggle away the consequences of wrong-
doing. This earth life if worthily lived was
enough without a God or a hope of heaven. He
fully appreciated the difficulty of his doctrine,
however. "How can any one become fanatic for

a negation?" says Dr. Hjerrild in *Niels Lyhne*.
"Fanatic for the idea that there is no God! But
without fanaticism no victory!"

The omnipotence of law and the sacredness of
truth—both conceived in terms of scientific knowledge—were the principles in the new era that
Jacobsen appropriated and made peculiarly his
own. They shaped his work—partly to its detri-
ment perhaps; for one can not help speculating
on how his lyric gift would have blossomed had
he not checked it so sternly, and what heights his
finely-touched spirit would have attained had he
flown a banner of less negative device.

Very different elements drew the allegiance of
Jacobsen's contemporary, Holger Drachmann.
He was no philosopher and had no interest in
problems except as they appealed to his heart, but
he was attracted by the social theories of the new
movement. Though himself a child of the upper
bourgeoisie, he had, as a strolling artist, lived
much among the poorer classes and was deeply
concerned for their welfare. He had faith in the
social revolution which he firmly believed to be
coming soon. Drachmann contributed to the fiction of the day a breezy, outdoor element with his
stories of sailors and fishermen, but he was first
and foremost a lyric poet, and was never quite at
home among the Realists. He had no palate for

Introduction

what he termed their "lenten fare." "The menu
of the day called for stockfish," but his taste was
for wine and meat. He not only chafed against
the restrictions of realism, but he felt with the instinct of a poet that literature must, when all is
said and done, draw its inspiration from ageless
values that have nothing to do with "issues" and
"problems" and are neither modern nor old-
fashioned.

Sophus Schandorph was quite in the spirit of
the new age when he satirized the professional
class, especially the clergy, and exalted workers in
more practical fields.

Karl Gjellerup was attracted to the Brandes
faction largely because of its hostility to the
Church. He had studied theology, but had been
disillusioned, and before even taking his degree
had turned into a fanatic atheist. Afterwards,
however, he became as violent an opponent of
Brandes as he had once been an ardent admirer.
His ethical sense rejected the naturalistic conception of love, and he finally adopted an ideal of
self-renunciation which approached the principles
of Buddhism. Gjellerup's achievements as novelist, dramatist, and lyric poet were recognized by
the bestowal of the Nobel prize for literature,
which he shared with Pontoppidan in 1917. His
voluntary expatriation, by many years of resi-

dence in Germany and absorption in German intellectual life, kept him somewhat outside the trend of Danish development.

Gjellerup's contemporary, Herman Bang, resembled him in his hatred toward that exaltation of sex which was the product in part of the new scientific knowledge, in part of the free thought which played havoc with all fixed standards. But unlike Gjellerup, Bang was himself in temperament and mental attitude, as well as in literary style, a product of his age—in some respects a victim of its upheavals and confusion. His tremulous and delicate art is the expression of a nature born to suffer. Sensitive and morbid, he lacked the stoical courage with which Jacobsen faced a world bereft of illusions. Through his own quivering nerves he felt the pain of others, and was oppressed, almost driven to despair, by his consciousness of universal human suffering. He was especially aware of the misery and degradation caused by sex, and had a terror not only of its perversities but of its normal impulses.

For his style, Bang acknowledged his debt to Jonas Lie. He resembles Lie in his almost feminine intuition, in his close observation of minute details, and his impressionistic manner of using them to reveal the nature of his characters. He lacks, however, the genial warmth and clear, ringing timbre of the Norwegian. His key is lower;

Introduction

his humor is often sardonic, and his pity not un-
mixed with contempt.   Occasionally he can write
an almost perfect short story without a jarring
note.

Henrik Pontoppidan in his early works advo-
cated social reform and attacked the ruling classes
with a more concentrated bitterness than perhaps
any of his contemporaries.   Yet he never believed
that salvation lay in party slogans, or that ex-
ternal reforms could effect the betterment which
could only come by slow transformation from
within.

Disillusionment is perhaps the word that best
describes Pontoppidan.   He is pessimistic to the
core.   While he is too good an artist to draw a
picture all in black, and has too much knowledge of human nature to fill his world with fools
and knaves, there is even in his noblest characters
—nay, especially in them—a curious barrenness
and futility.   We see this, for instance, in the
idealist, Emanuel Hansted, in *The Promised
Land,* a clergyman who tries to live in imitation
of Christ, but ends with failure and religious madness.   Among the women, Ragnhild and Jytte—
both aristocrats, and the latter of especially fine
caliber—are somehow entangled in the complexities of their own nature.   They have lost the
simplicity that might have brought happiness.

Qualities of real vitality, Pontoppidan thinks,

Introduction

are more apt to be found in the people who have
risen from the depths and have still a good deal
of the mud clinging to them. Of such is the unfrocked minister in *The Kingdom of the Dead,*
and, in the same book, the Liberal leader who,
lacking all the instincts of a gentleman, has nevertheless elements of real greatness. These men
attain a measure of success, but here again the
author's pessimism reminds us that it is only for
a short time. The next generation, which in-
herits civil and religious freedom without a struggle, is indifferent. Conditions have changed, but
the people remain the same, or have even deteri-
orated in the liberty which they do not know how
to use.

Pontoppidan is impatient of oratory and fine
phrases, whether political or religious. He be-
lieves in struggle and suffering, persecution and
even hatred as necessary to a healthy development.
Very characteristic is the flash of illumination that
comes to Emanuel Hansted when he sees his own
efforts frustrated. The man who has come in
his way is a weaver who by his own strength has
risen from the worst elements in the rural population; and Hansted remembers how, while they
were still friends, the weaver told him that he had
all his life been goaded on by a terrible memory
of his childhood—the sight of his father being
beaten by the young lord of the manor. Hansted

suddenly realizes that in the life of this man hatred has accomplished what his own love has failed to achieve. And yet there is at the end of the book a suggestion that Emanuel Hansted's sacrifice has not been entirely fruitless.

Pontoppidan now stands as the old master in Danish fiction, the only one yet living of the brilliant group who were young in the seventies and eighties. Through a long life he has persistently maintained the high standards set by the early leaders in the Realist school, unaffected by the process of deterioration which set in even before the end of the nineteenth century.

Jacobsen had in *Niels Lyhne* created a hero type which was destined to produce many imitations. Niels Lyhne is a dreamer and self-doubter who "can not find a handle to life," but he is a nature essentially sound and of fine instincts. In the treatment of Herman Bang the type became neurasthenic, and at the hands of younger writers it underwent a still further process of deterioration. The popular hero was a decadent who claimed kinship with Niels Lyhne only through his failure to fit himself into organized society. Literature became a matter of the cafés and boulevards and of the alcoves.

In the same period there were strong elements in the Scandinavian literary world turning toward Neo-Romanticism and Symbolism. In Sweden the romantic nineties produced Heidenstam, Selma Lagerlöf, and several other writers of the first rank. In Norway the chief name was Knut Hamsun. Denmark had its parallel movement, but it did not produce any great writer of fiction. Chief among its leaders were the lyric poet, Johannes Jörgensen, whose opposition to the preceding era was chiefly on a religious basis; and the dramatist and essayist, Helge Rode, who is still one of the most determined opponents of the Brandes influence.

In the domain of fiction the reaction against the nineteenth century Realists came at the beginning of the present century and was directed not against their realism, but against their cosmopolitanism, their intellectual arrogance, and the assumption that intellectual life in Denmark began and ended in Copenhagen.

Brandes had broken down national inhibitions and forced the Danes to receive the ideas current in contemporary Europe. Where he and his followers were lacking was in comprehension of Danish folk life.

The new men came from the provinces, usually from the peasantry, and were proud of their origin. Typical is the attitude of Jeppe Aakjær, who is a farmer's son and has chosen to remain a farmer, while he interprets the life of his neighbors in lyric verse. Aakjær and most of the

other members of the group are natives of Jutland, Denmark's mainland, which has been less
exposed to foreign influence than the islands, and
has preserved more of Northern characteristics.
The "Jutlanders," as they call themselves, have
an aggressive leader in Johannes V. Jensen, un-
questionably the dominant figure in Danish contemporary literature.

In the Jutland group we must count Jakob
Knudsen, a somewhat older man, a former folk
high school teacher, whose fiction falls chiefly
within the present century. Humor and ripe
wisdom have won for his novels deserved popu-
larity. Other Jutland writers are Marie Bregendahl, Johan Skjoldborg, and, among the younger,
Thomas Olesen Lökken, and Harry Söiberg.
Aakjær and Skjoldborg have used fiction in the
service of social reform and have painted dark
pictures of the life led by the lowest agricultural
laborers. Aakjær is, however, greatest in his
poetry, while Skjoldborg is a master of virile
prose. He has in some of his books described the
struggle for existence of those who live among
the treacherous sand dunes by the fierce Western
Sea, a region where nature has a harshness usually
unknown in Denmark. The same subject has
been treated by Olesen Lökken in forceful and
original fiction, and in a region near by Söiberg finds the background for his stories of reli-

gious stirrings among the peasants and fishermen.
Marie Bregendahl has painted charming domestic
interiors and has created some magnificent types
of peasant women.

The Jutlanders cultivate what is known as
Heimath literature (*Hjemstavns Digtning*),
common also in Norway. They have each identified themselves with a particular locality, studying its people, their dialect, characteristics, and
habits down to the minutest detail. In thus cir-
cumscribing their field, they impose stern limita-
tions on their art. They confine themselves to
portraying people with a limited range of thought
and feeling and shut themselves out from the
mental horizon of the more sophisticated classes.
Moreover, it can not be denied that there is something depressing in that picture of hard, rough
living conditions which is again and again unrolled
before us. What these authors lose in variety,
however, they gain in solidity and genuineness.
They have shown the continuity of racial heritage,
and have produced a literature that is both of and
for the people.

Johannes V. Jensen is a *Heimath* writer, in so
far as he takes for his point of departure the
place where his family has lived for generations—
Himmerland in Jutland. This region is supposed
to have been the original home of the Cimbri who
formed the vanguard of the barbarian hordes that

attacked Rome.   Whether or not this hypothesis
can be substantiated by scholarship, it has a certain poetic significance, for it is Johannes V. Jensen's distinction that he has linked local patriotism
with the larger life of the race.   In his modern
Himmerland people he has found traits that strike
roots down through the centuries to a primitive
time.   Their passions, their fierce vengeance and
stolid endurance, and their—more rare—bucolic
humor seem to belong to the Stone Age.

In his novel cycle, *The Long Journey,* Jensen
has essayed to trace the evolution of the Northern
race from prehistoric times to the beginning of
the modern era.   This imposing work has been
characterized as Darwinism grafted on *The
Poetic Edda,* Norse mythology, anthropology,
geology, and history, all blended in a poet's imagination.   There may be exception taken both to
his history and his science.   Although he has
made painstaking studies, Jensen is too much of a
creative genius to confine his imagination within
the stockade of known facts.   Possible discrep-
ancies seem of little consequence, however, compared with the grandeur of his conception and
the poetic beauty of his images.

Unforgettable is the description of the night
when northern Europe entered into the Ice Age,
when all the wild animals, big and little, oblivious
of old fears and enmities, rushed madly, hip by

Introduction

haunch, through the darkness, fleeing before the insidious foe that breathed upon them from the oncoming glacier. The people had already fled before the numbing rain and cold, but a single youth set his face to the north to go and conquer the new enemy. From him, and the girl he found on the glacier, the Northern people are descended. But the memory of the balmy land in which the childhood of the race was spent lives in their dreams as a lost Eden or as the Blessed Isles. This yearning for a lost land has made them vikings and explorers. It was present both in the migration of peoples that broke the strength of the Roman Empire, and in the great discoveries that initiated the modern era.

In his return to the primitive and heroic Jensen breaks with the realistic school of the late nineteenth century, but he borrows nothing from the romantic era that preceded it. Between Oehlenschläger's chivalrous gods and heroes and Jensen's grim, savage primitive man lies Darwinism and all that it imports. In his style Jensen is a thorough modern. It is vigorous and quick, even at times jerky in its nervous strength.

In Martin Andersen Nexö the city proletariat has found its spokesman. The peasant writers, dealing with what is proverbially the most conservative element in any population, see the individual as a part in a solid structure of inherited

beliefs and customs. Nexö takes the individual
man or woman without antecedents, to whom
everything is possible. Other authors have
dowered their heroes with a large heritage of
family position, schooling, and worldly goods.
In *Pelle the Conqueror,* Nexö creates a hero who,
in the author's own words, "springs naked out of
nothing and conquers the world." In *Ditte:
Daughter of Man,* the feminine counterpart of
Pelle, Nexö goes still further in vindicating
the sacredness of the individual human being.
"Every second a human soul is born into the
world. . . . That which has never been becomes
flesh and blood. No human being is a repetition
of any that has gone before or will ever be repeated in the future. Every new being is like a
comet which only once in all eternity touches the
earth's orbit—a phosphorescence between two
eternities of darkness. Then no doubt there is
joy among men at every newly lit soul?"—The
story of Ditte is far darker than that of the radiant Pelle. She is a poor servant girl who is se-
duced, maltreated, and done to death, who conquers only in that she preserves the unquenchable
goodness of her soul.

Nexö has himself lived the life of the very poor
and knows that they can and often do preserve
their human worth under conditions that would
seem deadening to all finer impulses. His dere-

licts have not only the traditional virtues of the poor, kindliness and loyalty, but they have kept their sense of humor, their capacity for enjoyment, and even some of the graces of life.

The graciousness and sweetness in *Pelle* helped to win for its author international appreciation. It can not be denied that in his later books the author yields to the temptation of throwing proletarian virtue into relief against the impossible vileness of the bourgeoisie, and that he sins especially in picturing conditions long since past as if they still existed. Nexö would answer that he is not interested in the story of a closed incident, but in the fight which is for ever being waged between those who have and those who have nothing.

Even a short survey of tendencies in modern Danish fiction can not close without mentioning the longing for a positive religion over and above the religion of humanity which Nexö preaches and the mystic devotion to the race which Johannes V. Jensen has exalted into a kind of religion. J. Anker Larsen's novel *The Philosopher's Stone* is a direct attempt to answer some of the questions that arise in the modern mind and to evolve a definite religious theory. While it cannot be claimed that the book is altogether successful either as art or as exposition, it is of interest as showing one important strand in the complex web

Introduction

of Danish literature to-day. In the peasant writers the religious feeling is more thoroughly interwoven with the texture of their work, inasmuch as they describe people to whom moral and spiritual experience has always come by means of their inherited faith and colored by its dogmas. Of great appeal is Harry Söiberg's monumental novel trilogy, *The Land of the Living,* which reflects the currents and cross currents of religious experience, and in its entire tendency shows the strongest possible reaction against the negative skepticism of the nineteenth century.

In the selection of the stories in this volume I wish to acknowledge my indebtedness to Mr. Julius Clausen of the Royal Library in Copenhagen, and other Danes, who have kindly assisted with their advice.

HANNA ASTRUP LARSEN

HANS CHRISTIAN ANDERSEN

THE SHEPHERDESS AND THE CHIMNEY-SWEEPER

HANS CHRISTIAN ANDERSEN (1805–1875) was born in Odense as the son of a servant girl and a poor journeyman shoemaker. His origin was not only lowly, but the erratic tendencies that in Andersen took the form of genius were present among his forbears as insanity and vice. His own parents, however, seem to have possessed qualities that enabled them to hold his affection. His father and his grandmother—whom he used to visit in the charitable institution where she lived—fed his desire for stories.

From his childhood Hans Christian was convinced that he was to become famous, and he thought the road to fame lay through the theater. Possessed by this illusion, he left Odense for Copenhagen when in his fifteenth year. His persistence in handing in to the Royal Theater one impossible play after another attracted the attention of one of the directors, Mr. Jonas Collin, who took the boy out of his miserable, disreputable environment and sent him to school. After passing his examinations, Andersen set out to make his living by writing. As a playwright he was never extremely successful, though his opera *Little Kirsten*, with music by J. P. E. Hartmann, is still popular. Among his novels *The Improvisator* and *Only a Fiddler* are best known.

Not until his thirtieth year did Andersen find his true field in the fairy tale. The first small collection contained tales based on folk-lore, but gradually he evolved the story built up entirely in his own imagination, often resembling a miniature novel, such as *The Shepherdess and the Chimney-Sweeper*.

Andersen suffered intensely from the hostility of the critics and from the social disability that clung to him even after he was the friend of princes. He never experienced a happy love and never married.

H. C. Andersen

THE SHEPHERDESS AND THE CHIMNEY-SWEEPER

HAVE YOU ever seen a very old wooden cupboard, quite black with age, and ornamented with carved foliage and arabesques? Just such a cupboard stood in a parlor; it had been a legacy from the great-grandmother, and was covered from top to bottom with carved roses and tulips. There were the quaintest flourishes upon it, and from among these peered forth little stags' heads with antlers. In the middle of the cupboard door an entire figure of a man had been cut out: he was certainly ridiculous to look at, and he grinned, for you could not call it laughing; he had goat's legs, little horns on his head, and a long beard. The children in the room always called him the Billygoat-legs-Lieutenant-and-Major-General-War-Commander- Sergeant; that was a difficult name to pronounce, and there are not many who obtain this title; but it was something to have cut him out. And there he was! He was always looking at the table under the mirror, for on this table stood a lovely little Shepherdess made of china. Her shoes were gilt, her dress was neatly caught up with a red rose, and besides this she had a golden hat and a shepherd's crook; she was very lovely. Close by her stood a little Chimney-Sweeper, black as a coal, but also made of porcelain; he was as clean and neat as any other man, for it was only make-believe that he was a sweep; the china-workers might just as well have made a prince of him, if they had been so minded.

There he stood very nattily with his ladder, and with a face as white and pink as a girl's; and that was really a fault, for he ought to have been a little black. He stood quite close to the Shepherdess: they had both been placed where they stood; but as they had been placed there they had become engaged to each other. They suited each other well. Both were young people, both made of the same kind of china, and both equally frail.

Close to them stood another figure, three times greater than they. This was an old China-man, who could nod. He was also of porcelain, and declared himself to be the grandfather of the little Shepherdess; but he could not prove his relationship. He declared he had authority over her, and that therefore he had nodded to Mr. Billygoat-legs-Lieutenant-and-Major-

[4]

General-War-Commander-Sergeant, who was wooing her for his wife.

"Then you will get a husband!" said the old Chinaman, "a man who I verily believe is made of mahogany. He can make you Billygoat-legs-Lieutenant-and-Major-General-War-Commander-Sergeantess: he has the whole cupboard full of silver plate, besides what he hoards up in secret drawers."

"I won't go into the dark cupboard!" said the little Shepherdess. "I have heard tell that he has eleven porcelain wives in there."

"Then you may become the twelfth," cried the Chinaman. "This night, as soon as it creaks in the old cupboard, you shall be married, as true as I am a Chinaman!"

And with that he nodded his head and fell asleep. But the little Shepherdess wept and looked at her heart's beloved, the porcelain Chimney-Sweeper.

"I should like to beg of you," said she, "to go out with me into the wide world, for we cannot remain here."

"I'll do whatever you like," replied the little Chimney-Sweeper. "Let us start directly! I think I can keep you by exercising my profession."

"If we were only safely down from the table!" said she. "I shall not be happy until we are out in the wide world."

And he comforted her, and showed her how she must place her little foot upon the carved corners and the gilded foliage down the leg of the table; he brought his ladder, too, to help her, and they were soon together upon the floor. But when they looked up at the old cupboard there was great commotion within: all the carved stags were stretching out their heads, rearing up their antlers, and turning their necks; and the Billygoat-legs-Lieutenant-and-Major-General-War-Commander-Sergeant sprang high in the air, and called across to the old Chinaman—

"Now they're running away! now they're running away!"

Then they were a little frightened, and jumped quickly into the drawer of the window-seat. Here were three or four packs of cards which were not complete, and a little puppet-show, which had been built up as well as it could be done. There plays were acted, and all the ladies, diamonds, clubs, hearts, and spades, sat in the first row, fanning themselves with their tulips; and behind them stood all the knaves, showing that they had a head above and below, as is usual in playing-cards. The play was about two people who were not to be married to each other, and the Shepherdess wept, because it was just like her own history.

[6]

"I cannot bear this!" said she. "I must go out of the drawer."

But when they arrived on the floor, and looked up at the table, the old Chinaman was awake and was shaking over his whole body— for below he was all one lump.

"Now the old Chinaman's coming!" cried the little Shepherdess; and she fell down upon her porcelain knee, so startled was she.

"I have an idea," said the Chimney-Sweeper. "Shall we creep into the great pot-pourri vase which stands in the corner? Then we can lie on roses and lavender, and throw salt in his eyes if he comes."

"That will be of no use," she replied. "Besides, I know that the old Chinaman and the pot-pourri vase were once engaged to each other, and a kind of liking always remains when people have stood in such a relation to each other. No, there's nothing left for us but to go out into the wide world."

"Have you really the courage to go into the wide world with me?" asked the Chimney-Sweeper. "Have you considered how wide the world is, and that we can never come back here again?"

"I have," replied she.

And the Chimney-Sweeper looked fondly at her, and said—

[7]

"My way is through the chimney. If you have really courage to creep with me through the stove —through the iron fire-box as well as up the pipe, then we can get out into the chimney, and I know how to find my way through there. We'll mount so high that they can't catch us, and quite at the top there's a hole that leads out into the wide world."

And he led her to the door of the stove.

"It looks very black there," said she; but still she went with him, through the box and through the pipe, where it was pitch-dark night.

"Now we are in the chimney," said he; "and look, look! up yonder a beautiful star is shining."

And it was a real star in the sky, which shone straight down upon them, as if it would show them the way. And they clambered and crept; it was a frightful way, and terribly steep; but he supported her and helped her up; he held her, and showed her the best places where she could place her little porcelain feet; and thus they reached the edge of the chimney, and upon that they sat down, for they were desperately tired, as they well might be.

The sky with all its stars was high above, and all the roofs of the town deep below them. They looked far around—far, far out into the world. The poor Shepherdess had never thought of it as it really was; she leaned her little head against the Chimney-Sweeper, then she wept so bitterly that the gold ran down off her girdle.

"That is too much," she said. "I cannot bear that. The world is too large! If I were only back upon the table below the mirror! I shall never be happy until I am there again. Now I have followed you out into the wide world, you may accompany me back again if you really love me."

And the Chimney-Sweeper spoke sensibly to her—spoke of the old Chinaman and of the Billygoat-legs-Lieutenant-and-Major-General-War-Commander-Sergeant; but she sobbed bitterly and kissed her little Chimney-Sweeper, so that he could not help giving way to her, though it was foolish.

And so with much labor they climbed down the chimney again. And they crept through the pipe and the fire-box. That was not pleasant at all. And there they stood in the dark stove; there they listened behind the door, to find out what was going on in the room. Then it was quite quiet. They looked in—ah! there lay the old China-man in the middle of the floor! He had fallen down from the table as he was pursuing them, and now he lay broken into three pieces; his back had come off all in one piece, and his head had rolled into a corner. The Billygoat-legs-Lieutenant-and-

Major-General-War-Commander-Sergeant stood where he had always stood, considering.

"That is terrible!" said the little Shepherdess. "The old grandfather has fallen to pieces, and it is our fault. I shall never survive it!" And then she wrung her little hands.

"He can be mended! he can be mended!" said the Chimney-Sweeper. "Don't be so violent. If they glue his back together and give him a good rivet in his neck he will be as good as new, and may say many a disagreeable thing to us yet."

"Do you think so?" cried she.

So they climbed back upon the table where they used to stand.

"You see, we have come back to this," said the Chimney-Sweeper; "we might have saved ourselves all the trouble we have had."

"If the old grandfather were only riveted!" said the Shepherdess. "I wonder if that is dear?"

And he was really riveted. The family had his back cemented, and a great rivet was passed through his neck; he was as good as new, only he could no longer nod.

"It seems you have become proud since you fell to pieces," said the Billygoat-legs-Lieutenant-and-Major-General-War-Commander-Sergeant. "I don't think you have any reason to give yourself such airs. Am I have to have her, or am I not?"

And the Chimney-Sweeper and the little Shepherdess looked at the old Chinaman most piteously, for they were afraid he might nod. But he could not do that, and it was annoying to him to tell a stranger that he all the time had a rivet in his neck. And so the porcelain people remained together, and they blessed Grandfather's rivet, and loved one another until they broke.

STEEN STEENSEN BLICHER

THE PARSON AT VEJLBY

STEEN STEENSEN BLICHER (1782–1848) was born in Jutland as the son of a country parson. He spent ten years in Copenhagen studying, and prepared himself for the Church, but it was some time before he obtained a charge in the poorest heath district. Later he was removed to a better living, in a more fertile part of Jutland, where he remained for the rest of his life. He was very unhappily married to a woman who had attracted him by her beauty and liveliness, but who turned out a household tyrant.

Blicher sought relief from the miseries of his home, partly in a most unclerical devotion to the bottle, partly by long walks over the heath with his gun and his dogs. On these hunting trips he discovered people and conditions yet unknown to literary treatment. In those days the interior of Jutland seemed very remote from the capital. The less fertile regions were sparsely peopled, but the inhabitants were a vigorous and original race. Country squires, clergymen, and peasants were masters of the land, and lived very much as their forefathers had done. Gypsies and other vagrants roamed the heath unrestrained. The author himself sometimes figures in his stories as the hunting parson, talking with peasants and gypsies—envying them their freedom from conventional restraints.

The Parson at Vejlby is based on an actual occurrence. In 1625 a clergyman, Sören Jensen Quist, was executed for a murder which, it was afterwards found, he had never committed. Blicher has, however, made very free use of his material. The moral and spiritual conflict in the minds both of victim and judge are entirely of his own devising.

Steen Steensen Blicher

THE PARSON AT VEJLBY

I

Judge Erik Sörensen's Diary

IN THE NAME of Our Lord, Jesus Christ!
Now at last, by the will of God, and through
the generosity of my dear patron, I am elevated,
all unworthily, to the office of County Sheriff and
Judge over this people. May He who judgeth
all men vouchsafe me wisdom and grace and uprightness so to fulfill my duties that I may find
favor in His sight.

"Every man's judgement cometh from the
Lord." Proverbs, 29, 26.

It is not good for man to be alone. Inasmuch
as I can now keep a wife, ought I not to look about
me for a helpmeet? The daughter of the pastor
at Vejlby is well spoken of by all who know her.
Since the death of her mother she has managed
the household affairs of the parsonage with thrift

and good sense; and as there are no other children with the exception of one brother, now a student at the University, it is likely that she will come into a tidy fortune when the old man passes away.

———

Morten Bruus from Ingvorstrup was here this morning and wanted to give me a fatted calf; but I remembered the warning of Moses, "Thou shalt take no gift," and refused it. This Bruus is much given to lawsuits, I am told, and is more-over contentious, and a great braggart; I will have nothing to do with him outside of my office as judge.

———

I have now taken counsel with my Heavenly Father and with my own heart, and it is clear to me that Mistress Meta Qvist is the one person with whom I wish to pass my life unto death. Yet will I observe her quietly for some time. Favor is deceitful, and beauty is vain. Never-theless, she is without a doubt the fairest woman I have seen in all my days.

———

This Morten Bruus is to me a most odious person, though I am scarce able to say why. He somehow reminds me of a bad dream, but so hazy and indistinct is the memory that I cannot even say whether I have ever really dreamed

[16]

about him.   It may well be that it is an evil omen.
He came here again this morning to offer me a
pair of blooded horses—splendid animals, dappled gray, with black manes and tails and black
fetlocks.   I know that he bought them separately
at a cost of seventy dollars for the two.   Perfectly matched as they are, the pair are well worth
a hundred, yet he offered them to me for seventy.
It was this very cheapness that gave me pause.
Is it not a bribery?   I am sure that he must have
some lawsuit in mind.   I do not want his dappled
grays.

————

To-day I visited the pastor at Vejlby.   He is a
God-fearing and upright man, but hot-tempered
and choleric, and intolerant of any opposition
to his will.   And he is close-fisted besides.   When
I arrived at the parsonage, there was a peasant
there who wanted his tithe reduced.   The fellow was a sly one, for his tithe was not too high,
and Pastor Sören seemed well aware of it, for he
talked to the man so that a dog would not have
taken a piece of bread from his hand; and the
more he scolded, the angrier he himself became. . . .   Well, Heaven knows, every man has
his faults.   Qvist means no harm by his outbursts,
for immediately afterwards he directed his daughter to give the man a piece of bread and butter

and a good glass of beer. . . . She is assuredly a comely and well-behaved maiden. When she saw me, she greeted me in a manner so kindly and yet so modest that I was strangely moved, and scarce able to say a word to her.

My farm steward worked at the parsonage upward of three years before he came to me. I shall question him skilfully and find out how she treats the domestics and anything else he may know of her. One may often get the most trustworthy information about people from their servants.

————

Zounds! My man Rasmus tells me that this Morten Bruus not so long ago went courting at Vejlby parsonage, but was refused. The parson was willing enough at first—for Bruus is a well-to-do man—but the daughter would have none of him. I understand that in the beginning her father took her sternly to task, but when he saw that she was unalterably opposed to the match, he let her have her own way. It was not pride on her part; for Rasmus says that she is as humble as she is good, and does not hesitate to admit that her own father is peasant-born as well as Bruus.

————

Now I understand what the Ingvorstrup horses were to do here in Rosmus; they were to draw me from the straight path of justice. It is a mat-

ter of Ole Andersen's peat-bog and adjoining
meadow. That prize was no doubt worth the
value of the horses. . . . Nay, nay, my good
Morten, you do not know Erik Sörensen. "Thou
shalt not wrest the judgement of the poor."

———

Pastor Sören of Vejlby was here for a short
visit this morning. He has hired a new coachman, one Niels Bruus, brother to the Ingvorstrup
farmer. This Niels, the parson complains, is a
lazy fellow and impudent and quarrelsome besides. Pastor Sören wanted him punished in the
stocks, but he lacks the necessary witnesses and
evidence. I advised him rather to dismiss the
unruly fellow at once, or else to try to get along
with him somehow until his time is out. At first
he answered my suggestions very shortly, but
when he had heard me to the end and weighed my
argument a little, he admitted the strength of my
reasoning, and thanked me warmly for my advice.
He is a hot-headed, quick-tempered man, but not
difficult to reason with when he has had time to
cool a little and compose himself. We parted
very good friends indeed. Not a word was
spoken about Mistress Meta.

———

This day I passed most agreeably at the Vejlby
parsonage. Pastor Sören was from home when
I arrived, but Mistress Meta greeted me warmly.

She was spinning when I came in, and it seemed to me that she blushed deeply. . . .

It is curious how long it took me to find some subject of conversation. When I sit on the bench in my judicial robes, I seldom lack for words; and when I cross-examine a prisoner, I can think of questions enough to ask; but before this gentle innocent child I stood as confused as a chicken-thief caught red-handed. At last it occurred to me to speak of Ole Andersen and his lawsuit, his peat-bog and meadow; and I do not know how it came about, but the talk turned from meadows to roses and violets and daisies, until finally she conducted me out into her garden to see her flowers. Thus pleasantly we passed the time until her father returned home, and then she retired into the kitchen and did not appear again until she came to bid us to supper.

Just as she stepped into the doorway, her father was saying to me, "I presume it is high time for you also to enter into the state of matrimony." We had just been talking about a magnificent wedding which had been celebrated at Höjholm manor. Hearing this last remark, Mistress Meta blushed as red as a rose. Her father smiled slyly, and said, "One can see that you have been bending over the fire, my daughter."

I have taken the good pastor's advice to heart, and, God willing, it shall not be long now before

I shall go courting at the parsonage, for I consider her father's words a subtle hint that he
would not be averse to having me for a son-in-
law. And the daughter? Why did she blush,
I wonder. Dare I take that as a favorable sign?

————

And so the poor man is to keep his peat-bog and
his meadow after all. . . . But assuredly the
decision made the rich man my mortal enemy.
Before the judgement of the Court was read,
Morten Bruus stood and stared scornfully at Ole
Andersen. At the words, "It is the verdict of
the Court," he looked around the court-room and
grinned slyly, as if certain of a favorable decision.
And that he was, indeed, for I was told that he
had remarked, "It's foolish for that beggar to
think he can win against me."

Yet that is just what happened.

When Bruus heard the verdict, he shut his
eyes and pursed his lips together, and his face
was white as chalk. But he managed to control
his rage, and said to his opponent, as he went out
of the court-room, "I wish you joy, Ole Andersen.
Losing that peat-bog won't beggar me, and the
Ingvorstrup oxen will doubtless get what hay they
need elsewhere."

But outside we heard him swearing to himself
and cracking his whip over the horses' backs, so
that it echoed and re-echoed in the woods.

Denmark's Best Stories

The office of a judge is indeed a heavy burden. He makes a new enemy with every verdict he pronounces. But if we can only keep on good terms with our own conscience . . . "Endure all things for conscience's sake."

———

Yesterday was the happiest day in my whole life; my betrothal to Meta Qvist was celebrated at Vejlby parsonage. My future father-in-law spoke from the text, "I have given my maid into thy bosom," Genesis, 16, 5. He spoke very movingly of how he was giving to me his most precious treasure in this world, and of how he hoped I would be kind to her. (And that I will, so help me God!)

I had scarce believed that the grave, even stern old man could be so gentle and tender. When he concluded, his eyes were filled with tears, and his lips trembled. My beloved wept like a child, especially when he referred to her sainted mother; and when he said, "Thy father and mother shall foresake thee, but the Lord shall take thee up," I too felt my eyes filling with tears, for I thought of how God had watched over me and guided me and showered me with His blessings after I had lost my own dear parents.

When we had plighted our troth, my sweet bride gave me her first kiss. May God bless her! She loves me fondly.

Steen Steensen Blicher

At the table the merriment was unrestrained. Many of her mother's kinsfolk were present, but none of her father's, for they are but few and live far up by the Skaw. There was food and wine in abundance, and after the tables were cleared there was dancing until well-nigh dawn. The neighboring parsons from Aalsö, Lyngby, and Hyllested were all present; the last became so tipsy that he had to be put to bed. My father-in-law also drank mightily, but did not seem the worse for it; he is as strong as a giant, and could doubtless drink all the parsons in the county under the table. I noticed, too, that he thought it would be good sport to see me a little fuddled, but I took good care that he should not. I am no lover of strong drink.

Our nuptials will be celebrated in six weeks. May God give His blessing thereto!

———

It is a pity that my father-in-law should have got this Niels Bruus in his service. He is a rough fellow, a worthy brother to him of Ingvorstrup. He ought to be given his wages and shown the door; that would be far better than to soil one's fingers in a fray with such a brute. But the good parson is hot-tempered and stubborn, and two hard stones don't grind well together. He is determined that Niels shall serve his time out, even though it means daily vexation for himself.

[23]

64348

The other day he gave Niels a box on the ear, whereupon the rascal threatened that "he would see to it that the parson was paid back." But to all this there were no witnesses. I had Niels up before me, and both admonished and threatened him, but I could do nothing with him. There is evil in the man.

My betrothed, too, has entreated her father to rid himself of the fellow, but he will no more listen to her than to me. I scarce know how things will go when she moves from her father's roof to mine, for she shields the old man from a great deal of trouble and knows how to smooth over everything.

She will be to me a tender wife, "as a fruitful vine by the side of thy house."

———

It was an unlucky business—and yet lucky too, for Niels has run away. My father-in-law is angry as a German, but I rejoice silently that he has thus got rid of this dangerous person. No doubt Bruus will try to avenge his brother at the first likely opportunity, but thank Heaven we have law and order in this land, and the law will protect us.

It seems that Pastor Sören had set Niels to digging in the garden. When he came out a little later to see what progress had been made, he saw the fellow stand resting on his spade and cracking nuts which he had picked off the bushes. He had done no work at all. The parson upbraided him. Niels answered impudently that he was not to be ordered about by any one, whereupon he got a blow on the mouth. At this he flung away his spade, and berated his master foully. Then the old man's fiery temper burst out, he seized the spade, and clouted him with it over the head. He should not have done so, for a spade is a dangerous weapon, especially when lifted in anger and in the hands of a strong man. The rascal let himself fall as if he were dead, but when the parson became frightened and attempted to lift him, he jumped up, ran across the garden, leaped the hedge, and disappeared into the woods just back of the parsonage. . . . So my father-in-law himself described the unhappy affair.

My betrothed is much distressed about it. She fears that Niels will avenge himself in some way or other—that he will work some harm on the cattle, or even set fire to the house. God helping, I think there is small danger.

Only three weeks more now, and then I can lead my bride into my home. She has already been here and taken stock of everything, both within and without. She seemed well pleased and complimented us on the orderliness and neatness everywhere. The only thing she seems to regret is that she will have to leave her father; and he will surely miss her. Yet I will do whatever I can to compensate him for his loss. I will exchange for his daughter my own good Aunt Gertrude, a very capable woman, alert and active for her age.

My betrothed is indeed an angel! Every one speaks well of her—I am sure I shall be a most happy man. God be praised!

————

What can have happened to that fellow! I wonder if he has fled the country. In any event it is a sorry tale, and people around in the parish are beginning to gossip about it. I am sure that these calumnies must have their source back in Ingvorstrup. It would be a pity for my father-in-law to hear of them. . . . Had he only followed my advice and rid himself of the surly fellow! For the wrath of man worketh not the righteousness of God. Yet I am but a layman, and should not presume to rebuke one of God's servants, especially one so full of years and dignity. . . . We can only hope that all this talk will die away of itself.

To-morrow morning I will go to Vejlby, and I shall soon learn whether he has heard aught of the slanders.

The goldsmith has just been here with the pair of bracelets that I ordered; they are very handsome, and will, I am sure, give pleasure to my dear

Meta. If only they fit her . . . I took the measurement of her wrist hastily and in secret with a blade of grass.

———

I found my father-in-law quite depressed; indeed I have never seen him in such low spirits before. Busy tongues had already brought him some of the stupid rumors which, more is the pity, are common talk in the neighborhood. Morten Bruus is reported to have said, "The parson will have to bring back my brother Niels, even if he has to dig him up out of the ground."

It may be that the fellow is in hiding at Ingvorstrup. At any rate, he is gone, and no one has seen hide or hair of him since he ran away. My poor betrothed is allowing it to prey too much on her mind; she is disturbed by portents and bad dreams.

———

Lord have mercy upon us all! I am so overwhelmed with sorrow and terror that I can scarce guide my pen; a hundred times already it has slipped from my hand. My heart is full of fear and my mind so distracted that I scarce know how to begin. The whole thing has burst upon me like a thunderbolt. Time has ceased to have any meaning for me, morning and evening are as one, and the whole terrible day is like one jagged stroke of lightning which has burned down in a

[27]

moment my proud temple of hope and ambition.

A venerable man of God accused of murder, in jail and in chains! Of course there is always the hope that he may be innocent, but, alas! that hope is but as a straw to the drowning, for the circumstantial evidence against him seems very heavy indeed. And to think that I, miserable wretch, should be his judge! And his daughter my promised bride! . . .

It was early yesterday morning, about half an hour before sunrise, that Morten Bruus came here to the house, bringing with him one Jens Larsen, a crofter from Vejlby, together with the widow and daughter of his former shepherd. Bruus declared to me at once his suspicion that Pastor Qvist had killed his brother Niels. I answered him that I, too, had heard gossip to that effect, but that I regarded it all as a silly and vicious slander, unworthy the attention of honest men, inasmuch as the pastor had told me that Niels had risen and run away.

"Had Niels actually run away, as Parson Qvist says," Bruus retorted, "I am sure that he would have come to me at once, and told me all about the affair. But that the real cause of his continued absence is quite another, these good people"—he indicated his three companions—"can bear witness, and I therefore ask you, as judge, to examine them."

"Bethink yourself well, Bruus," I warned him, "and you, good folk, bethink yourselves well before you bring accusations against your venerable and honorable spiritual guide. If, as I strongly suspect, you are unable to prove your charges, then it will go hard with you."

"Parson or no parson," Bruus cried wrathfully, "it is written, 'Thou shalt not kill,' and it is also written that the Government beareth not the sword in vain. We have law and justice in this land, and a murderer cannot escape his just punishment—even if he had the governor for a son-in-law."

I ignored the sneer, and replied with dignity, "Very well, be it as you will. What do you, Kirsten Madsdaughter, know of this crime of which Morten Bruus accuses your pastor? Tell me the truth, as you would tell it before the great judgement seat, and as you may be required to tell it to the Court later on."

Thus admonished she told the following story:

Shortly after noon of the day when Niels Bruus was said to have run away, she and her daughter, Elsa, had passed along the path outside the parsonage garden. Just as they came about midway by the stone fence which encloses the east side of the garden, they heard a voice call "Elsa!" It was Niels Bruus. He was standing just inside the hazel hedge that borders the stone fence, and had bent the bushes aside to ask Elsa if she wanted some nuts. Elsa took a handful of them, and asked him what he was doing there. He answered that the parson had told him to spade the garden, but that he would rather pick nuts; the garden could take care of itself for a while. At the same moment they heard a door slam, and Niels said, "Listen, now we're going to have a sermon." Being curious, they waited for a moment, and they soon heard the pastor and Niels brawling. One word led to another, and at last they heard the pastor cry out, "You dog, I will teach you to be impudent! You shall lie dead at my feet!" Whereupon they heard a couple of smart blows, as when one receives a slap on the mouth. At this they heard Niels Bruus revile the pastor, calling him a hangman and a coward and much besides, from which they concluded that the pastor had struck him. To all this stream of abuse the pastor answered not a word, but Kirsten and her daughter heard two dull blows, and saw the blade and part of the handle of a spade fly up in the air a couple of times; but whose hand it was that wielded the spade they were unable to see, for the hedge was thick and high. After that all was quiet within the garden, but the shepherd's widow and her daughter had become so thoroughly frightened that they hastened away to their cattle out in the pasture.

The girl Elsa confirmed her mother's story in every circumstance. I asked them if they had not seen Niels Bruus come out of the garden, but they both denied this, though they assured me that they had looked back a number of times.

All of this agreed completely with what the pastor had already told me. That the witnesses had not seen Niels coming out was to be explained by the fact that the woods were just as near the south side of the garden, and, according to the pastor, it was in this direction that he had fled. So, after weighing the testimony of Kirsten and her daughter, I declared to Morten Bruus that their tale threw no new light on the case, inasmuch as the pastor had already told me the whole story himself.

At this Bruus smiled bitterly, and asked me to examine his third witness, which I proceeded to do.

Jens Larsen, after I had admonished him as I had the first two witnesses, told the following story:

Late one evening—not the evening of the disappearance of Niels Bruus but, as far as he could remember, the following night, he was returning home from the neighboring hamlet of Tolstrup, and walking along the path which ran by the east side of the parsonage garden, when he heard from within the sound of some one digging. There was a bright moon that night, and, though somewhat frightened, he decided to see who it was that was digging, and what he could be doing at so unusual an hour. So he took off his wooden shoes, scrambled up the stone wall, and made a little peep-hole through the thick hedge with his hands. There in the garden, flooded in moonlight, stood the figure of the pastor in his long green robe and his white cotton nightcap. He was smoothing the surface of the ground with the back of a spade. Suddenly the pastor turned, as if conscious of being watched, and Jens Larsen, being frightened, slid hastily down the wall and ran home.

Although I thought it strange that the pastor should be out in his garden at that time of night, I was still unable to find any valid grounds for suspicion of the imputed murder. This conclusion I communicated to Morten Bruus with a solemn warning, not only to retract his baseless charges, but to put an end to the rumors by a public declaration of his retraction. To this admonition Bruus merely replied, "Not until I know what the parson was doing in his garden at that hour of night."

"By that time," I warned him, "it may be too late; you are gambling your honor and welfare on a very dangerous chance."

"I owe that much to my brother," he rejoined.

"I hope that our rightful rulers will not refuse me the aid and support of the law."

Such a demand I could not ignore, and so I was forced to investigate Bruus's charges. I hastily made what preparations were necessary and, accompanied by Bruus and the three witnesses, drove over to Vejlby. Heavy of heart I was, and sore depressed, not from fear that I should find the fugitive Niels in the garden of the parsonage, but at the thought of subjecting the pastor and my betrothed to such vexation and indignity. All during the trip my thoughts dwelt on how I might make the defamer of innocence feel the full weight of the law. Ah, Thou merciful Heaven, what a shock was in store for me!

I planned, as soon as I arrived, to take the pastor aside and forewarn him, thus giving him time to compose himself. But Morten anticipated me, for, as I drove up to the parsonage, he rode past me on his horse, dashed up to the door, and, as the pastor opened it, cried out:

"Folks say that you killed my brother and buried him in your garden. Here's the judge come with me to search for him."

This rude announcement so disconcerted the pastor that he was unable to say a word before I jumped out of my carriage, and, hurrying to him, seized his hand, and said:

"Now you have heard the charge, and without

palliation. I am sorry that I, as judge, am bound to do this man's bidding. But your own honor now requires that the truth be brought to light, and the mouths of the slanderers stopped."

"It is indeed hard," Pastor Qvist replied, "that a man in my office should be required to refute so abominable an accusation. . . . But enter if you will, my garden and my house are open to you."

We passed through the house and into the garden at the back. There my betrothed met us, but when she saw Bruus behind me she trembled with fear, and her eyes looked to me appealingly.

"Be not alarmed, dear heart," I whispered to her hurriedly. "Go into the house, and fear nothing, your enemy is rushing headlong to his ruin."

Morten Bruus led the way to the hedge over toward the east. I and the witnesses followed him, then came the pastor with his servants whom he had himself ordered to bring spades. The accuser stood still for a moment, looking around until we came up to him; then he pointed to a place on the ground, and said:

"That looks as if it was dug up not so long ago. Let us begin here."

"Dig, then," the pastor ordered angrily.

His men set to work with their spades, but after a few moments Bruus, who was watching their progress with obvious impatience, tore the spade from the hands of one of the men and joined in the work with tremendous energy. When they had spaded about a foot beneath the surface, they came to ground so hard that it was clear it had not been disturbed recently—probably not for years.

All of us—with one exception—were vastly pleased, the pastor most of all. He began already to triumph over his accuser, and taunted him with the sneer—"Well, you slanderer, did you find anything?"

Bruus did not vouchsafe him an answer, but stood thoughtfully for a moment, and then, turning to Jens Larsen, asked, "Jens, where was it you saw the parson spading that night?"

Jens, who had stood all this time with folded hands watching while the others worked, looked up with a start at this question. He let his gaze wander slowly around the garden, and finally pointed to a corner two or three fathoms from where we were standing.

"I think it was over there," he said.

"What is that, Jens?" the pastor exclaimed with some asperity. "When did you ever see me spade?"

Without heeding this interruption, Morten Bruus beckoned us all over to the designated corner. He brushed away some withered cabbage stalks, branches, and other rubbish, and ordered the digging to begin at once.

I stood quietly by, well satisfied with the course of events so far, discussing with my father-in-law the misdemeanor for which the accuser had made himself liable and the punishment which could be meted out to him, when one of the spaders screamed—"Jesus Christ!"

We glanced quickly over at them. The crown of a hat had been uncovered, and they were all staring at it in terror.

"I think we'll find what we're looking for right here," Bruus said. "I know that hat well, it belonged to Niels."

My blood froze in my veins, and I saw the whole structure of my life crumble to earth.

"Dig, dig!" the terrible blood-avenger bawled, redoubling his own efforts.

I looked over at my father-in-law; he was pale as death and trembling, but his eyes were wide open and fixed in a sort of fascination on the dreadful spot.

Another scream! They had uncovered a hand stretching up at them through the earth.

"Look," cried Bruus, "he is reaching up at us. Wait, brother Niels, you'll soon have your revenge."

Presently the whole body was uncovered, and it proved to be that of the missing Niels, beyond

any doubt. The face was scarcely recognizable
—the flesh had already begun to decay, and the
nose was broken and smashed flat; but the clothes,
especially the shirt with Niels's name sewed on it,
were immediately identified by his fellow-servants.
And in the left ear they even found the leaden
ring which Niels had worn constantly for several
years.

"Now, you man of God," Morten cried—
"come and lay your hand on the dead and deny
your guilt if you dare."

The pastor sighed deeply, and raised his eyes
in a mute appeal to Heaven. "Almighty God,"
he said, "Thou art my witness that I am innocent
of this crime. Strike him, that I did indeed, and
bitterly do I repent it now. Strike him I did, but
who buried him here, that Thou alone knowest."

"Jens Larsen knows it too," Bruus interrupted
with a sneer, "and perhaps we shall find others
besides. Sir Judge"—he turned to me—"doubtless you will wish to examine the servants, but I demand that you first place this wolf in sheep's
clothing under lock and key."

Alas, Thou merciful God! no longer dared I
doubt; the evidence was too plain. But I was
ready to sink into the ground with horror and
loathing. I was just about to tell the pastor that
he would have to submit to arrest, when he himself spoke to me. He was ghostly pale, and shak-

ing like an aspen leaf. "Appearances are against me," he admitted, "but surely this is the work of the devil himself, and I know that there is One above who will bear witness to my innocence. Come, Sir Judge, in chains and in prison will I await His disposition of me, poor sinner that I am. Comfort my daughter! Remember she is your promised wife."

Scarce had he finished speaking, when we heard a moan and then a body fall behind us. We turned quickly, and I saw that it was my betrothed who had swooned and lay prone on the ground. Would to God I might have lain down beside her and neither of us ever awakened again! I lifted her up and held her in my arms, thinking she was dead; but her father tore her from my grasp, and carried her into the house. At the same moment I was called away to inspect a wound in the head of the slain man, which, though not deep, had cracked the skull, and had clearly been caused by a spade or some such blunt weapon.

After this we all went into the parsonage. My betrothed had already regained consciousness, and when she saw me she rushed to me, flung her arms around my neck, and implored me by all that was sacred to save her father from the great danger which threatened him. Afterwards she begged me, for the sake of our great love, to allow her to go with him to prison, which request I granted her. I myself accompanied them to the jail at Grennaa, in what a state of mind God alone knows. During the whole of that melancholy ride none of us spoke a word, and I parted from them with a bursting heart.

The body of Niels Bruus has been placed in a coffin which Jens Larsen had ready for himself, and to-morrow it will be honorably buried in Vejlby churchyard.

To-morrow, too, the first witnesses will be heard. . . . May God strengthen my weakness!

————

Fool that I was to strive so eagerly for this office of county judge! Would that I had never obtained it! It is a dreary business to be a judge. I would fain change places with one of the talesmen!

When this servant of God was led into Court this morning, his hands bound and his feet in chains, I was reminded of our Lord before the judgement seat of Pontius Pilate, and methought I heard distinctly the voice of my sweetheart—alas, she is lying ill at Grennaa—whisper to me: "Have thou nothing to do with that just man."

Would to God that her father was such a one, but at present I cannot perceive the slightest possibility of his innocence. . . . Jens Larsen, the widow, and her daughter Elsa were the first witnesses. They reaffirmed on oath the entire story which they had previously told me, and that almost word for word. Nothing was retracted, nothing added. Besides these, three new witnesses appeared, Sören Qvist's two men servants and his milkmaid. The two men said that they had been sitting in the servants' hall the afternoon of the day of the murder, and that through the open window they had distinctly heard the voices of the pastor and Niels raised in angry altercation and that they had heard the former cry out, "You dog, you shall lie dead at my feet." Their testimony, therefore, coincided with that of the widow and her daughter. They affirmed further, that they had twice before heard the pastor abuse and threaten Niels, that when the pastor was angry, he did not hesitate to use whatever weapon came to hand, and that he had once struck a servant with a wooden maul.

The maid deposed that, on the same night when Jens Larsen had seen the pastor in the garden, she had been unable to sleep, and as she lay there wide awake she heard the door from the hall to the garden creak on its hinges. She sprang from her bed and went over to the window to see what it could be, and saw the pastor in his long robe and nightcap in the garden. She was unable to see what he was doing out there, but about an hour later she heard the garden door creek again.

When all the witnesses had been heard, I asked the defendant whether he had anything to say in his own defense, or whether he was prepared to make a confession. He folded his hands over his heart, and said solemnly, "I am speaking the truth, so help me God, and I swear by His holy word that I know no more of this matter than I have already confessed. I struck the deceased with a spade, he fell, sprang to his feet again, and ran out of my garden. What happened to him afterwards, or how he came to be buried in my garden, I do not know. As to the testimony of Jens Larsen and my maid that they saw me out in the garden at night, I can only say that, either they are lying, or else the whole thing is a phantom from hell. . . . But I can clearly see that I have no one to defend me here on earth, and if my Heavenly Father chooses to remain silent, then verily I know that I am lost, and I bow to His inscrutable will." When he had finished speaking, the old man heaved a deep sigh, and bowed his head upon his breast.

Many of those who were in the court-room could not restrain their tears, while others whispered that maybe their parson was innocent after all; but this was merely the natural result of the emotions and sympathies which he had aroused. My own heart, too, argued for his innocence, but the reason of the judge cannot be swayed by the counsels or pleading of the heart; neither love nor hate, reverence nor contempt, gain nor bereavement can weigh by so much as a grain of sand in the even scales of justice. My own well-considered judgement did not allow me to conclude other than that the accused had killed Niels Bruus, though not with deliberate intent or purpose. That he had threatened Niels several times before the murder did not appear to me evidence of deliberate intent; for he had been in the habit of making threats, though he had never before been known to carry them out. The murder had no doubt been a crime of passion; that the defendant now persisted in his denial was doubtless due to the instinct of self-preservation and the desire to vindicate his honor.

Morten Bruus (there is a churlish brute, ugly enough before and worse now since his brother's murder) began to talk about means to force confession from an obdurate sinner, but I shut him up quickly. God forbid that I should put so venerable a man on the rack! What is it after all but a trial of physical and mental strength; he who withstands the torture and he who succumbs to it may both be lying, and a forced confession can never be trustworthy. Nay, rather than resort to that, I would give up my office and the duties that have become so irksome to me.

Alas, my poor Meta, my dearest, I have lost her in this world, and yet I loved her with all my heart.

———

I have just gone through another heart-rending scene. As I sat reviewing this terrible case in my mind, trying to find some solution, the door flew open and the pastor's daughter—I scarce dare call her betrothed who will never be my wife —rushed in, threw herself at my feet, and embraced my knees. I lifted her into my arms, but it was some time before either of us could speak for tears. I mastered my emotion first, and said to her, "I know what you are come for, dear heart—you would ask me to save your father. Alas, God have mercy on us poor mortals, I can do nothing. . . . Tell me, dear child, do you yourself believe your father to be innocent?"

She put her hand on her heart, and said, "I do not know," and with that she began to weep again most bitterly. "Surely, he did not bury Niels in the garden," she went on, when she had recovered somewhat, "but I suppose the man died out in the woods from the blows that my father had given him—alas, it must be so."

"My dear girl," I said, "both Jens Larsen and your maid saw him out in the garden the following night."

[43]

She shook her head slowly. "Perhaps the foul fiend may have blinded them."

"Lord Jesus forbid that he should have such power over Christian folk," I replied.

She began to weep again, but after a little she said, "Tell me, my affianced husband, tell me frankly, if God does not vouchsafe further light on this matter, what verdict will you pronounce?" She looked at me full of fear, and her lips trembled.

"Were I not sure that any other judge would be more severe than I," I answered her, "I would resign my seat at once—yea, gladly lay down my office forever. But, since you demand an answer, I dare not conceal from you that the mildest sentence decreed by the laws of both God and the king is a life for a life."

At this Meta fell to her knees in despair, but in a moment she was on her feet again. She retreated a few steps, and then advanced toward me, crying, as if distracted, "Will you murder my father? Will you murder your betrothed?" She held her hand up to my eyes, "Do you see this ring?" she asked me. "Do you remember what my unhappy father said when you placed it on my finger?—'I give my maid into thy bosom'— But you—you pierce my bosom."

Merciful God, every word she said pierced my own bosom. "Dearest child," I sighed, "say not

[44]

so! You tear my heart with red-hot pincers. What is it you want me to do? Do you ask me to set free one whom the laws of God and man condemn?"

She was silent for a moment, lost in thought, and I continued, "One thing I will do, and if it is wrong, then I pray God not to lay this sin to my charge. Listen, dear child. If this trial is concluded, then we both know that your father's life is forfeited. There is no escape but in flight. If you can evolve any plan of escape, I promise to shut my eyes and keep silence. . . . Nay more, I will give you every assistance. Look you, as soon as your father was imprisoned, I wrote to your brother in Copenhagen, and we can expect him almost any day now. When he comes, let him help you, and meanwhile try to win the jailer for your plan; if you need money, all that I have is yours."

When I had spoken thus, her face flushed with hope, and she threw her arms around my neck, and cried, "God reward you for this advice! If only my brother were here now, then I know we should succeed." She stopped, and was silent a moment. "But where could we go?" she asked, "and if we were able to find refuge in some strange land, then I should never see you again."

She said this so plaintively that I thought my heart would burst. "Dearest child," I consoled

[45]

her, "I will find you and come to you, no matter how far you may travel. And if our resources are not sufficient for our support, then these hands of mine shall work for us all. They have wielded the axe and the plane before, and they can do it again."

At this she was exceeding happy, and kissed me many times. Then we prayed together that God might see fit to further our plan, and when she left me she was buoyed up with hope.

I too began to hope that we might find some way. But no sooner had Meta gone, than my spirits were assailed by a thousand doubts, and all the difficulties which seemed at the moment so easy to overcome now appeared like mountains which my weak hands could never remove. Nay, out of this darkness and terror only He to whom the night shineth as the day can lead us!

———

Morten Bruus was here this morning and announced two new witnesses with an air that boded little good for us. He has a heart as hard as flint and full of poison and gall. The new witnesses are to appear in court to-morrow, and I am as despondent as if it were myself that they were to testify against. May God give me strength!

———

All is over! He has confessed everything!
The Court was convened, and the prisoner was

led forth to hear the testimony of the new witnesses. They deposed: That, on the now famous night of the day after the crime, they were
walking along the road that runs between the
woods and the garden of the parsonage, when
they saw a man emerge from the woods with a
large sack on his back, walk quickly over to the
garden, and disappear behind the fence. The
man's face was completely concealed by the sack,
but the moon shone full on his back, and they saw
distinctly that he was clad in a long green robe,
and that he wore a white nightcap.

No sooner had the first witness completed his
testimony than the pastor's face went ashen gray,
and it was with the greatest difficulty that he
stammered in a weak voice, "I am ill." He was
given a chair and sat down heavily. Bruus
turned to the spectators, and said, "That helped
the parson's memory, didn't it?" The pastor
either did not hear the sneer or ignored it. Instead he beckoned to me, and when I came over to
him, he said, "Let me be taken back to prison. I
want to talk to you." It was done as he requested.

We drove off to Grennaa, the pastor riding
with the jailor and the clerk, and I alone. As we
opened the door to the prison, there stood my betrothed making her father's bed. On a chair at
the head of the bed hung the tell-tale green robe.

[47]

When she saw us entering together, she gave a cry of joy, for she concluded that her father had been freed, and that I was coming to release him from jail. She dropped the bed-covering, rushed over to her father, and flung her arms around his neck. The old man wept so that his eyes were blinded with tears. He did not have the heart to tell her what had just happened in the court-room, and instead sent her on some errands in town.

Before she left us, she ran over to me, took my hand and pressed it to her heart, and whispered, "Have you good tidings?" To conceal my own confusion I kissed her on the forehead, and said merely, "Dearest, you shall know everything later on. I cannot tell yet whether what has happened is of great importance one way or the other. Go now, and fetch us what your father asked for."

Alas! what a change from the time when this innocent child lived, carefree and happy, in the pleasant parsonage, to the dreary present here in this dismal prison.

"Be seated, my friend," the pastor said to me as he himself sat down on the edge of the bed, folded his hands in his lap, and stared down on the floor as if lost in thought. At last he roused himself, sat up, and fastened his eyes upon me. I waited in breathless silence as if it were my own doom I was about to hear—as indeed in a sense it was.

"I am a great sinner," he began at last, "how great I do not myself know. God alone knows, and I am firmly convinced that he wishes to punish me here in this world so that I may receive grace and eternal blessedness hereafter. Praise and glory be unto Him!" With this he seemed to gain more quietness and strength, and he proceeded as follows:

"From my earliest childhood, as far back as I can remember, I have been of a quarrelsome nature, proud and hasty, impatient of opposition, and always ready to resort to blows. Yet have I seldom let the sun go down on my anger, neither have I borne malice toward any man. When I was but a half-grown boy my ungovernable temper led me to commit a deed which I have often since bitterly repented and which, even now, I cannot recall without pain. Our watch-dog, a gentle beast who had never harmed any living creature, ate up my lunch which I had for the moment laid on a chair. I flew into a rage and kicked him so hard with my wooden shoes that he died the next morning in terrible agony. That time it was only a dumb animal who was the victim of my passion, but it should have been a warning to me not to lay violent hands on any creature. Again, some years later, when I was a student at Leipzig University, I picked a quarrel with a Bursch, called him out on the field of honor, and gave him a wound in the chest that came within a hair's breadth of killing him. So you see I have these many years deserved what I am now to suffer, but now my punishment falls with tenfold weight on my sinful head: An old man, a pastor and messenger of peace, and—a father, O merciful God, that is the deepest wound of all!" He sprang to his feet and wrung his hands so that I could hear the joints creaking. I would have said something to console him, but could find no words.

When he had regained control of himself, he sat down again, and continued, "To you, formerly my friend and now my judge, I am about to confess a crime which I can no longer doubt having committed, but which I still do not fully understand."

I started in surprise and wondered what he meant, for I had prepared myself for a full and open confession.

"I want you to pay the closest attention to what I am about to relate," he continued, "and try to understand me. I have already confessed all that I know: that I struck Niels with a spade —whether with the edge or the flat side I cannot remember—and that he fell down, jumped up, and ran away into the woods. The rest, alas! has been told by four witnesses: that the boy died in the woods, and that I fetched the body and buried it in my garden the following night. And though of all this I know nothing myself, I am forced to accept it as the truth, and you shall hear my reasons.

"On three or four occasions earlier in my life I have walked in my sleep. The last time I know of having done this was some nine or ten years ago; it was the night before I was to hold funeral services for a man who had met a very sudden and painful death. I remember it all distinctly. . . . I remember that I was at a loss for a suitable text, when the words of one of the Greek philosophers occurred to me: 'Call no man happy before he is dead.' But to use a heathen text for a Christian service would never do, and I was sure that I should be able to find the same idea somewhere in the Bible. I hunted diligently, but without success, and since I was already tired from other work, I undressed and went to bed, and soon fell asleep. The next morning when I went to my study to find a proper text and outline my talk, I was dumbfounded to see, lying on my desk, a piece of paper with the words: 'Call no man happy until his days are told,' written in large clear letters. But this was not all; beside it lay a funeral sermon, brief but well-constructed—and all in my own handwriting. No one had been in the room. The door was bolted on the inside, because the lock was worn and easily sprang open. No one had come through the window, for it was

frozen fast to the casement. I had composed
and written the whole thing in my sleep.

"Nor is this the only instance of its kind. It
was indeed but a few months previous to this that
I had, while sound asleep, gone into the church to
fetch a handkerchief which I distinctly remember
having left on my chair behind the altar.

"And now, my friend, it must all be plain to
you. When the first witness was giving his testimony this morning in court, I suddenly remembered these earlier occasions of walking in my
sleep, and I remembered, too, another incident
which, until that moment, had completely slipped
my mind: when I awoke on the second day after
the flight of Niels I found my green robe, which
I always hang over the back of a chair beside my
bed, lying on the floor. . . . The poor victim of
my ungovernable temper must have fallen dead in
the woods, and I must have found him there,
brought him to my garden, and buried him—all
in my sleep. Yes, God have mercy upon me, it
must be so."

He ceased speaking, and buried his face in his
hands. As for me, I was utterly astounded and
full of misgivings. I had from the beginning believed that the murdered man had died on the
spot where he was attacked, and that the pastor
had hastily covered him over with some dirt—

though how he was able to do this in broad daylight without being seen was a mystery to me—
and later had buried the body deeper in the
ground. Now the last witnesses had just testified
that they saw the pastor carrying a sack from the
woods. This struck me as most extraordinary,
and it had occurred to me at once that their testimony might conflict with our earlier version of
the case, and the man's innocence thus be demonstrated. But now, alas, all the facts fitted together only too well, and his guilt was established
beyond the shadow of a doubt. Only the curious
aspect which his sleep-walking had given the case
continued to perplex me. That he had committed the murder was certain, but whether the
last and the less important half of the crime was
carried out in a waking or a sleeping condition
remained a puzzle to me. The pastor's whole
conduct, his testimony in court, all bore the hall-
mark of truth; yea, for truth's sake he sacrificed
his last hope of life. Yet perhaps he still hoped
to preserve a certain remnant of honor; or, on
the other hand, perhaps he was really telling the
truth. Such spells of sleep-walking are not unknown, nor is it beyond the realm of possibility
that a man who was mortally wounded could
have run as far as Niels must. . . .

The pastor paced quickly to and fro, then

stopped in front of me. "You have now heard my full confession," he said, "and I know that your lips will be forced to pronounce sentence on me and to condemn me, but tell me, what says your heart?"

"My heart," I replied, though I could scarce speak for pity, "my heart bleeds for you, and it would gladly cease beating at this moment could it thus save you from a shameful and terrible death." Our last resort—flight—I dared not even mention.

"You cannot save me," he said hurriedly. "My life is forfeited, my death just, and I shall serve as a terrible warning to succeeding generations. . . . But promise that you will not abandon my poor daughter. . . . I had hoped, once, to give her to you in marriage." At this the tears welled up in his eyes, but he mastered his emotion, and continued, "That hope I have myself destroyed, for you cannot wed the daughter of a malefactor! But promise me that you will take care of her as a second father."

Mournfully I gave him my hand.

"I presume you have not heard from my son of late?" the pastor continued when we had both recovered our composure. "I hope that he may remain in ignorance of this misery until it is all over, for I do not think I could bear to see him."

[54]

He buried his face in his hands, turned and rested his forehead against the wall, and sobbed like a child. It was some time before he was able to speak.

"Now, my friend, leave me—and let us not see each other again until we meet in the house of stern justice. And then—give me one last token of your friendship—let my sentence be pronounced soon, to-morrow if possible, for verily I long for death. I hope that through the grace and the infinite mercy of Christ it will mean but the beginning of a happier life than this, which is now one long night of anguish and terror. Farewell, my kind and sympathetic judge, let me be brought before you to-morrow. And send at once for my friend Pastor Jens in Aalsö, for I want him to minister the last sacrament to me. Farewell, God bless you and preserve you." He averted his face, but stretched forth his hand to me. I stumbled out of the prison, scarce knowing what I did.

I should perhaps have ridden home without speaking to the daughter, had she not been awaiting me outside the prison wall. She must have read the death sentence in my face, for she paled and seized my arm. She looked at me imploringly, as if begging for her own life, but could not ask—or dared not.

"Fly, fly—save your father!" was all that I could say. I threw myself on my horse, and was home before I knew it. To-morrow, then . . .

The sentence has been pronounced, and the guilty man heard it with greater fortitude and composure than his judge possessed. Every one in court, with the exception of his obdurate enemy, showed the most profound sympathy for the condemned, and there were those who whispered that it was a cruel sentence. Yea, cruel it is indeed, for it deprives one man of his life and three others of their happiness and peace of mind forever. May the merciful God judge me more leniently than I, poor sinner, dare judge my fellow-man.

This morning she was here and found me sick in bed. There is no longer any hope. He refuses to escape.

Everything was arranged. The jailor had been won over. A fisherman, a nephew of her mother, had promised to transport them all to Sweden, and had his fishing smack in readiness; but the repentant sinner was not to be persuaded. He will not flee from the sword of righteousness, for he is firmly convinced that through his own death and his Savior's, he will find salvation hereafter . . . She left me as unhappy as she came, but without a single unkind word. God help her, poor child, how will she ever live through the terrible day! And here I lie, sick in body and in soul, unable to give comfort or aid. . . . Her brother has not yet arrived.

Farewell, bride of my heart! Farewell, in this dreary world until we meet again in a better one. . . . May it not be long, for I am wearied of this life and ready for death. Would that I might pass over the border ahead of him whom stern duty forces me to send thither.

"Farewell, my beloved," she said to me. "I leave you without bitterness, for I know that you did only what was your stern duty; but farewell, now, for we two can never meet again." She made the sign of peace over me, and left me.

Merciful God, where will she go? What are her plans? Her brother is not yet here—and to-morrow—at Ravens' Hill . . .*

(At this point the Diary of Judge Erik Sörensen comes to an abrupt end. For the elucidation and exposition of this terrible tragedy we can refer to the written account of the parish pastor at Aalsö, neighbor and friend of the lamented Sören Qvist, which follows below.)

* The knoll on Aalsö meadow just outside of Grennaa, where Pastor Sören Qvist was beheaded, is still called Ravnhöj (Ravens' Hill).

II
The Narrative of the Aalsö Pastor

In the seventeenth year of my pastorate there occurred in this neighborhood an event which filled all men with terror and consternation and reflected shame and disgrace upon the cloth. The pastor at Vejlby, the Reverend Sören Qvist, in a moment of anger killed his coachman and buried him at night in his garden. He was duly tried in the regular court, and, after hearing the damning testimony of several witnesses, confessed the dreadful crime, and was sentenced to be beheaded. This sentence was carried out here in Aalsö meadow in the presence of thousands of spectators.

The condemned man, whose spiritual adviser I had formerly been, requested that I be allowed to visit him in prison and bring him the solace of religion, and I can truthfully say that I never administered the last sacrament to a more repentant and believing Christian. He confessed with deepest contrition that he had hardened his heart and been as a child of wrath, for which God had humbled him deeply and covered him with shame and bowed him with sorrow, that he might again be raised up through Christ. He maintained his composure to the very end, and, standing on the scaffold, spoke to the assembled throng a few words full of power and grace,

[58]

which he had composed during his imprisonment. His homily dealt with anger and its terrible consequences, and was replete with moving reference to himself and the great sin into which his anger had led him. His text he took from the Lamentations of Jeremiah, chapter two, sixth verse, "The Lord hath despised in the indignation of his anger the king and the priest." Upon the conclusion of his moving discourse, he disrobed, tied the cloth before his eyes, and knelt down with folded hands, and as I said the words— "Verily I say unto thee, to-day shalt thou be with me in paradise," the sword fell, and his head was severed from his body.

That which made death most bitter to him was the thought of leaving his two children. The elder, a son, was away at the time of the execution and only arrived in the evening of the day on which his father paid the supreme penalty. The daughter—who, to the still more heartrending woe of herself and her lover, had been affianced to the judge who sentenced him—I took home with me, more dead than alive, after she had said a last farewell to her father. When I returned home from what was the most painful duty of my whole life, I found her fairly composed, and busied with preparing her father's shroud—for it was permitted him to be buried in consecrated ground if the interment were conducted in quiet and privacy. She no longer wept, but neither did she speak. I too was silent, for what indeed was I to say to her, I who was myself bowed down with sorrow and foreboding?

About an hour after my return home, my carriage arrived with the body, and shortly afterwards a young man on horseback dashed into the yard. It was the son, whom we had thought in Copenhagen, but who had been all this time in Lund. He threw himself upon his father's body, and thereafter into his sister's arms; brother and sister clasped each other in a long embrace, but neither of them was able to say a word.

That afternoon a grave was dug hard by the side door of Aalsö church, and there, at midnight, were laid the last mortal remains of the former Vejlby pastor. A stone with a simple cross, which I had earlier prepared for myself, marks the grave, and reminds every church-goer of the sinfulness of man and his ultimate salvation through the Cross of Christ.*

The next morning both the children had disappeared, and no one has since been able to discover any trace of them. God alone knows in what secluded corner they have hidden themselves from the world.

* This marker is still standing in the Aalsö churchyard.

The county judge continues to ail and is not expected to live. I myself am sore afflicted by sorrow and anguish, and I feel that death would be the greatest boon to all of us together. We are in the hands of God. May he suffer us to be governed by His wisdom and His mercy.

Lord, how inscrutable are Thy ways!

In the thirty-eighth year of my pastorate, and just twenty-one years after my brother pastor, the Reverend Sören Qvist of Vejlby, was sentenced to death and beheaded for the murder of one of his servants, it happened that a beggar came to my door. He was an elderly man with grizzled hair, and walked with the aid of a crutch. None of the maids were present at the time, so I went out into the kitchen myself to give him a bite to eat, and, while he was munching his bread, I asked him whence he came. He sighed, and replied, "From nowhere."

I then asked him his name. He looked timidly around, and said, "They used to call me Niels Bruus."

I felt a cold shiver run down my spine, and said to him, "That is an ugly name; a fellow of that name was murdered here about a score of years ago."

He sighed even more deeply, as he muttered,

[61]

"I ought to have died then; it has gone badly
with me ever since I left this country."

I could feel my hair stand on end, and I shook
with terror; for now it seemed to me that I recognized him, and further, it was as if I saw standing before me the living image of Morten Bruus
whom I had buried three years earlier. I started
back and made the sign of the cross, for I thought
that this must be a ghost.

My visitor seated himself heavily on the edge
of the fire-place, and said, "Alack-a-day, parson,
I hear my brother Morten is dead. I went to
the farm at Ingvorstrup, but the new owner
didn't know me and drove me away. . . . Is my
old master, the Vejlby parson, still alive?"

Then suddenly the scales fell from my eyes,
and I understood the meaning of this whole miserable affair; but I was so profoundly shocked
that I quite lost the power of speech for several
minutes.

"Heigh-ho," he was saying, as he greedily ate
his bread, "it was all Morten's fault. But did
any harm befall the old parson?"

"Niels, Niels," I cried, full of horror and
loathing, "you have a bloody crime on your conscience. On your account an innocent man lost
his life at the hands of the executioner."

The beggar started back so that he almost
fell into the fire; the bread dropped from his

hands, and his crutch rattled to the floor. "God forgive you, Morten," he groaned, "God forgive you and me, but it was none of my doing. . . . But tell me," he looked at me appealingly, "it's not true? You're only trying to scare me. I have come here from far on the other side of Hamburg, and not a word of this have I heard on the way. No one has known me, except you, parson, but when I passed through Vejlby I asked if the pastor was still alive, and they said Yes."

"That is the new pastor," I told him, "not he whom you and your wicked brother did to death."

At this the poor fellow began to wring his hands and moan and whimper with such evident sincerity that I could clearly see that he had been but a blind tool in the hands of the devil. He even aroused my pity, and I invited him into my study, where I spoke to him a few words of comfort until he was somewhat quieted, and was able to tell me, brokenly, the whole story of their hellish machinations.

The brother Morten—a man of Belial—had conceived a deadly hatred of Pastor Sören Qvist at Vejlby from the day that the pastor had refused him his daughter in marriage. When therefore the pastor rid himself of his coachman, Morten told his brother Niels to seek the position. "And have a care now," he told Niels, "when the chance comes we'll play a trick on the black man, and you shan't be the loser by it." Niels, who was rough and stubborn by nature and was egged on by Morten, was soon quarrelling with his master, and the first time the pastor struck him he hurried over to tell his brother at Ingvorstrup.

"Just let him strike you once more," Morten said, "and he shall pay dear for it. If he does, you come to me and tell me at once."

It was shortly after this conversation that Niels picked a quarrel with the pastor out in the garden, and when the pastor had felled him with a blow from the spade, he ran without delay to Ingvorstrup. The brothers met outside the farmhouse, and Niels told Morten what had just happened in the parsonage garden. "Did any one see you on your way over here?" Morten asked him. Niels thought not. "Then," said Morten, "we will give the parson a fright that he won't recover from for a fortnight."

Morten then led Niels by a secluded way to the farmhouse and concealed him there until night. As soon as every one was in bed, the brothers stole forth to a corner in the meadow where, two days earlier, they had buried the body of a youth about the age, size, and general appearance of Niels. (He had worked at Ingvorstrup, and hanged himself in his room, some said in desperation over Bruus's tyranny; others, in grief over an unhappy love affair.) This body the brothers now dug up, despite the protest of Niels, and carried back to the farmhouse which was nearby. Then Niels was compelled to take off all his clothes, and the dead body was dressed in them, piece for piece, even to Niels's earring. When this work was completed, Morten gave the corpse a blow on the face with a heavy spade, and one over the temple, and then threw the body into a sack until the following evening, when they carried it into the woods just outside the parsonage at Vejlby.

Time and again, Niels assured me, he asked his brother what all this ado was about, but the latter always replied, "That is none of your affair; you leave all that to me." Now when they were come to the woods, Morten said to him:

"Run over and fetch me one of the parson's gowns—try to find the long green robe I have seen him go around with in the morning."

"I dare not," Niels replied, "his clothes are all hanging in his bedroom."

"Then I dare," said Morten, "and I will do without you. Now you go away at once, and never show your face here again." He drew a bag from his pocket. "Here is a purse with a hundred dollars; that ought to last you until you get to the South—but remember—far away—

where no one will know you or recognize you. Take another name, and never set foot on Danish soil again. Travel by night, and hide in the forests by day. Here is a bag with food enough for you until you get out of the Kingdom. . . . Now don't come back if you value your life."

Niels, who was accustomed to obeying his brother, did as he was told, and there the brothers parted, nor did they ever see each other again. Niels had suffered much in foreign lands. In Germany he was conscripted for the army and served in many campaigns in which he lost his health. Poor, weak, and miserable, he resolved to revisit his birthplace before he died, and after encountering much hardship and suffering he had managed to make his way back to this neighborhood.

Such, in brief, was the story which this unhappy wretch told me, and I was forced to accept its veracity. Thus it was revealed to me that my unfortunate brother pastor had fallen as a sacrifice to the infamous villainy of his mortal enemy, to the delusion of his judge and the witnesses, and to his own too ready self-deception. What, indeed, is man that he dare set himself up to judge his fellow-men! Who dares say to his brother, "Thou art deserving of death!" Judge not, that ye be not judged. Vengeance is mine, I will repay, saith the Lord. Only He who gives life can take it away. And may He compensate you for the bitter martyrdom which you suffered here with the gift of everlasting life!

I did not feel disposed to surrender this broken and repentant sinner to the law, all the less as the judge, Erik Sörensen, was still living, and it would have been cruel to let him know of his terrible mistake, before he left this world for one where all things are to be revealed. Instead, I strove to give the returned prodigal the solace of religion, and exhorted him by all that was sacred to conceal his real name and the real story of the Vejlby crime from every one. On this condition I promised him a refuge and care at the home of my brother, who lives far away from here.

The next day was a Sunday. When I returned home late that evening from my parish of ease, I found that my beggar had gone, and before the evening of the following day his story was known all over the neighborhood. Driven by his uneasy conscience, he had hurried over to Rosmus and there revealed himself as the real Niels Bruus before the judge and all his household. The judge was so deeply affected that he suffered a stroke and died before the week was out. And on Tuesday morning they found Niels Bruus lying dead outside the door of Aalsö church, across the grave of the sainted Sören Qvist.

MEÏR ARON GOLDSCHMIDT

AVROHMCHE NIGHTINGALE

Meïr Aron Goldschmidt (1819–1887) was a member of a Jewish merchant family. He was brought up in Copenhagen, in the home of an uncle who was an orthodox Jew, and the prayers and ceremonies in which he was taught to take part made a profound appeal to the boy's imagination. They were destined to appear later in his works.

First, however, Goldschmidt entered upon a journalistic career. He founded and edited the weekly *Korsaren* (The Corsair) in which he tried to introduce some of the great international ideas that later inspired his younger compatriot, Georg Brandes; but, unlike Brandes, he was much given to personalities, with the result that he spent much of his time in jail or defending himself against suits for libel.

While still engaged in editorial work, Goldschmidt wrote his novel *The Jew,* in which he espoused the cause of his own people with an impassioned plea for justice. The Jews in Denmark were still discriminated against in many ways; it was only a few weeks before Goldschmidt's birth that the last persecution took place. His shorter stories, *Avrohmche Nightingale, Maser,* and others, are charming and sympathetic but non-polemical pictures of life in the Jewish communities. In the popular novel, *The Raven,* the Jewish element is less marked.

Goldschmidt was a transition type, midway between Romanticism and Realism. Nevertheless he may be called the first modern novelist of Denmark, the precursor of that brilliant group in which J. P. Jacobsen was the first.

Meïr Aron Goldschmidt

AVROHMCHE NIGHTINGALE

THIS is a story about a poor old Jew who hanged himself for love, was cut down, and decided to hang on anyway.

Since it is only fair to tell such a story in detail and to start at the beginning, it would be well to say a few words concerning Leizer Suss.

Probably there are not many people who remember Leizer Suss, partly because he died many years ago, and partly because he was not officially known by the name of Suss. He was called Lazarus, which is the same as Leizer. Either he must have inherited the name of Suss or obtained it by chance; for it means a horse, and he was by no means what one might call stupid. In the congregation he was respected for his piety, or rather his orthodox observance of all ceremonies. In consideration of this as well as of his poverty, he had been given the duties of a *schauchet,* that is a butcher and dealer in meat which the congregation could eat with all assurance of its orthodox preparation.

Besides this, there is not much to be said about

him. He died almost unnoticed, leaving an
elderly widow and six children—one daughter
and five sons. According to the Jewish law, the
latter had been educated until their thirteenth
year, after which they supported themselves as
apprentices in various business houses, one in
Altona, the others in Copenhagen.

Years passed, and the family lived happily,
according to the Latin rule: *Bene vixit qui bene
latuit*—he lives well who lives unnoticed. The
mother was aging, being about sixty years old,
but healthy, active, and a trifle domineering.
The daughter, Gittë, at this time nearing the
forties, was still unmarried, either because she
was poor and the daughter of a *schauchet* (de-
fects which her beautiful brown eyes could not
offset) or because she was unable to look after
her own interests. There were probably various
reasons which, grouped together, were called the
will of God. Her brothers tried to make up
for her loss through placid kindness, gifts, and
occasional jokes. They were hard working and
thrifty. Thus their earnings and consequently
their contributions to the support of their mother
and sister increased yearly. The four sons who
lived in Copenhagen met in their mother's house
every Friday evening just as regularly and un-
failingly as she lighted and blessed the Sabbath
candles.

Besides the slowly and modestly increasing prosperity, one more change had come into the family after the father's death; the brothers had slightly altered their last name. Michael, the oldest son who was living in Altona, had introduced this alteration. He was to be made a partner in the "House"—a haberdashery store —and one day the owner, whose name was also Lazarus, said to him, "Your name is Lazarus. Well, that is a good name—it is not for me to deny it. But one can get too much of a good thing. Lazarus and Lazarus—say what you like, that does not look right on a sign."

"But Lazarus and Co.—" said the future partner modestly.

"Lazarus and Co.? And if somebody asks, who is the Co.?—Lazarus!—Turn it as you like: Lazarus and Lazarus!"

"Well, but—" said Michael, and stopped here without courage to express his thought, "Then perhaps you do not want me for a partner?"

After a slight pause the owner continued, "Tell me, had not your lamented father another name than Leizer?"

Michael blushed and did not answer.

"Of course it is between us, and that is not going to disturb your lamented father in his grave. But wasn't he sometimes called Leizer Suss?"

[73]

"That may well be," answered Michael.

"Well, there you are! Who says you are to keep every letter of your father's name, especially when he never bore it willingly! We shall change the *u* to an *a*. Lazarus and Sass—that isn't bad! That sounds nice!"

Thus the matter was decided, and as Michael, the head of the family, called himself Sass, one after the other of his brothers and, finally, his mother adopted the name. At first they did so with some apprehension, but as nobody objected, they made no further ceremony about it. It is possible or even probable that the congregation joked a little about the change; but as above said, no one objected.

The only person who did not like the new name was Avrohmche Nightingale. From his earliest youth he had been a friend of the family. He appeared at the Friday evening meetings as regularly as any of the sons. He had seen all of them grow up—he was eight years older than the oldest son—he had played with them, shared sorrow and joy with them. Once the possibility of his marrying Gittë had been considered, but it had passed away without causing any disturbance. Now, when along with the new name appeared several new pieces of furniture and a certain new atmosphere fraught with greater pretensions, he had a vague, uncertain sense of losing his hold. It was as if he did not "belong" as completely as formerly, as if his humble trade were noticed more than before. But nothing was tangible; it was only an indefinite perception which appeared one moment and vanished the next. Still this was why he did not like the name of Sass, but he took good care not to say so.

Here the reader will ask, "But what was his humble trade?" Permit me to lead up to this information by describing the circumstances that decided his profession for him.

His father was called in the congregation Reb Schaie, with the surname of Pollok. He was one of the last men here with a long beard, a caftan, and a fur cap. Although his appearance thus reminded one of a "Polish vagabond," he was an intelligent and active member of society, and carried on a rather extensive business in fur and hides. He kept accounts—of which most business people in those days had a very incomplete knowledge—and was altogether a most exact, serious, and severe man. Of course he wanted his son to take up his business. But his Abraham (Avrohom, diminutive Avrohmche) developed a steadily increasing passion for music and singing. Not only did he insist on hearing good music as often as the chance offered itself, but once in a while he would give vent to utter-

[75]

ances which indicated his wish, or rather enthusiastic hope, to perform in public some day—to go on the stage. For a time his father treated this as childishness, as a dream that would vanish when once he was working in the business. Contrary to his custom, he would even joke about the matter, and say with obvious sarcasm, "Avrohmche may still become a *hrasan*" (cantor in the synagogue). But one evening he happened to enter his son's attic room. There he came upon Avrohmche dressed in tights, with a feathered cap on his head, and singing a bravura to which the old music teacher Leibche Schwein, also called Levin Snus, played the accompaniment on his guitar. Reb Schaie chased Leibche Schwein down the stairs, and said to Avrohmche, "Knitted underwear and a feathered cap! Why not the Grand Cross of Dannebrog? That my eyes have to see such a *meschuggas!* Do you realize how mad you are? I shall say only one word to you —listen: Those of the audience who will not hiss you for your long nose and your crooked mouth—do you know why they will hiss you?"— "No, Father."—"For your crooked legs."

These cruel but not quite unfair words destroyed an ideal, a hope, a goal in the heart of Avrohmche. He was only nineteen years old, but from this moment he was no longer young. He did not show his desperation. He complained to nobody. A spring had been broken in his soul, and it was as if even the memory of this spring had vanished. But at the same time he had lost a part of life itself. However, one deep and still passion remained—the passion for music. As his father from now on gave him a still smaller allowance than formerly, to prevent him from engaging a music teacher, the idea occurred to him to rent a box in the theater and sell the tickets, thereby being enabled to get in for nothing himself. For some time this worked very well; but just as a plant needs a certain degree of warmth in order to blossom and bear fruit, so any business undertaking, no matter how modest, needs a certain amount of time and care. Not all theater tickets sell like hot cakes at all times. One must be enterprising. There are competitors, chances, conjunctures to be met, and Avrohmche was often cruelly torn between his duties to his father's business and his own. The result was that he neglected both. Without knowing the true reason, his father found more and more cause to be displeased with him, but finally the whole matter came to light. Avrohmche had contracted debts which amounted to much more than a single theater subscription would have cost, and his creditors turned to his father. Reb Schaie paid the debts, gave Avrohmche a sum of money, and said in a low voice

[77]

in which the German-Hebrew with its mysterious, execrating timbre had a power that could not be expressed in Danish, "Leave my house! Your theater madness will some day make you look for a nail to hang yourself on! You are useless and good for nothing on this earth! Out with you!"

At this time Leizer Suss and his wife turned out to be Avrohmche's best and perhaps only friends. The occasion made Leizer Suss do something very remarkable for him: He went straight to Reb Schaie to remonstrate with him about his harshness to his son and to bring about a reconciliation; but he returned very crestfallen and never mentioned what had happened. Then he said to Avrohmche, "You are not going to suffer want so long as I have a piece of meat." He and his wife both did what they could to help the young man plan for the future. As there was no hope of his conquering his passion, it was deemed best for him to devote his life to the theater—not to the stage itself, but to the renting of several boxes. His experience and some perseverance would enable him to earn his living —to cut the matter short, he became a ticket speculator. Now it is out, and after this introduction it does not seem so very bad, and will not lessen the reader's sympathy for Avrohmche Nightingale.

But you will ask, "Whence came the surname of Nightingale?" That was given him because of his unfortunate attempt to sing. The Jews have a remarkable talent for a particular kind of ironical surnames, and Mrs. Sass sometimes used the name with a certain malice which did not indicate any ill will, but only showed that her friendship had not made her blind to her protégé's shortcomings.

Leizer Suss died, and was followed shortly after by Reb Schaie, who left a small fortune to his son. The inheritance was smaller than expected, but still sufficient to have enabled Avrohmche with his modest wants to retire from business and live on his income. But art, even in the farthest corner of its court, has a fascination which few that have ever felt it can resist; and besides it is always hard for a man to give up his activity and his habits. Even the game of a ticket speculator has its emotions. There come triumphs which, although small, gladden his heart; on some evenings he rises to a certain importance, takes part in the life which pulsates so strongly on the stage, reflects in his face the fire of the drama. He could not find openings for other work, or perhaps had neither the wish nor the strength to strike a new path. So Avrohmche Nightingale remained a ticket speculator.

Perhaps at one moment he could have given

up his profession. Shortly after his father's death, he thought it his duty to show his gratitude toward the Suss family by offering Gittë his hand and his inheritance. But Gittë refused him, and her mother did not try to influence her, perhaps because she still had other hopes for her daughter. Proposal and refusal were exchanged in all friendliness, and Avrohmche's relations with the family remained the same.

He lived in Pilestraede, where he had rented a room on the fourth floor of a house across the yard, close to the workshop of a carpenter. This gave his clothes a faint but persistent smell of shavings which made his competitors call his box the coffin. Occasionally he retorted wittily and maliciously, but preferred to mumble his pertinent remarks quietly to himself with a faint smile, instead of uttering them aloud. He was satisfied with the consciousness that he could retaliate if he wished. As an orthodox Jew and a man who had become a ticket speculator from necessity and not from choice, he felt an inner dignity which raised him above all criticism and even above his very profession.

Whoever met him at this point of his life— about his fiftieth year—saw a rather round-shouldered man, pale, with a gentle, fixed smile; with his hands crossed and hidden in his sleeves; with a curious little motion of his head to one side, as if continually and secretly beating time; while a wink or a twisting of his eyelids kept time with his nodding. He wore a long frock coat in summer and an equally long heavy overcoat in winter. People would have thought that the man's destiny was completed, that he was quietly and peacefully covering the longer or shorter distance to his grave.

Not at all! The crisis in Avromche's life was yet to come and was brought about by one single thoughtless word, or rather the thoughtless use of one single word: Suss.

One evening when he arrived at the Sass home, the door was opened by a strange servant girl. Seeing her face he understood at once that the family had changed servants, and in the same instant the old grudge against the name of Sass, with which he could never become familiar, gave him the malicious idea to ask, "Is Mrs. Suss at home?" The word slipped out of his mouth almost without his knowledge. He did not really mean to tell the maid that her mistress should rightfully be called Suss. Perhaps he hardly wanted her to hear the word; yet in that moment of deviltry he needed a confidant, just as King Midas's barber had to betray the secret of his donkey-eared master to somebody, even if only to a little tuft of grass in the field. He rejoiced in pronouncing the word, thus giving vent to his feelings. But the next moment, when the girl answered quietly, "Yes, Mrs. Sass is at home," he regretted it, partly because he felt the answer as a well merited rebuke, and partly because he was afraid that the girl would report his remark to her mistress. But now it was too late. It would make matters worse to ask the maid to keep still, and moreover he had no time. The next moment he was shown into the living-room.

During the whole evening and the following days he was miserable. He said to himself, "Next time I go there I know how I shall be received. Mrs. Sass will pretend not to see me, and should I sneeze she will ask, 'Who is that? Oh, it's Pollok'—for she will not say Avrohmche. And if in the course of the evening she cuts an orange, she will pass the pieces round the other way, so that there will be nothing left when my turn comes. What do I care for the orange? But the expression of her face! The airs she will give herself! My insides shake with fright. That is the way she will treat me for a week or ten days, or perhaps longer, until a good play comes along, and I ask her to go. Then she may say, 'Well, I think Mrs. Suss might just as well go to the theater for once!' And she will give me a look that will prick my heart like two needles! That is what I get for my cursed talk!"

He did not dare to go to his friends, and yet did not dare to stay away. At last he had to go. He was received in the same natural, almost indifferent way as usual, and thought at first that it was the calm before the storm, staged purposely by the family so as to heighten the effect of the sudden and crushing thunderbolt. But it was soon beyond doubt that the barometer indicated fair weather, and he felt immensely relieved and grateful to Heaven as well as to the maid who had evidently kept quiet. One evening he found some pretext for going there, and brought a penny Christmas cake as a present for the maid. In those days maids and Christmas cakes were probably better than they are now, for she accepted the gift with thanks. Later, when she had to light him downstairs and open the street door for him, she thanked him again.

"You are very welcome," said Avrohmche; "you are a good girl. I am not going to tell you why you are a good girl, but you are. What is your name?"

"Emily."

"Emily! That is a nice name. How old are you?"

"Nineteen."

"Nineteen," said Avrohmche, for the first time looking straight into her pretty and fresh young face. He added naïvely, "You look like a good

[83]

girl, too. Where is your home? Here in Copenhagen?"

"No, Sir, I am from Nakskov."

"From Nakskov? What was your father's business?"

"He is a currier."

"He is still living? Why did you not stay at home?"

"Father married again, and my stepmother wanted me to leave."

"Poor girl! You are a good girl—keep on being good!"

"Yes, Sir," she answered; but it is doubtful whether both meant the same thing. Avromche meant that she should keep on being silent about the word Suss.

Without quite being able to account for it, Avrohmche felt that evening and the following days that something unusual had happened. To be sure, he had been relieved of a great worry and danger; but it was not that alone. Although the conversation with the maid had been most insignificant, yet it was a quite new experience in his life. When did he converse with anybody except about tickets or the commonplace trivialities that were discussed in the Sass home? When did he ask an interested question, and when did the answer awaken such a gentle joy in his mind as these simple remarks from a girl who was content and glad by virtue of her youth? There comes a time in the life of every man when youth acquires a power over him of which he had no idea during his own youth. But this power was felt so much more strongly by Avrohmche because ordinarily nobody looked at him or spoke to him in such a friendly way, least of all any one as pretty as this girl. A ray of joy shone into the soul of the old man, as if in some strange way he had met a sister whom he did not dare acknowledge, and also did not want to acknowledge; for it was far from any thought of his that there might be a more intimate or even cordial relation between him and a Gentile servant girl.

And yet it was a new joy to him every time the girl lighted him downstairs, and they exchanged a few words which always were almost identically the same as on the first evening. As he only wanted to hear her voice and occasionally glance at her fresh face, it hardly mattered to him what he asked her and what she answered, and he did not realize that he was making himself ridiculous by always repeating the same words—"You are from Nakskov?"—"Yes."— "And your father is a currier?"—"Yes."—"And your stepmother does not want you at home?"— "No."—"You are a good girl. Good-night."— And her clear, laughing voice, returning his good-night, kept ringing in his ears and made him very happy.

Something had entered his ordinary prosaic life, something to think of and long for, and this made him appear younger. He carried himself straighter. He met people with greater confidence and no longer displayed the bad temper which had come over him in his later years and which often had made him lose customers. He bought a new coat; and although he had every reason to do so (the old one was very shabby) this created quite a sensation among his business associates as well as in Kompagnistraede, where Mrs. Sass lived. "What has come over Nightingale?" people asked. If any one else, even a man in his nineties, had changed this way, one would have said, at least jokingly, "He is in love, he is courting somebody." But nobody thought of making such a joke about Avrohmche, although this was actually the case; and Avrohmche himself did not have the faintest suspicion of the truth. For the first time in his life he enjoyed living. For the first time since his early youth he felt a longing which at the same time gave him happiness. The spring which his father had broken had in its own strange way regained its resilience. This had happened so gently and slowly, with such calmness and innocence, that he himself did not notice it except for his general feeling of joy. Perhaps this is the way the forest feels on a spring-like sunny day in November.

That winter "Svend Dyring's House" *—made its first appearance, and called forth not only great applause but also strong emotion, especially from the fair sex in the audience. It was said that several ladies had fainted from excitement. The following Friday evening the Sass brothers, who had all seen the play, expressed their delight with it or their approval of the public opinion; but all agreed that Mrs. Sass ought not to see it, the emotion would be too much for her. Avrohmche took a decidedly impartial stand. The play filled the boxes to overflowing—so far so good. But on the other hand it did not appeal to his ear because it was not an opera, and the music in it was not to his taste. His heart was just then filled with admiration for "Massaniello" which was given during the same season, and even more for the "Slumber Aria"; and he considered the general enthusiasm for "Svend Dyring's House" a passing fad. Yet he wished Mrs. Sass to go and see it from his box and share the delight of her sons. Now more than ever he wanted to give pleasure to this family, and

* A romantic drama by Henrik Hertz, based on the old folk-song motif of the dead mother who visits her neglected children.

[87]

for the moment make himself a man of importance by giving tickets to Mrs. Sass and her daughter and escorting them to and from the theater. For these reasons he protested with unusual energy against the brothers' assertion that their mother would not be able to stand an emotional scene.

"Stand it?" he said, "what is there to stand? What reason is there to faint? I do not see it. A woman next to my box fainted, to be sure. But why did she faint? Because she was a fat brewer woman, and Henriksen had packed the box too full. Henriksen is a *Retseiach*.* But am I going to pack my box too full when I am inviting a good friend, and will Mrs. Sass not get a good seat in the first row and without any crowding from the front or the back or the sides? Stand it?—Nonsense!"

But one of the sons insisted that the plot of the drama justified their fear. He quoted not incorrectly:

> *"Every mother full well will know*
> *What milk in my breasts to thee can flow."*

"How can mother stand that?" he added.

"Why not?" cried Avrohmche. "Does anybody have to be a woman to understand that?

* An inconsiderate brute.

[88]

Am I a woman, or don't I know that a dead and buried mother who is nothing but a ghost has no milk in her breasts? If I know it, your mother knows it too, and is not going to faint over it."

Another son said gently and gravely, "Mother will think of our lamented father, *olov ha scholaum*.* When the dead woman goes away, and Dyring stretches his hands out to her and asks her to stay, Mother will think of our lamented father in his shroud."

"The Lord forbid!" cried Avrohmche. "I would not have that happen to save my soul! But is not your mother an intelligent woman? Will she not be sensible and say to herself: One of those women will have to go away, or the man has two wives, and who is to go? Who else than she who is dead and buried?"

Perhaps Avrohmche's eloquence would have had no effect if the sons had not themselves chosen an argument which resulted in the opposite of what they had expected; for it is a well known fact that women enjoy emotion, although they do not admit it openly. Mrs. Sass said with dignity, "I shall not think of your lamented father, *olov ha scholaum*. Why should I? A man's wife has died and comes back—what is that to me? I am going."

* Peace be with him.

During this discussion the servant girl had come and gone, and as she had never been inside a theater, her ideas about plays in general and "Svend Dyring's House" in particular were even hazier than those of the ordinary country girl. If possible, the mysterious repulsion and vast fascination of the play were increased when Mrs. Sass came home accompanied by Gittë and Avrohmche, and was received by all the sons as if returning from a journey. As soon as she entered, she cried proudly, "Did I faint? Was I sick? You tell them, Gittë. I did not even weep—what is there to weep about? But for the sake of appearances I wiped my eyes and blew my nose when the others wept. It certainly was fine—But wasn't she madly in love? Well, I suppose those times were different!— But I did not understand that about the baked apple—" *

"The baked apple?" cried Avrohmche.

"Well, baked or roasted! What is the difference? Doesn't he roast an apple? What becomes of it? That is not explained—"

She realized from the embarrassment on her sons' faces and Avrohmche's twitching mouth that she had made a blunder, but she had no idea

* The hero in "Svend Dyring's House" cuts love runes in an apple. The word *riste* in the combination *riste runer* means to cut. It also means to roast.

what it was, and maternal dignity did not permit her to dwell upon her mistake. She could not in the presence of her children allow her mind to be improved at the cost of her self-esteem. The subject was changed, and the actors, costumes, knights, the wicked Guldborg, and the poor children were discussed.

It seemed to the servant girl that it would be worth years of one's life to see something so wonderful. But how could it be done, how would it be possible to go there? Because Avrohmche Nightingale had given her a Christmas cake it did not at all follow that it was his duty to give her a ticket to the theater. It is true that his portentous secret was in her hands; but she did not even know it. She had not heard, or at least not understood, the profound difference between Suss and Sass, and even if she had known the secret she would hardly have thought of using it to obtain a ticket. In Avrohmche's mind, however, the feeling of his indebtedness was not only unimpaired, but had even grown stronger. Unconsciously the silver of gratitude had been interspersed with the gold of love. A few evenings later, when to his great happiness she was again lighting him down stairs, he said, "Do you know what it is to *rist* runes?"

"Yes, it is to cut them."

"Not to roast them, is it? Well, then you

may go and see the play. Will you? Would you like to have a ticket?"

"Oh, Mr. Nightingale!" she exclaimed, and in an unconscious gesture of clasping her hands nearly dropped the candle.

"Well, my name is not really Nightingale. It is Pollok. But never mind. If you want to say Nightingale, do so; but it really is Pollok."

Probably the girl did not notice any improvement by the change, but she said, "I beg your pardon, Mr. Pollok! But oh, how kind you are!"

She said this with such heartiness in her voice and look that, if Avrohmche had been a young man without the fatal resemblance to the description of him given by his father, he would have been justified in believing that also in her case the silver of gratitude was mixed with a more precious metal. Avrohmche did not see himself but only her, and with the words, "We shall see about it," he went away happy.

The matter turned out to be more difficult than he had imagined, but the difficulties gave reason for joyful excitement. There was much to be considered and discussed. Emily could only go out every other Sunday. She hardly knew how to find the theater, still less the box. It was therefore natural that Avrohmche offered to come for her, wait at the door, take her to the theater, and afterwards see her home. If her own mother had lived, she could not have wished a more innocent escort for her daughter, and for Avrohmche it was a late but veritable rendezvous with all its yearning and secrecy— he was at last young and happy!

Emily had dressed as for a dance, in a low-cut jaconet dress, but with a little silk kerchief laid modestly round her neck. She looked so pretty and almost ladylike that Avrohmche was quite proud to take her to the box. To protect her from too much attention he gave her a seat in the second row. He placed himself behind in the third row and kept bending over her, explaining the proceedings on the stage or preparing her for what was coming. Polite and grateful for his attention, however tiresome it was, she turned toward him as often as possible, whereby the little silk kerchief slipped down unnoticed in the heat of the theater. With the feeling that something was being revealed to his eyes which they had not an honest right to see, Avrohmche gently and conscientiously put the kerchief back in its place every time it fell. This manœuver very soon attracted the attention of a young man in the box next to Emily, whose eyes were not so discreet as Avrohmche's. He thought at first that it was a jealous old husband who had brought his wife to the theater.

Soon, however, he recognized Nightingale, and the matter became quite incomprehensible and interesting to him. It seemed to be a nice coquettish young girl whom the ticket speculator volunteered to shield. After the fall of the curtain he addressed a remark to Emily, and since she did not think it right to reveal her position as a stranger among all these charming people who seemed like a big assembly of friends, she answered pleasantly and gratefully, which, however, was quite misunderstood by the young man. Avrohmche could not forbid her to answer, neither could he give her any advice or hint. At the same time he felt all the pangs of jealousy, whether the young man spoke to her or merely looked at her. He wished for the strength and courage of ten men so as to choke the intruder or at least throw him out.

The curtain was again raised, and the progress of the play affected Avrohmche in a hitherto entirely undreamt of way. A deeply hidden poetic instinct stirred suddenly in his soul, revealing to him that the spirit or mood developing on the stage and taking hold of the audience (we call it romance) was something that he had outgrown long ago or in which, rightly or not, his soul was denied a part, whereas Emily and even the odious young man had the sanction of the world to enjoy the emotion to its full extent. He felt this

with unspeakable anguish, as if hearing his own
death-warrant or being present at his own funeral.   Never had any play impressed him as this
one did.

"All the little pictures turned to the wall—"

The knights and ladies and young lovers suddenly remembered his father's words, and said
to him, "Why will they hiss you? For your
crooked nose and your crooked mouth and your
crooked legs!"   And he saw himself answering
to this description, repulsive and a stranger among
the others, miserably rejected.   But the music,
which he had scorned because it was different
from that of "Massaniello," came upon him now
and took hold of his organism, gave him arti-
ficial youth, tossed him around as if he "belonged," although he knew that he was an out-
cast.

Why should he not be happy? He could
marry the girl. Yes, of course, he could offer
his hand to the currier's daughter! He would
be excommunicated, but within his soul he would
remain a Jew!—And what if they did excom-
municate him! What had his life been but a
cold, clammy fog! After all, whether as a blessing or a curse, this woman was the only ray of
light in his existence—it seemed rank insanity

[95]

to let her be snatched away from him. He did not have to remain in Copenhagen. He could move to the country and live with her in some quiet, hidden, and cheap place. At least he was an honorable man. Could that be said about the cad in the other box? He would be happy, he was bound to be happy! His decision only needed words to be irrevocable—and here the curtain fell.

Where was his real life? In the box with the girl and the tenderness and jealousy called forth by her? Although he was so close to her, he could not find one fitting word to say, but heard with disgust his own voice saying—"Is it all right? Are you having a good time? Do you like it?" Whereas he wanted to say, "Speak to nobody! Look at nobody! Become my wife!"

Or was real life on the stage where the last act was beginning, where he again was suffering on account of his age, again became young, again made his decision? Verily, the tempest had seized Avrohmche Nightingale. Oh, you sympathetic souls, you would have wept to look into him and laughed to look at him.

Stunned by so many emotions, he left the box with Emily after the end of the play, as a ship leaves the stormy sea for the port. But the young man walked close to them, and at the foot of the stairs, when the collision with the audience from the pit caused a confusion in the crowd, he succeeded in pushing Avrohmche aside and offered his arm to Emily. Avrohmche cried out— his words can be explained only by the storm that had just passed over him, or perhaps by a wish to arouse sympathy, securing some rights for himself. He cried, "Stop! Help! He is stealing my wife!" The young man slipped away like an eel. In the same instant several hundred eyes were turned toward the well-known speculator, and in the sudden silence after his words he had in a flash furnished people with a story to be told at the supper-table or elsewhere.

A few moments later they were in the street. Avrohmche crossed the square silently. The moment had come for him to speak, but there were still too many people around them. He wanted to reach Vingaardstraede before he asked her to sign the document to which he had put his seal. But when he was about to speak and turned toward her, he saw that she was crying.

"What is the matter?" he exclaimed in dismay. "Why are you crying?"

"Because you disgraced me by calling me your wife."

He did not understand that every young girl who is publicly and against her will represented as being married may feel this as a disgrace, and that the country girl felt bitterly that she had been the center of a small scandal. He interpreted her words as the declaration that she considered a marriage with him, the Jew, as a disgrace, and in the same moment he had fallen from his own heaven, even though he was still uncured. He said no word, not even good-night when they parted.

Neither did he say good evening to the carpenter's journeyman who as usual came out on the stairs and handed him a small lantern, for according to tradition no one was allowed to carry an uncovered light in or near the workshop. The journeyman lived there and was the night-watchman.

As soon as Avrohmche was in his room he gave vent to his feelings.

*"Ausgefallene Schtrof'! * I* must have sinned in my mother's womb so as to be made not only *meschugge* ** but *meschugge metorf!* *** To call that out to everybody! Where were my senses? Did I ever have any? Am I born blind and deaf and mad? *Schema Jisroel!* That will be the death of me! How can one live after having been such a cursed fool? How can one? *Oi! Oi! Oi!* They all heard it, and they heard still more! To-morrow they will tell

* Punishment from Heaven.
** Crazy.
*** Stark crazy.

[98]

that I have children around here, and how can I prove that it is fiction and lies, that I belied myself? Should I ask her to state—*sau m'hrulle und sau m'hrulle* *—no, that way is still worse than the other—if only she had been willing! But I was willing, I scoundrel, I scoffer of Israel! Can I ever forget? I can *never* forget it!— Avrohmche, Avrohmche, one minute has made you an unhappy man! *Oi! Oi und Weh!*"

On this occasion a strange thing happened. He realized his misfortune, but could not quite understand it. Something in his head snapped whenever he tried fully to see and comprehend the double curse upon his fate. He had disgraced himself before the public and the congregation for the sake of happiness, but this happiness had changed to misery and humiliation. The disgrace remained and became intensified. His mind circled wildly round his dilemma, trying to get at the center of it, but screamed with pain before reaching its goal, and rushed back to the circumference.

All this did not take place in silence. Through the thin wall the journeyman heard him rush back and forth, speak to himself, curse and moan; and having noticed his haggard face on the stairs, the young man came up to his room.

* I am ruined one way as well as the other.

"Are you sick, Mr. Pollok?" he asked, looking in.

Avrohmche grasped his head and said, "Toothache! Yes, toothache! Terrible!"

"Is it a molar?" asked the journeyman and came nearer.

"A molar? It is worse than that! It is a *schikse!*" * answered Avrohmche, finding a certain relief in confiding in another person without betraying himself.

"Then it is a dog-tooth?"

"No, I wouldn't say that. But I feel like a dog myself. I am tormented like a dog, oh! oh!"

"But where does it hurt?" asked the man, holding the lantern up to Avrohmche's face.

"It is rheumatism. I am getting old. I am an old horse and a big ass, I ought to be dragged out to Amager like the other old horses. Well, they are going to drag me out—just wait and see!"

"Well, I suppose you must have it out; but that cannot be done until to-morrow."

"To-morrow! I wish to-morrow would never come!" answered Avrohmche with a shudder.

"Come, come, Mr. Pollok!—Don't you want to take something for it?"

"Take something?—What is there to take?

* Gentile girl.

What do you know about it? A young and good-looking man like you is happy—I mean," he added, getting better hold of himself, "a young man with such good, fine teeth."

"Still I have been through it."

"You have? What did you do? I tell you, you have *not* been through it!"

"Yes, I poured some brandy on the tooth."

"Brandy on the tooth," said Avrohmche slowly. Instinctively he felt the need of warmth and cheer, and the advice seemed good to him. "Where can I get it? have you a little?"

With the quiet satisfaction felt by laymen whose remedy for some ailment is being accepted, the journeyman went to his room and brought back a blue flask and a thick, broadfooted glass.

Taking the glass, Avrohmche wanted to say a Jewish prayer, but there came over him a ghastly feeling of having forfeited the right to do this, of having in thought and intention forsaken his God and his people. In despair, he emptied the glass without further ceremony. After the first shock of the unaccustomed drink, he felt warmed through and through, and said, "That was good just the same!"

"It did not quite get to the tooth," said the journeyman.

Avrohmche answered with a strange laugh, "It did not get to the tooth, and still it got there."

"Well, it does you good anyway," said the man, pouring out a glass for himself and emptying it.

"How could it get to the right tooth?" continued Avrohmche. "If it could get to the right tooth, I should not be here, and you would not be here, and there would be no need of it."

The journeyman did not understand this dark, talmudistic speech and answered simply, "Take one more little drink."

"Well, a very small one."

Avrohmche took another swallow and admitted gratefully that he felt much better now. The journeyman bade him good-night and went away.

But when he had gone, the human sympathy and temporary distraction had also vanished, and the dreadful reality burst forth anew, combining with the drink to lash Avrohmche's consciousness to the fever point. The facts seemed impossible to him, yet he could not deny them. It was as if there were some creature in the room with him which now hid in a corner, now would jump at him, seize his throat, throw him down. Meanwhile his thoughts and memories chased around as in the wild whirl of madness, and he saw conflicting events in simultaneous action: Emily, gliding away from the square like a shadow; the young man from the box, laughing to his face;

the crowd in the vestibule immeasurably far below him. The air was full of buzzing and laughter, of the ringing music of "Svend Dyring's House" and the rebel scene of "Massaniello"; and in the midst of it all soared his father, pale as death and saying to him, "Your theater madness will some day make you look for a nail to hang yourself on! You are useless and good for nothing on this earth!"—When this horror vanished for a moment, the horror of the morrow rushed out of the corner in the shape of another ghost.

It was unbearable; still he could not shake it off. He could not even utter a shriek, but remained groping in the middle of the darkened room as in a nightmare, with only one vague longing—to slip away from life which held no refuge for him.

What awakens the thought of suicide? The doctors call it a disease, a sort of insanity. But when and how is the harmony of our mysterious secret organism transformed into the discord which reveals insanity and gives us the impulse? And how can insanity make a man hang himself, an undertaking which in the eyes of normal people is difficult and requires a good deal of intelligence? We have some kind of experience in all other ways of suicide. Everybody has sometime in his life cut himself, wounded himself with a pointed instrument, or drunk something nauseating. Those that kill themselves by shooting have previously handled guns or pistols, but no one has had experience in hanging himself on a nail or a hook. And still people do this very thing at the critical moment with an assurance which seems a weird stroke of genius piercing insanity.

How did it occur to Avrohmche to hang himself? He was standing on the brink of insanity, but he had not yet tumbled down. His dead father was pointing to the nail that he was to hang himself on, yet Avrohmche had never taken this for more than a figure of speech. He wanted to have done with life, but had not yet lost the instinct of self-preservation, of love for himself as a living being. A seeming trifle decided his fate. During his terrible delirium he saw something on the wall that had a human shape. It was his old coat hanging on a nail. Suddenly it was as if he had a companion, a fellow-being near him, and he was filled by a great desire to approach this fellow-being. After what seemed an infinitely long time, he managed by exerting his whole strength to take a step toward this friend in need and seize him—only to find that it was a mere empty shell of a man, perhaps of his own father. Through his disappointed or frightened fingers a sensation rose to his brain and completed the madness. With incredible haste and clearness he remembered that the maid had lately stretched a new clothes line outside the window. Then he was certain of having seen a big nail under the ceiling. In an instant he had hauled in the clothes line and had hung himself.

But again he had made more noise than he was aware of, and hardly had he accomplished his deed before the journeyman was in the room and had cut him down.

Thus Avrohmche did not kill himself, but was nevertheless more dead than living. The journeyman called for help, and the patient was taken to the hospital.

In the city the strange rumor about his marriage was spread almost simultaneously with the news that he had been taken to the hospital delirious or insane. The latter news swallowed up the former. When a man is overtaken by a commonplace misfortune he ceases to be interesting. Only the Sass family did not quite feel this way. To be sure, their sympathy with him on account of his illness had a hard struggle with their indignation over his secrecy and slyness in getting married. Still his very marriage called forth the conception of something grandly preposterous and inconceivable. The most reliable information from all around the city threw no light on the subject. At his lodging it was said that he had been out of his head and had tried to commit suicide, but the journeyman as well as his master and the whole family were greatly surprised when the question about his wife came up. In the vestibule of the theater he had been seen and his exclamation heard, but nobody in the crowd had noticed his wife. Even though somebody had seen Emily among other women near him, she was the last person in the world to be taken for his companion through life. Some people said indifferently that it was probably no one else than Gittë Sass whom he had married. When the Sass family tried to identify his wife around town, they were to their great surprise directed to their own home. It did not occur to them that her home really might be said to be in their kitchen, and that a single question to their servant girl would have put them on the trail of the truth.

Meanwhile he who could have given the best information, if he had been so minded, was in the hospital. For some time it was not known whether or not his mind was clear, and therefore no visitors were allowed. He was lying there protected against the world by his very illness and the inviolability of the hospital. When his convalescence began, accompanied by the usual state of happiness, impotence, and renewed life, the previous events stood before his mind without pain, veiled in a strange haze. He realized with delight that he was not married and had not forsaken the congregation. Let whoever wanted to do so come and investigate. Even if he had said so himself, it was nevertheless not true. But why had he said so? Here his head began to swim again. He hoped that Emily would keep silent about his love, as she had kept silent about the word Suss, but still this point worried him the most. He did not know that he had never betrayed the secret of his love to her or anybody else.

By this time Mrs. Sass had had an opportunity to reflect and overcome her first indignation over his slyness. She began to doubt it and consider many possibilities. Even if he had not married, he might still do so. Worse things had been known to happen; there were plenty of widows or elderly maids who might be suggested to him by the Jewish matrimonial agent. People knew very well that he had money. How could she have forgotten it, overlooked it with her eyes wide open? His new coat! If not a sign of his marriage—all things considered that was not likely—it was a sign that he was not averse to change. She did not understand herself. She had only herself to blame if he had married. She would have deserved the annoyance of seeing him and his money annexed by another family, by people who had never been good to him and would not have opened their home to him when his own father had turned against him. But was he really married or not? For the present all depended on this.

At last the moment came to find out. She was sitting at his bedside and asked him—or rather did not ask him but remarked, "Avrohmche, people say that you were taken ill because you have nobody to care for you and are neglecting yourself altogether."

"Who should take care of me?" asked Avrohmche languidly, and purposely with great innocence. But at once he became frightened. She might answer, "Perhaps our servant girl, Emily?" His anxiety made him look so deathly pale and livid that Mrs. Sass, fearing that he was feeling worse, broke off the conversation. But at home she said, "He is no more married than my cat!"

At her next visit she said, "Avrohmche, are you strong enough to discuss your future with me?"

He had no objection to the future, if one would only leave the past alone. So he answered, "The future will be that I shall be buried!"

"Stuff and nonsense! There is nothing the

matter with you. You never looked better than now!"

Avrohmche did not trouble himself about the true meaning of this ambiguous compliment; he was listening as quietly as a mouse.

She continued, "We have spoken of your future before—do you remember? When my lamented husband was living?"

"Gebenscht soll er sein! * If anybody is in *Gan Eiden* ** it is he."

"Please God, yes. Do you know what he would say if he were alive?"

Avrohmche was again overcome by fear. He expected her to say, "My dear Leizer would say that you ought not to make a fool of yourself with our servant girl."—He managed to say, "He would speak gently."

She nodded slowly and significantly as she answered, "Yes, he would speak gently. He would say, Avrohmche, you are too good to go around in the rain and cold every evening, and be taken ill and die in the hospital. You must have somebody to live with you and take care of you and be good to you in your own home. You ought to marry, Avrohmche."

It was coming—now it was only as much as a hair's breadth away from him, and in a second

* May he be blessed.
** Paradise.

the scornful, crushing remark would have reached
him, "You ought to marry our servant girl."
He groaned, "It is all over with me," and closed
his eyes to the lightning.

"Nonsense, Avrohmche! It is never all over.
—Do you believe that my son Isaac is an honest
and honorable and decent and hard-working
man?"

What was that? She was speaking of her
son! Her thoughts were not where he had
feared! He opened his eyes.

"Do you believe that?" she repeated.

"Do I? Indeed I do!"

"And do you believe that he understands his
business?"

"*Kol Iisroel* * ought to have sons like Isaac!
Can I say more?"

"Well, Isaac wants to go into business for himself. You put your little capital into his business, and the Lord will provide for the rest!"

Now Avrohmche understood perfectly. He
realized that he was saved and felt it as a miracle, and in return for the marvelous concealment
of his dissipation he thought it only fair that he
should marry Gittë.

He addressed hurriedly a blessing to the Lord,
and asked almost without thinking, "But what is
Gittë going to say?"

* All Israel.

"Gittë," said Mrs. Sass, "is a sensible girl and past her childhood. And am I not here?"

The next day Gittë came alone.

Without any preamble she said, "Pollok, Mother says that you and I must marry."

Avrohmche answered, "She said the same to me."

She continued, "We are no longer children, Pollok. You would get a poor old maid. Well, you know that. But I must ask you something."

"If I can answer you, go ahead, Gittë."

"You can answer. You are the only one that can and the only one that must. Is it a sin to be fond of a Gentile—I mean really to love, to be in love with a Gentile?"

Avrohmche had thought himself perfectly safe; now the question overwhelmed him so that he nearly fainted. But he managed to collect himself and raise a small barricade. "Sin?" he said. "There are greater sins."

"But suppose I had been in love with a Gentile, what then?"

"You!" cried Avrohmche, and a new thought was born in him. He was a man, the lord and judge of women. But at once he wavered. Was it a trap? Or what kind of a tale was this? He dared say no more.

She did not heed him, but went on, "Of course

it would be a sin against the Lord if I were going to hide something from the husband He is giving me."

She seemed to be in earnest, and the thought took hold of Avrohmche.

"Who is he?" he cried. "What kind of a man is he? Where did you meet him?"

"He was an officer."

"An officer! Soldiers exist because of our sins, and officers because of our great sins! An officer! How did you meet an officer?"

"I don't know, Pollok. I suppose it was *g'sardin.** I was walking in the street, and all at once his eyes were looking into mine. I had never seen him before. It was something quite new. It was as if both of us had been created that very moment."

"One pays no attention to such a person—an officer! One simply walks past him."

"Did I not walk past him? I almost went into the wall of the house to make way for him. I turned into air, I turned into nothing, and I passed him."

"Well; past is past. That was the end of it—wasn't it?"

"No. One day as I was sitting at the window, suddenly he stood in the street, looking up. I

* Decreed by Fate.

[112]

thought I should fall out of the window. I could not help it."

"*Ausgefallene Schtrof'!*" cried Avrohmche with a bitterly humorous pun. "I understand— then you began to meet him in the street."

"Then I began to meet him in the street."

"What did he say?"

"For God's sake, Pollok! How could he have addressed me?—I should have screamed! I should have died! Speak to an officer in the street! I never looked at him any more!"

"Well," said Avrohmche with a faint smile, "if you neither spoke to him nor looked at him—"

"Pollok, I am going to tell the truth. That is why I came. I did not speak to him, but I thought of him, and when I met him I felt that he knew it."

"And you say you did not look at him?"

"I did not look at him."

"*Schkorum,*" * murmured Avrohmche and turned half against the wall.

"I did not look at him, and I stayed at home and never went out alone."

"That is good. Very good."

"But he wrote to me."

"He did not speak, but he wrote?—What am I to hear, Gittë? Why beat about the bush?

* Lies.

[113]

You had much better tell me the whole story straight out."

"But I am telling you that he wrote to me."

"What did he write?"

"He wrote—what does one write to a young girl? He wanted to see me and speak to me; he wanted to meet me."

"That is what they always write. One does not pay any attention."

"One does not pay any attention! Pollok, when you took Mother and me to the theater to see 'Svend Dyring's House' and they began to speak of runes, I understood what runes were; but you did not understand it, Pollok."

"Much she knows about it," murmured Avrohmche to himself. After a short silence he went on. "Runes. In the play she runs after him."

"I did not run after him. How could I? How could I have escaped from Mother and my brothers?"

"That is so. You are a good girl, Gittë. You stayed at home. And then at last it was over, really over?"

"Then one Friday afternoon I received a letter in which he told me that he was going away Sunday morning, and now he had a wish as urgent as that of a dying man; he wished to see me just once, and I was to decide myself what time

[114]

Meïr Aron Goldschmidt

I could come on Saturday evening.—And I
could have gone, for Mother was going to the
theater, and my brothers were not coming home.
And he implored me like a man before his
death!"

"Runes," said Avrohmche, "that *verschwärzte*
writing! Those cursed runes! The Lord curse
him who invented them! *Omein!* *—Well, then
you went?"

"No, for when I was going to write and set
the time and place, it was *Eref,*** and Mother
had lighted the Sabbath candles, and of course
then one is not allowed to write."

"And so you really did not write?" asked
Avrohmche, although he found it very natural.

"I had the pen in my hand; but when I was
going to put it to the paper and for the first time
in my life break the Sabbath, my father arose
before me in his shroud."

"Well?"

"Well. And Saturday evening when I could
write again, it was too late, and it was all over.
And I thanked God."

"When did this happen? How long ago?"

"That was when you proposed to me the first
time, twenty years ago."

"Twenty years!" cried Avrohmche, and sat up

* Amen.
** Sabbath eve.

in bed. "Gittë! In the name of the Almighty God! I have been in love with a *Schikse,* not twenty days ago!"

"You, Pollok?—Poor Avrohmche!"

"Will you pardon me, Gittë?—It was for her sake that I wanted to hang myself—I was mad, raving mad; but that is why I am lying here! But now it is all over, Gittë; will you bear with me and pardon me?"

"Poor Avrohmche, my husband before God! Let us remember the dead and keep together until *Bal Hamoves* * comes!"

————

Some time after, Avrohmche turned up in his old lodgings to move his belongings to another place, which had been prepared for him. He looked just as he had before his great adventure, only paler, but this was rather becoming. The journeyman came to say good-bye, and said to himself that Avrohmche looked as if he had been whitewashed inside, but both men were embarrassed. At last Avrohmche cut the matter short and said, "Well, I was mad, raving mad, and wanted to take my life. You saved me and cut me down—still I hung on! But now I am hanging on to myself in the right way!"

* The Angel of Death.

JENS PETER JACOBSEN

FRU FÖNSS

JENS PETER JACOBSEN (1847–1885) was born in the small town, Thisted, in Jutland, as the son of a merchant in moderate circumstances. His mother instilled into his mind the idea that he was to be a poet, but he was almost equally drawn to the study of botany, which had then just been introduced into the school curriculum. At the University he won a gold medal by his thesis on a certain microscopic marsh plant. Unfortunately, however, in his excursions after specimens—often wading barefoot through the marshes to save shoe-leather—he laid the foundation for the dread disease that rendered his entire productive period a fight against physical handicaps, and ended his life at the age of thirty-eight.

Jacobsen's first story, *Mogens,* created a sensation by the daring originality of the style, which had some of the same verbal quality that had seemed so startling in Hans Christian Andersen. The style in the historical novel, *Marie Grubbe,* for which Jacobsen drew on a store of archaic words and phrases, was even more colorful.

As his most important work Jacobsen regarded the modern novel, *Niels Lyhne,* which is in part autobiographical, and reflects the intellectual currents of his generation. The closing pages in the book, where Niels Lyhne dies faithful to his atheism, were no doubt written by Jacobsen to steel himself for the ordeal of his own approaching death; just as the beautiful letter of Fru Fönss to her children expressed his longing to be remembered. When his fatal illness could no longer be fought down, he went home to his mother in Thisted, where he died as quietly and bravely as he had lived.

Jacobsen's complete works include only the two novels mentioned, a few shorter stories, and a sheaf of exquisite poems.

Jens Peter Jacobsen

FRU FÖNSS

IN the formal garden behind the old palace of the popes in Avignon there stands a bench from which one may look out over the river Rhone, over the flower beds of Durance, over hills and fields, and over a part of the city.

On this bench two Danish women were sitting one October afternoon—a widow, Fru Fönss, and her daughter, Ellinor.

Although they had been several days in Avignon, and had become familiar with the scene before them, they were still wondering that Provence should look like this.

Was it really Provence! A clayey river with patches of boggy sand, long banks of stone-gray gravel, pale brown fields without a blade of grass, pale brown hills, dust-gray roads, and here and there, near the white houses, groups of black trees—absolutely black trees and bushes! Over all this a whitish heaven, trembling with light that made everything paler, dryer, brighter, and still more fatiguing, with not a glimpse of suc-

culent and satiated color anywhere, only fam-
ished, sun-tortured tints! And not a sound in the
air, not a scythe cutting grass, not a cart rumbling along the roads! The city on either side
seemed built up of silence, with all these noon-
hushed streets, and all these deaf-mute houses
with every shutter closed, tightly closed on every
one, houses that could neither hear nor see!

Fru Fönss had only a resigned smile to offer
this lifeless monotony, which made Ellinor plainly
nervous, not irritated and vexed, but whimpering
and tired, as from a day-long drizzle when lugubrious thoughts pour down with the rain; or
from the stupidly condoling ticks of a clock when
one is bored; or from the flowers on the wall-
paper when the same chain of dreams reel around
in one's brain against one's will, and link and
break and link again ad nauseam. It sapped
her physical strength, this landscape, and almost
made her faint. For to-day the view conspired
with reminiscences of a hope that had burst, and
with sweet, delicious dreams which now were
sickening and loathsome dreams that made her
blush with shame, but which nevertheless she
could not forget. Why should the landscape
here arouse her memories, when the shock had
come far from here, in homely environments,
under light-green beeches near the glittering
Sound? Yet every pale-brown hill whispered her

secret, and every green-shuttered house stood there and kept silent about her.

It was the old grief of young hearts that had befallen her. She had loved a man and had believed in him, but he had suddenly chosen another. Why? What had she done to him? How had she changed? Was she not the same as she had been? The old eternal questions over again! She had not said a word to her mother, but the mother had divined it all and had been very solicitous about her. Ellinor could have screamed under this solicitude which knew and yet was not supposed to know. This, too, the mother had understood, and so they had gone abroad. The purpose of the whole journey was only to make her forget.

Fru Fönss did not have to make her daughter uneasy by watching her face in order to read her thoughts. She need but keep an eye on the nervous little hand that reached out along the bench-bars with listless despair, shifting every moment, like a feverish patient tossing about in bed. If she only looked at that hand, she knew how wearily the young eyes gazed into space, how poignantly the delicate face trembled at every breath, how pale it was in its agony, and how sickly blue the veins appeared beneath the transparent skin of her temples.

She grieved so for her little girl; and she

yearned to have the child lean against her so that she might breathe down over her all the comforting words she could think of. But she had the belief that there are sorrows which must die in secret and must not be allowed to cry out in words, lest some day under new conditions when all would change to joy and happiness these same words may become burdensome and binding; because the one who uttered them would hear them whispered in another's mind and fancy them looked at and turned over in another's thought.

Moreover, she feared to harm her daughter by paving the way to her confidence. She would not have Ellinor blush before her. No matter now much it might give relief, she would not aid her in humiliating herself by throwing open the most secret chambers of her soul to another's eye. On the contrary, although it was harder for both to bear, she was pleased to find in her young daughter a certain sound stubbornness, akin to the dignity of spirit she herself possessed.

Once upon a time, many years ago, when she herself was such a young girl of eighteen, she too had loved with all her soul, with every nerve in her body, every hope in life, and every thought. But all in vain. He had only had his fidelity to offer and to test out in an endless betrothal; and there were conditions in her home that could wait no longer. Then she had taken the man they had given her, the one who was master of those conditions. They were married, and the children came, Tage, the son who was with her in Avignon, and the daughter who sat beside her. And her marriage had really turned out much better, both brighter and happier, than she had expected. Eight years it lasted; then her husband died. She had mourned him sincerely, for she had learned to feel affection for this refined, thin-blooded nature, who, with tense, egoistic devotion, loved almost morbidly that which by family ties belonged to him, and who cared about nothing in all the world save its consensus, only that, nothing else.

After her husband's death she had lived for her children; but she had not lived in seclusion with them. She had taken part in social life, as was natural for a young and wealthy widow. Her son was now twenty-one; she herself was not many days shy of forty and still beautiful. There was not a gray streak in her massive, dark-blond hair, not a wrinkle to mar her large, dauntless eyes; and her figure was slender in its shapely fullness. Her strong, delicately drawn features were emphasized by the darker and more colorful complexion which the years had given her. But there was a sweetness in the smile on her curved lips, an almost youthful promise in the soft, dewy glow of her brown eyes that made her face gentle again, and kind. Yet there was also the full, somber cheek and the firm chin of the mature woman.

"Here is Tage, I think," remarked Fru Fönss to her daughter, when she heard laughter and a Danish exclamation on the other side of the thick hedge.

Ellinor pulled herself together.

Yes, there they were, Tage and Kastager from Copenhagen, with his sister and daughter. Fru Kastager was ill in bed at the hotel.

Fru Fönss made room for the two women. For a moment the men tried to converse, standing, but soon were enticed by a low gray stone wall that enclosed the place of observation. They sat thus, saying little, for the newcomers were tired after a short railroad trip through rose-blushing Provence.

"Look there!" exclaimed Tage suddenly, and slapped his palm flat against his light trousers.

They looked.

On the brown landscape appeared a dust cloud, over it a cape, and between these a horse became visible.

"It's that Britisher I spoke about, who has just come," said Tage to his mother. He turned to Kastager. "Have you ever seen anybody ride like that? He reminds me of a Gaucho."

"Or Mazeppa," answered Kastager.

The rider vanished.

They rose and started for the hotel.

Fru Fönss and her children had met the Kastagers in Belfort, and since they were taking the same route through the south of France and along the Riviera, they were keeping company for the present. Both families had stopped here in Avignon. Fru Kastager suffered from an old malady, and Ellinor needed rest.

Tage was delighted at this arrangement; for day by day he fell more incurably in love with the pretty Ida Kastager. Fru Fönss was disturbed about it. Although Tage was quite sure of himself and was mature for his age, there was no hurry about an engagement. And then, this Kastager! Ida was a splendid little girl; the mother was a cultured woman of excellent family; and the father was both able and wealthy, but there was a ludicrous air about him; when his name was mentioned, it brought a smile to people's lips or a twinkle in their eye. For he was so fiery and so extremely enthusiastic, so loud and garrulous and open-hearted, that it required much discretion to associate with such an enthusiast. Fru Fönss disliked the idea that people should mention Tage's father-in-law with a twinkle in their eye or a smile on their lips. She therefore treated the family rather coolly, which greatly distressed the ardent Tage.

The next morning Tage and his mother made a visit to the small museum in the city. They found the gate open, but the door to the collection was locked, and ringing the bell proved fruitless. The gate admitted them into a small yard which was surrounded by a newly white-washed archway of short, thick-waisted columns, braced by black iron rods.

They walked around and viewed whatever fragments were displayed along the wall: Roman tombstones, pieces of sarcophagi, a draped headless figure, two vertebrae of a whale, and a row of architectural details.

There were fresh traces of the whitewash brush on the whole collection.

Soon they were back at the starting point again.

Tage climbed the rear stairs to ascertain whether there was anybody in the house, while Fru Fönss strolled back and forth in the archway.

As she approached the gate, there appeared, right before her at the end of the path, a tall, bearded man with a sunburned face. He carried a tourist handbook and seemed to be listening for something, then glanced at her.

At once the Britisher of yesterday came to her mind.

"Pardon me, madam," he said inquiringly, and bowed.

"I am a stranger here," replied Fru Fönss. "There seems to be nobody in charge, but my son ran up to find out . . ."

These words were exchanged in French.

At that moment Tage returned. "I've been all around," he said, "even inside the living-room, but there wasn't even a cat to be seen."

"I hear," remarked the Britisher, this time in Danish, "that I have the pleasure of being among countrymen."

He bowed again and withdrew a few steps, as if to suggest that he had spoken only to let them know that he understood what they were saying. But suddenly he stepped near, with a tense, agitated look in his face, and asked, "Is it possible that you and I, madam, are old acquaintances?"

"Are you Emil Thorbrögger?" she exclaimed, and held out her hand.

He grasped it. "I am," he said joyfully. "And it is really you!"

Tears almost rose to his eyes as he looked at her.

Fru Fönss introduced her son.

Tage, who had never in his life heard of Thorbrögger, thought only of the Gaucho who had

[127]

turned out to be a Dane, and, as there was a pause, and some one had to say something, he could not refrain from breaking the silence. "And I said yesterday you reminded me of a Gaucho!"

Yes, answered Thorbrögger, that was not far from the truth, since he had lived on the prairies of La Plata for twenty-one years, and during all those years had been more on horseback than on his feet.

Had he returned to Europe for good?

Yes, he had sold his ranch and sheep and had come back to look over the Old World, where he belonged, though, frankly, he had often found himself very much bored with roving about just for pleasure.

Perhaps he was homesick for the prairies?

No, he had never pined for any clime or country and fancied that he was only missing his daily work.

Thus they conversed, and at last the custodian came, overheated and out of breath, with heads of lettuce under his arm and fiery red tomatoes in his hand. He opened the little stuffy exhibit of paintings where they received but the vaguest impression of old Vernet's yellow storm clouds and black waters, while they learned far more about each other's life and fate from the time they had parted long ago.

[128]

For it was him she had loved, the time she was bound to another. During the following days, when they were much together, and when the others—mindful that such old friends must have many things to tell each other—often left them alone, in those days they soon realized that, no matter how much time had changed them, their hearts had forgotten nothing.

Perhaps he was the first to grow aware of this, for all the timidity of youth, its romance and plaintive yearnings, overwhelmed him at once; and he suffered thereby. It distressed the mature man thus suddenly to lose the poise and self-reliance he had acquired through life, and he wished his love were moulded otherwise; it should have been more dignified, more composed.

Fru Fönss did not feel younger, but it seemed as though within her soul a dammed up stream of tears had burst open again and had begun to flow. It was so joyful and soothing to weep. She found a treasure in her tears, and felt herself richer and everything else worth more to her—a feeling of youth at last.

One night she sat alone in the hotel. Ellinor had retired early, and Tage had escorted the Kastagers to the theater. She had been sitting there in her tedious chamber and dreaming in the twilight produced by a pair of candles, until her dreams, by a ceaseless coming and going, had reached their vanishing point. She was tired, but with the pleasant, genial fatigue that is diffused through us when happy thoughts begin to slumber in the mind.

She could not sit here idle the whole evening, without so much as a book; and the play would be on for another hour yet. She began to pace up and down the room and stopped before the mirror to smooth her hair.

She might drop into the reading room downstairs and look through the periodicals. At this hour of the evening it was always empty.

She threw a large black lace scarf over her head and went down stairs.

Yes, it was empty.

The small room was packed with furniture and glaringly illuminated by half a dozen broad gas jets. It was hot in there, and the air was dry, almost parching. She pulled the scarf down over her shoulders.

The white pages there on the table, the folders with their large gold letters, the empty velvet chairs, the regular squares of the rug, and the pleated folds of the curtains, all looked so mute in the strong light.

She still dreamed, and dreaming she stood and listened to the long-toned singing of the gas jets.

The heat made her almost dizzy.

Jens Peter Jacobsen

Slowly, to support herself, she reached for a heavy bronze urn that stood on a console by the wall, and grasped its flower-moulded edge.

It was comfortable to stand thus, and the bronze was delightfully cool against her hand. But as she stood there, another element entered her mood. She began to feel the plastic beauty of the pose into which she had fallen as satisfying to her limbs, to her body. Her realization of the charm that had come over her at that moment, and of how well her pose became her, together with the mere sensuous harmony of her body, merged into a feeling of triumph that filled her like a strange and solemn ecstasy.

She felt herself so strong at that hour. Life lay before her like a great and glorious day; no longer as a day tilting toward the quiet, lugubrious hours of dusk, but as a vast and vigilant span of time, with feverish pulses beating every second, with the joy of light, with speed and vigor, with infinity pointing outward and inward. She rejoiced at the fullness of life, and yearned for it with a feverish glow and dizziness.

A long while she stood thus, captivated by her thoughts, forgetting everything around her. Suddenly she seemed to hear the silence, the long-toned singing of the gas jets, and she let her hand drop from the urn, sat down at the table, and began to turn the pages in a folder.

Some one passed by the open door; she heard the steps return, then she saw Thorbrögger entering.

They spoke a few words, but as she seemed occupied with the pictures, he also began to look through the periodicals. They did not seem to interest him, for when she glanced up, her eyes met his, which looked searchingly at her.

He was just on the verge of speaking, and there was a nervous, determined twitch about his lips that told her clearly what his words would be. She blushed, and intuitively, as though to keep his words back, she handed him her magazine across the table, pointing to a drawing of some cowboys who were hurling their lassos at wild bulls.

He was almost lured into jesting at the artist's naïve conception of the art of lassoing. This, to be sure, was a temptingly easy subject to discuss, in contrast with the one that filled his mind. But he firmly thrust aside the magazine and bent slightly over the table.

"I have thought so much about you of late," he said. "I have always thought so much about you—in Denmark long ago, and over there also. For I have always loved you; and when sometimes I feel as if I had never loved you before now that we have met again, it isn't true, great

[132]

as my love for you is now, for I have always loved you, always. And if now I might call you mine, you can not understand what that would mean to me, if you, who were taken away for so many years—if you would come back!"

He was silent a moment, then he rose and approached her.

"Oh, but say something! I am standing here, talking blindly, talking to a stranger, to an interpreter, who again must render my words to the heart I am appealing to. I don't know . . . stand and weigh my words . . . I don't know how far or near . . . I dare not utter the prayer of worship that overflows my heart—or dare I?"

He slipped down on a chair beside her.

"If only I dared, I should fear nothing. . . . Is it true! Oh, God bless you, Paula!"

"There is no longer anything to keep us apart," she said, with her hand in his. "Whatever comes, I have a right to be happy once, to live a full and natural life, to fulfill my dreams and desires. I have never resigned myself to fate. Just because happiness failed to come to me, I never believed life to be all dullness and duty. I knew that people could be happy in this world."

Silently he kissed her hand.

"I know," she mused sadly, "that those who will judge me most gently will allow me the joy of knowing that you love me; but they will say that this ought to be enough for me."

"But it would never be enough for me, and would you have the right to drop me like that?"

"No," she said. "No."

A moment later she went up to Ellinor.

Ellinor was asleep.

Fru Fönss sat down at the bedside and watched the pale child, whose face could be seen but dimly in the yellow, meager glow of the night lamp.

For the sake of Ellinor they must wait. In a day or two they would part from Thorbrögger and go to Nice to remain there alone. The whole winter she would live for Ellinor. But to-morrow she would have to tell them what had happened and what was to be expected. No matter how they would take the news, she could not bear to be together with them day after day, locked out from their hearts by such a secret. And they would also need time to familiarize themselves with the idea; for there would be a parting of the ways, how complete would depend upon the children themselves. They should have full freedom in whatever policy they adopted toward her and Thorbrögger. She would demand nothing. It was for them to give.

She heard Tage's step in the parlor and went in there to meet him.

He beamed and at the same time appeared so nervous that Fru Fönss instantly knew that something had happened, and she also surmised what.

But he, who wished to find a fitting introduction to that which he had on his mind, chatted distractedly about the theater; and not until his mother went over and stroked his forehead and compelled him to look at her, did he confide his secret, that he had proposed to Ida Kastager and had been accepted.

They talked a long while about the engagement, but the mother had the feeling all the time that she spoke with a certain reserve, which she was unable to overcome. Because of her own excitement, she feared to chime in too much with Tage; then besides, she could not bear to have her suspicious thoughts make the faintest shadow of connection between her cordiality to-night and her own confession to-morrow.

Tage, however, was not aware of her reserve.

That night she found very little sleep, her thoughts kept her awake. How strange that he and she should meet again and be as fond of each other now as in the old days!

Old days, especially for her! She was not young any more; she could certainly not pose as a young girl. The future might prove that he would have to bear with her and get used to the fact that it was many years since she was eight-

een. Still she felt young. She was young in
many ways; yet she was aware of her age, realized it clearly in a thousand subtle movements,
in mien and gestures, in the manner in which
she would respond when called, in her way of
smiling at an answer. Ten times a day she
would make herself old in these things, because
she would lack the courage to be as youthful in
her manner as she was in her mind.

Thoughts came and vanished, but always the
same question about her children remained.
What would they say?

It was late in the forenoon on the following
day when she approached the subject.

They were sitting in the parlor.

She said she had something important to tell
them, which would alter all their lives greatly,
and which would surprise them very much. She
begged them to listen as calmly as possible and
not be carried away by their feelings, for they
must know that what she had to tell them was
irrevocable. Nothing could change her decision.

"I want to marry again." And she told them
how, before she knew their father, she had been
in love with Thorbrögger, how they had been
parted, and how they had found each other again.

Ellinor wept. Tage rose from his chair, all
bewildered, and came over to his mother, kneeled
down, and caught her hand. He pressed it ten-

derly to his cheek, confused and half choking with emotion.

"But mother! What have we done to you? Did we not always love you? When we were with you or away from you, we yearned for you as for the dearest in the world. We never knew father except through you. You taught us to love him. If Ellinor and I are fond of each other, it is because you showed the one what was worth loving in the other. And the same with every person we came in contact with. Everything we have is from you, and we adore you, mother. If you knew . . . You have no idea how we yearned for you. You taught us to control ourselves, and we have never dared to come as near to you as we desired. And now you say you want to leave us, thrust us aside entirely! It's impossible. Could anybody ever hurt us more than that? And you don't want to hurt us, you want to do us good. Tell us it isn't true! Say, it isn't true, Tage; it isn't true, Ellinor."

"Control yourself, Tage! Don't make it hard for yourself and others."

"Hard!" he said. "Hard, hard! I wish it wasn't worse than that; but it's frightful—unnatural! It's enough to drive one mad. Do you really know what you have given us to think about? My own mother accepting a stranger's caresses! My mother the object of a man's pas-

[137]

sion, embraced and embracing again! That's a thought for a son, worse than the worst insult.— But it's impossible; it must be impossible. Is there no power in a son's prayers? Ellinor, don't sit there crying! Help me beg mother have pity on us."

Fru Fönss tried to silence him with a gesture of her hand. "Let Ellinor alone," she said. "She is tired enough; besides I have told you that nothing can be altered."

"I wish I were dead," remarked Ellinor. "But it's true what Tage says, mother. You have no right to give us a stepfather at our age."

"Stepfather!" cried Tage. "I hope he doesn't for a moment dare . . . You're mad, mother. Where he enters, I shall take my leave. No power on earth can make me tolerate any kinship with that man. You will have to choose between him and us! If the happy pair are headed for Denmark, we remain in exile; if they stay here, we depart."

"Is that your last word, Tage?" asked the mother.

"I hope you don't doubt it! Imagine the family life; Ida and I sitting out there on the terrace at night, and some one whispers behind the laurels, and Ida asks me, 'Who is whispering?' and I answer her, 'It's my mother and her new husband.'—No! I should not have mentioned this; but you see the effect already, the harm it has done me. And it will have the same effect on Ellinor too, you may be sure."

Fru Fönss let the children withdraw, and remained alone.

Tage was right, the news had done no good. How far they had drifted away from her already during that short hour! How they looked at her, no longer as *her* children, but as their father's! How ready they were to drop her the moment they found out that her whole heart no longer belonged to them. But after all, she was not only her children's mother; she was an individual apart from them, with her own life to live, and with hopes that had nothing to do with them. But perhaps she was not so young as she had believed. She had realized this during her conversation with them. Had she not been sitting there trembling and almost felt herself encroaching on the rights of youth? The selfishness and naïve tyranny of youth echoed through all they had said.—We alone have the right to love; life is ours; yours is the duty to live for us.

She began to understand that old age might be a blessing. Not that she wished to be old, yet old age smiled to her faintly as a far away peace, now after all the excitement, and at the prospect of so much strife. For she did not believe her children would change their minds, and yet she must talk to them again and again, of course, before she gave up hope. It was best that Thorbrögger should go away at once. If he were not at hand, perhaps the children would be less irritable, and she might succeed in showing them how eagerly she sought their welfare. Their first bitterness would then have time to wane, and all—no, she did not believe all would end well.

It was decided that Thorbrögger should go to Denmark to arrange their papers and remain there, temporarily at least. Yet very little seemed to be gained by this. The children shunned her; Tage was forever with Ida or her father, and Ellinor found a way of keeping the sick Fru Kastager company. And when, at last, they all happened to be together, where then were the confidential chats of the good old days? What had become of the thousand and one topics for conversation? If they found a topic, what became of its interest? They sat there discoursing distractedly like hosts and guests who were parting after having enjoyed each other's company—those who left, thinking of the journey; those who remained, thinking of their daily routine when the guests should have gone.

No longer had they anything in common; they had lost their feeling of kinship. They spoke of how they should arrange things next week, next month, one month later even; but it did not in-

terest them as in the old days when they were
planning for days of their life. Now it meant
only a way of filling up the days of waiting, days
that had to be endured one way or another; and
all three asked themselves, What next? They
were no longer secure in life, for they had no
foundation to build on, till that which separated
them had been definitely settled.

Day by day the children forgot what their
mother had been to them, as children do when
they believe an injustice has been done them—a
thousand benefits for a single grievance.

Tage was the more tender of the two, but also
the one most deeply wounded, because he had
loved her most. Many a long night he had
grieved over the mother whom he had not been
able to keep as he wanted her, and there were
times when his memory of her love for him
numbed all other emotions within him. One day
he had gone to her and prayed and begged her to
be theirs alone, but got No for an answer. And
this No hardened him and made him cold too, a
coldness which at first frightened him because it
was accompanied by a terrible emptiness.

Ellinor took it differently. She had in some
strange manner mainly felt that an injustice had
been done her dead father, whom she remembered
very dimly. She painted him so vividly in her
imagination, digging up all she had heard about

him, asking Kastager and Tage about him, kissing a medallion with his portrait every morning and evening, and longing, somewhat hysterically, for his old letters that were kept at home, and for things that had belonged to him.

As the father rose in her esteem, the mother sank. The fact that she had fallen in love lowered her in the eyes of the daughter; she was no longer the mother, the perfect and wise, the supreme and most beautiful of human beings. She was a woman like other women—not exactly like others and, because of that, still more to be censured, criticized, and found wanting. Ellinor was pleased that she had kept her unhappy love affair to herself. She did not know how much her mother had aided her in her reserve.

The days passed, and this mode of life grew more and more unbearable. They all realized that a compromise was hopeless; and instead of coming together again, they were torn further apart.

Fru Kastager, who was well by now, but had been secluded from all that had happened, understood the problem best, because she had heard every side impartially. She had a long talk with Fru Fönss, who was happy to find a friend who would listen calmly to her plans for the future. Fru Kastager proposed that the children should accompany her to Nice, that Thorbrögger should return to Avignon, and that they should be married. Her husband could very well remain here and act as witness.

Fru Fönss wavered for some time. It was not possible for her to learn what the children thought of the scheme. They received the news with a dignified air of silence; and when they were pressed for an answer, they had only this to say that they were obliged, of course, to comply with whatever their mother decided upon.

At last she took Fru Kastager's advice. She bade her children good-bye, and they left. Thorbrögger came, and they were married.

Spain became their home. Thorbrögger chose it because of the sheep culture there.

To Denmark neither of them wanted to go.

And so they lived happily in Spain.

Twice she wrote to her children, but in their first impulsive anger they returned the letters. Later they regretted this, no doubt, but pride prevented them from writing to her; and thus all intercourse ceased between them, though they heard about each other now and then through friends.

Five years passed, and Thorbrögger and his wife lived happily together. Then she was suddenly taken ill. The malady was swift and wasting and inevitably meant death. Her strength vanished hour by hour; and one day when the grave no longer was far away, she wrote to her children.

"Dear Children," she wrote. "I know that you will read this letter, for it will not reach you until I am dead. Do not be afraid, there are no reproaches hidden between the lines. If only I were able to fill them with enough love!

"When people love each other, Tage and Ellinor—little Ellinor—then the one who loves the most must always be the humblest; and therefore I come to you once more, as in my thoughts I shall come to you every hour of the day, as long as I am able. The one who must die, dear children, is so very poor. I am so poor now, for the whole beautiful world that has been my rich and blessed home these many years is to be taken away from me; my chair will be empty; the door will be locked on me; and I shall never put my foot into the world again. I therefore look at the world with the prayer in my eyes that it be fond of me; and therefore I come to you, praying that you will love me with all the love you once bestowed on me; for bear this in mind: to be remembered is the only morsel in the world of man that from now on will be mine. Only to be remembered, that and nothing else.

"I have never doubted your love; I realized so well that it was your great love which caused your great anger. If you had loved me less, you would more readily have let me go. And therefore I want to say this: if some day it happens that a man, broken down with sorrow, comes knocking at your door to talk to you about me, to talk about me for the sake of his own grief, then remember, no one has ever loved me as he did; all the joy that ever shone from the heart of man came from him to me. And soon, at the last great hour, when darkness comes, he will hold my hand, and his words shall be the last I hear.

"I bid you good-bye, but this is not my last good-bye to you; for that I want to send as late as I dare. All my love shall be in it, my yearnings of so many years, my memories from the time you were small, and a thousand wishes and thousands of thanks. Good-bye, Tage; good-bye, Ellinor. Good-bye, till my last Good-bye!

"YOUR MOTHER."

SOPHUS SCHANDORPH

STINA BECOMES A FARMER'S WIFE

Sophus Schandorph (1836–1901) was extremely popular in his own day and is still liked for his good-natured humor. He was a native of Ringsted in Zealand. At the University he specialized in Romance philology, but though he attained a high, even a distinguished, level of intellectual culture, he always hankered for the homely environments of his youth. When the new parole of realism was given by his friend, Georg Brandes, Schandorph perceived with satisfaction that he could use his knowledge of simple country life as literary material.

He satirized the members of the official or academic class, who, up to that time, had regarded themselves as repositories of all culture, but his touch is sometimes so heavy that he defeats his own purpose. In the novel *Common Folk* he expresses his sympathies for the hard-working people of the lower middle class. Schandorph is at his best in the short story, especially when writing of Zealand peasants, whom he described with massive realism and jovial good humor.

Sophus Schandorph

STINA BECOMES A FARMER'S WIFE

SINCE Midsummer Day not a drop of rain had fallen, and now August was nearing its end. The road looked like a trail of spilled flour winding through bare fields. The stubble land was cracked with drought. The fallow fields gleamed yellow against crumbling grayish white soil. The low ditches were lined with ugly dusty grass, like long tangled wisps of hair. All growing things were drying up in an abandonment of despair. The light blue cloudless sky had tortured them too long. The sun, with its self-complacent smile, had scorched them so mercilessly, so continuously, that now, in spite of their burning thirst, they had grown too listless to implore the heavens for a drop of water. In all the dazzling whiteness of the landscape there was not a spot of deeper color to rest the weary eye.

A peasant girl of short, broad stature came walking along the road. Every step she took raised the dust like a low, dense cloud of steam. She seemed as resigned as the plants, but with a

[149]

considerably greater vitality. No sentimental
pity for her floral fellow-creatures moved her—
at least she did not waste one glance on them.
Only when a cow began to prance in the field she
slightly turned her snugly kerchiefed head. She
never stopped or quickened her steps, but kept an
even pace with unchanging calmness, walking
along with her feet apart, like a sturdy, broad-
gaged wagon, while the thick, heavy soles of her
leather shoes made goodly tracks on the ground.
Drops of perspiration trickled from her white
forehead down her ruddy, freckled nose, but this
was the only movement in her big, sun-burned
face. She did not even blink in the sun. Her
mouth was slightly open, displaying a remarkably
strong and beautiful row of upper teeth. From
time to time she ran the tip of her tongue over
her lips, without, however, changing their position.

Stina had need to arm herself with patience;
she had already walked two miles from the town
where she was in service, and had fully four miles
more to go before reaching the village of her destination. Her mistress, the widow of the late
dean, had given her a whole day's leave. This
occurred twice a year, once at Shrovetide, and
once after the summer holidays, when the two
sons of the house had returned to their studies at
the University in Copenhagen.

Stina always took advantage of these two free days to visit her eight-year-old daughter. With some help from the parish, this child—unfortunately born out of wedlock—had been placed in the care of a cottager and his wife in Stina's native village. The father had worked on the same farm with Stina when she was twenty-two years old, but, upon learning that she was "in trouble," he had hastily left for America.

Stina's progress along the dusty road was very slow, just barely noticeable. One or two vehicles passed her. The first was a light cabriolet, on the back seat of which a fat country gentleman was sprawling, puffing at his cigar. On the front seat the coachman cracked his whip as the carriage whizzed by. Stina came near being struck by the tip of the lash. She even blinked a little at the threatening possibility. The dust stirred up by the wheels whirled around her like the steam from an engine and made her sneeze. Although there was plenty of room in the carriage, it would never occur to a "gentleman farmer" to give a peasant girl a lift, nor would she ever ask him to do so.

A little later she was overtaken by a butcher in his one-horse cart. Whoop-la! What a wild gallop, zigzag from one side of the road to the other, the wheels just escaping the ditches on either side, the springs bouncing and clanging!

The butcher was alone in his cart. He was wearing a striped blue and white linen coat, soiled with brownish blood stains, and was lustily whistling "Oh, Susannah." His straw hat was pushed back over his fiery-red, perspiring forehead. In the back of the cart, behind the seat, were two lambs, bleating indolently, as if only fulfilling an official duty. Without stopping, the butcher shouted to Stina, "Hey, lady, will you ride with me through the course of life? Hey?"

Stina did not respond to this address with so much as a glance. She said to herself, "Butchers always talk so silly."

Wrapped in a new cloud of dust, she sneezed again, patiently wiped her nose with the back of her cotton glove, then wiped the glove on her dress in the hollow of her arm.

From a distance she heard the noise of a third vehicle, but did not turn to look. It was a long time coming, and, judging by the sound, the horses were ambling. At last it overtook her. It was a small two-horse spring-cart with only one seat. This seat was occupied by a middle-aged man who looked well fed without being exactly stout. He wore a coat of thick black broadcloth with pockets and edges bound in wide wool braid. His head was covered by a light gray cloth cap, trimmed with numerous small buttons which were faded yellow and displayed their wooden skeletons un-

der the threadbare cloth covering. A short pipe
with a big wooden head lay thrust in a corner of
the seat. After spitting in the opposite direction
from Stina, the man stopped his horses with a
soft "Whoa!" and said slowly in the broadest Zealand dialect, "Maybe that girl would like a lift?"

"Many thanks," answered Stina.

She took hold of the dash-board, stepped on
the whipple-tree so heavily that it swung way out
to the side, and let herself down on the seat with
a thump that made the springs resound.

For a moment the owner of the cart peered at
her from the corner of his eye and looked as if he
were going to say something. But when his guest
did not by the faintest sign reveal any inclination
toward conversation or friendliness, and when he
saw her staring straight ahead, crowding as far
as possible away from him into the opposite corner of the seat, he sighed loudly, and exclaimed,
"Well, well, begosh ye—hm, hm!" He stopped
for a moment, wiped the perspiration from his
forehead, reached for his pipe, stuffed it from a
bladder-pouch, lighted it, touched the fat white-
maned sorrels lightly with the whip, and with a
"Gidap!" made them start an easy trot.

Always the same white road, edged by grass
and plantain leaves covered with a thick layer of
dust. Always the same stubbly fields, unending
stretches in woodless regions, interrupted only by

the square of some solitary farmhouse, or by a cottage half veiled by the poplar row around the garden. Here and there a dried-out pool with its cracked, wrinkled, and hard clay bottom bore witness to the monstrous drought of the summer.

"It sure is mighty hot," sighed the farmer after they had ridden quite a distance.

Stina nodded, continuing to stare straight ahead. The man could only see the profile of her nose move a bit. Again he was silent for a while before making a new attempt to exchange ideas with her.

"The crop got in very well this year. There was nothing to complain about. For the weather was right steady. But—eh—the grain don't weigh much, and we got a mighty big pile o' chaff."

These reflections awakened so much interest in Stina that she turned half toward the farmer, and murmured, "The hay wasn't any good either."

"No; if only we don't have to buy fodder for the cattle before winter is over."

"That might be bad enough," said Stina sullenly, and turned away from the man. Perhaps this discouraged him from further attempts at conversation. He turned toward her several times, clearing his throat and mumbling, "Well, well, begosh! Ye-e-es."—What was there to be said to that?—Then, as he did not receive the least response, he fell into a silence, perhaps into a reverie. He bent forward, placed his whip between his legs, the handle leaning against his right thigh, and left the two sorrels to do as they pleased. At their present pace it was out of the question for them to cover four miles an hour, and yet the perspiration formed big flakes of foam on their loins and backs.

No sound was heard except the heavy, monotonous creaking of the axles and a slight rattling of the harness when the horses shook themselves to get rid of the "blind flies" that buzzed around the carriage and sometimes, with a short, faintly snapping sound, hit the leather cover which protected the travelers.

The owner of the spring-cart was roused from his drowsiness by a motion of the girl beside him. Again he glanced sideways at her, and saw her untie the knot in the red and white dotted cotton kerchief which was covering the bundle in her lap. Inside was a parcel wrapped in a newspaper. She opened it, took out a big round of rye bread covered with smoked sausage, and broke the bread in two parts. With a nod she offered her host one of these, without, however, looking at him.

"Thanks to him who offers," murmured the farmer. Each devoured his half of the round with due composure. It was succeeded by another covered with green cheese. This slice was also broken in two by its proprietress who then repeated her silent invitation.

"Why, that's a darned shame," said the farmer. But when Stina continued holding the bread toward him, he took it with an attempt to be polite—"Those are really very fine sandwiches."

He half rose in the seat and began to fumble in his coat-tail pocket. As his arms were short, he had some trouble in hauling out a black, hammered pint bottle. A blue checked cotton handkerchief came out with it.

"Shall we make the nightingale chirp?" he asked, chuckling inwardly without moving his lips. He produced a strident noise by rubbing the moist cork against the bottle, which he then offered to Stina. She gave him an indignant glance and rejected the proffered bottle by a gesture. The farmer laughed as before, and said, "Why—it ain't brandy. It's sweet punch extract."

This information altered matters. Stina took a swallow from the bottle, and grunted something which was meant to be thanks. The man took a long pull, and exclaimed with voluptuous delight, "Ah—ah—that cools one off a sight in such a heat. It's a tidy drink."

Stina nodded and licked her lips. A much softer "Ah" than that of the man was evidence of the enjoyment which the sweet drink had given her.

They continued their ride over the white road, without the least change in the surroundings or the situation. A couple of times the farmer moved nearer to Stina, as if by way of experiment, but each time she squeezed farther into the opposite corner of the seat.

They came to a hill. Now the horses had to walk slowly. From the top of the hill a village could be seen, topped by the white church tower with tiled, white-washed step-gables. Here and there were some farms, separated from the road by dunghills and blackish brown pools of water.

"Whoa!" said Stina when they had reached a cottage with green window-frames and a wilted rose-bush growing along the wall.

"Oh, is that where it is?" said the farmer. "Whoa! Do you understand Danish, you red fox?"

This latter remark was addressed to the near horse, which had not been willing to obey orders at once, but seemed impressed by this appeal to its nationality.

A little girl in a pink calico dress appeared in the door, which consisted of an upper and a lower part, both open.

"Ma," she cried, tripping on the stone floor.

But when she saw the stranger and the fine cart she crept behind the door-post, and one could see nothing of her except a ruddy cheek and a flaxen curl. Soon after a middle-aged woman came out. She nodded, saying, "Good-day! It's Stina, is it? So you're coming in a carriage to-day!"

"I give many thanks for the ride," murmured Stina, offering the peasant a limp hand, which was received with a similar suggestion of a hand-shake.

Stina climbed down, again making the traces and the whipple-tree shake and rattle. The woman from the cottage nodded to the man simultaneously with Stina. He returned the greeting by touching the back of his cap, growled "Nah!" and drove away.

As said before, Stina had come to see her little girl. The cottager had gone to work. His wife and Stina exchanged few words during their dinner, which consisted of kale and bacon.

"That was Per Larsen from Orslovlille who gave you a lift," said the cottager's wife incidentally.

"Yes, I know him," answered Stina.

The girl was even more than usually taciturn that afternoon. As on former occasions, she played with her child in the little yard. Their game consisted of the little girl's catching hold of her mother's dress behind, while both of them

jogged back and forth at a slow trot, repeating
ad infinitum in a half singing, half reciting tone:

> *"Now we are driving to Copenhagen,*
> *To buy sweet chocolate."*

The cottager's wife stood in the door, shading
her eyes with her hand, and said, "How nice little
Marsina plays with her mother."

During her former visits Stina had been a trifle
livelier, and had interrupted the never varying
game by interludes of chatting with the peasant
woman. But to-day her

> *"Now we are driving to Copenhagen,*
> *To buy sweet chocolate—"*

went on without intermission, and she stared
straight ahead. To be sure, she sometimes kissed
little Marsina, who bore this queer name in memory of her unscrupulous father, Jens Madsen, but
somehow her caresses lacked heartiness. After
each kiss the child gave her mother a strange, dully
questioning look. Once when Stina squarely met
the glance of her child, she began to cry. The
peasant woman thought it her duty to say a word
of comfort, which took the following form:

"Yeh, men are foul trash, that's what they are,
sure! To think of that fellow Jens Madsen!
Well, there are enough of them, begosh. Himself is of course neither hot-headed nor runnin'

after the girls—mercy, no—but on the other hand he's most always drunk."

"I s'pose so," said Stina distractedly, "he was always keen on brandy."

"Yeh, what is one to say? If he neither scolds nor beats me, and he ain't doin' nothin' of the kind, one has to take it as it comes. But you ain't quite well to-day, Stina, I don't think. You're so queer."

"There's somethin' rumbling inside of me," said Stina.

"If only it ain't the ague," said the woman.

At five o'clock Stina had to leave. She walked the six miles back to town along the dusty road, but this did not trouble her much. It was as if she were altogether enveloped by the dust-clouds, and neither saw nor heard anything.

———

Stina had been working for Mrs. Aaby, widow of the dean, for five years. Her mistress was a plump, black-haired, and brown-eyed little lady of about fifty-five years who, after her husband's death, had moved back to the small city where she was born and where her father had been town judge. She was naturally merry and fun-loving, but during the twenty years of her married life her husband's superior position in the clergy had necessitated a serious and dignified demeanor on her part. Now she was eking out a scant living with a widow's pension. The friends of her youth were scattered in all directions far from her native town. She lived in the memories of her former opulent and hospitable home where the bishop, on his visits of inspection, was so well fed and cared for that he had never there been inclined to give the schoolmasters their usual dose of severe reprimand. The dean's widow spent her time knitting much woolen underwear for poor children, and reading all the novels of the circulating library. Only when dining with the town officials and a few wealthy merchants did she put on her aristocratic, churchly airs.

She had grown fond of the rural population where her husband had his charge. She had humor and heart enough to understand the peasants, and even though her sense of superiority occasionally compelled her to strut a little, this had not harmed her reputation for being "a real common woman." In fact, it pleased the peasants that the widow of the dean knew how to hold her own among the best people. The schoolmaster had long ago informed them that she was a real lady, whereas the wives of the neighboring clergymen, strictly speaking, were just like anybody else.

Her husband's former parishioners had not forgotten her in the course of time. Some farmers still sent her geese and ducks at the great church festivals. Even some well situated cottagers now and then sent her a score of eggs or a bottle of thick cream.

One day—not even a Sunday or holiday—a man brought her a big fat turkey. As people in a small town all know each other, she saw at once that the messenger was the hired man of Kristen Nielsen in Kirkegade who kept "Board and Lodgings for Travelers," and in whose house the peasants from her husband's former parish, Orslovmagle and its annex, Orslovlille, used to put up.

"From whom is that?" asked the widow.

"From Per Larsen in Orslovlille," answered the man.

"Is that so?" said the widow, and tipped the man. When he had gone, she said to herself, "I wonder what has come over that sullen and stingy fellow, Per Larsen. He never put his foot inside of the church and did not give a whit more in tithes than the law required."

She rose from her afternoon coffee, and holding the fat turkey by the wing, she went into the kitchen to express to Stina her surprise over this present from Per Larsen.

Stina stood at the kitchen table eating her meat and potatoes with the absent-minded, apparently thoughtful air with which servant girls consume their lonesome and cheerless repasts. When her mistress entered, Stina turned away quickly and raised her kitchen apron to her nose and eyes.

"Do you understand, Stina, what has come over Per Larsen in Orslovlille?"

"No-o," answered Stina, still turning her head away.

"Look at the huge turkey he is sending me!— Do look at it, Stina! We can invite the apothecary's and the Henningsens to dinner on it—but what is the matter, my girl? Why, you are weeping for all you are worth, Stina!—What is it?—Stina! Are you ill?"

"Yes, it pulls from way up in my throat down to my very heels," mumbled Stina in a voice that sounded as if she had a lump of porridge in her throat.

"Don't talk with your mouth full, my girl," said her mistress in a moralizing tone. She got a little attack of her clerical dignity now that she was quite relieved of any worry about the girl's health—for Stina regularly announced the above mentioned symptoms whenever she was in bad humor or had much to do.

Mrs. Aaby laid the turkey on the kitchen table, where she discovered a good-sized piece of cardboard lying wrong side up. She turned it over. On it was pasted a colored and shiny picture above some lines of verse. Stina collapsed on the kitchen chair, sobbing wildly. The picture represented an arbor in which a man dressed in a green coat, green breeches, and white stockings embraced a crimson, short- and narrow-skirted woman with a lemon-colored shepherdess hat. Above the treetops hovered three pink, winged naked creatures—angels or cupids—with yellowish-brown shadows along their backs. Underneath were the following lines:

> *Two hearts that tremble with earnest love*
> *To the bosom of nature find their way.*
> *The angels from Heaven soar above,*
> *Protecting the two from all dismay.*
> *Rejoice, O maiden! Look toward the light,*
> *The sun smiles down at your ardent bliss;*
> *And later, the stars of the tranquil night*
> *Send your anxious heart a comforting kiss.*

Mrs. Aaby read the verse, burst out laughing, and said, "Why, Stina! Where did you get that terrible stuff?"

"Yes, that's the worst nonsense I ever saw," answered the maid, "but the picture is real pretty, I think."

"Who gave you that? Have you a suitor? Eh, Stina?"

"Oh, that's some tomfoolery of that silly hired man from Kristen Nielsen. He's always up to some monkeyshines."

"Did he bring the card with the turkey?"

[164]

"I didn't see no turkey before Missus brought that big thing there. No, he threw it in when he passed the kitchen window."

"But what can be the matter with Per Larsen in Orslovlille?"

"Well, I'll be darned if I know that."

"Don't say 'darned,' Stina."

As soon as Mrs. Aaby had left the kitchen and could be supposed to be sitting in her living-room, Stina took the card, looked long at the picture, read the poetry in a whispering voice, and said, "To think that anybody can get up such lovely words!"

She opened her dress, hid the card in her bosom, and started to polish the kitchen utensils. As the metal grew brighter, and the sun began to shine warmly through the window, the thirty-year-old girl, usually so serious, seemed to acquire new life. She sighed a few times—was it with fatigue or content? Who knows?—and began to sing:

> *That men behave like drunken swine*
> *Is not at all uncommon,*
> *Instead of water they drink wine.*
> *This happened to a tailor.*
>
> *He drank and drank until he could*
> *Not see the flies upon the wall,*
> *And when he went into the field*
> *He had an ugly fall.*

His nose tore up the ground so black
With tar one thought 'twas painted;
A sow that stood and saw it all,
With fear she almost fainted.

She sang these words slowly and monotonously; she could not have sung a hymn more solemnly. When she had reached the interesting place in the ballad with which the above quotation ends, her mistress opened the door, and said with a surprised smile, "Are you singing, Stina?—No? Wasn't somebody singing?"

"No, nobody was singin'," answered Stina in a sullen and almost offended tone.

———

"What in the world can be the matter with Per Larsen?" exclaimed Mrs. Aaby in November when Kristen Nielsen's hired man brought her half a side of bacon with respectful greetings from Per Larsen of Orslovlille. "He sends me presents, but he never comes to see me. What do you think about it, Stina?"

"I don't think nothin' about it," answered Stina.

Toward Christmas Stina received a visit from her little girl's foster-mother. Before leaving, the woman asked permission to speak to Stina's mistress. This was granted her. Mrs. Aaby was drinking her ten-o'clock coffee, and thought it behooved her to be on her dignity.

"Well, Matty," she said, sitting in the middle of her sofa, with the bright-polished, steaming brass samovar on the table before her, "I hear that the little girl is doing well at school."

"Yes, she's smart enough at readin'," answered the peasant woman.

"Good—with the Lord's help she may become a joy and comfort to her mother. It was sad that Stina had to go through that bitter lesson in her youth."

"Yes, but *now* that's all the same."

"Is it—how is that?"

"Why, Stina's goin' to be married. She's leavin' the Missus on Mayday. This very day I brought a message to her from Per Larsen in Orslovlille."

"Good Heavens! What is all this, Matty?"

Forgetting her dignity, the clergyman's widow jumped up and burst into tears. The peasant woman joined her in this, and said in a stifled voice, "Per Larsen is waitin' for me in the street. I rode to town with him, and he'll take me home again. Dear me, yes! The Lord knows that a person has both joy and sorrow in this world."

"I must talk to Per Larsen," said Mrs. Aaby, going to the window and opening it.

True enough, there was his spring-cart standing in the street. Per Larsen, arrayed in a big fur cap and a coat with shoulder-cape and broad sheepskin collar, sat patiently waiting, bent forward, with the whip between his legs. When he heard Mrs. Aaby open the window, he looked up and lifted his cap. He put one foot on the hub of the wheel, jumped heavily to the ground, tied the traces, and approached the house after hauling something out from under the seat. This something turned out to be two geese. He appeared in the living-room with a goose in each hand.

"Well, well, Per Larsen!" said the widow. "While your old pastor, the dean, was living, we never saw you."

"And that's the truth," said the farmer calmly. "I couldn't afford to make my tithe bigger than I had to so long as I had both the old folks to look out for."

"But you never came to church either, Per Larsen."

"Ye-es! I went to church every time I had something to do there—when there was a funeral, or I was asked to be godfather, or such. I followed the poorest cottager to the grave, I sure did. But—er—I'd like to talk to the Missus about Stina. For howsomever you may be surprised, I mean to marry her."

Per Larsen uttered the last sentence with unusual energy, which he furthermore enhanced by the resolute way in which he placed the geese in an armchair.

"Mercy! they are greasy," said the widow, moving them to a newspaper on the table. "But—Per Larsen—you see, Stina has a—hm!—well, Matty knows that better than any one else."

"Why, of course I know that as well as Matty," said the farmer. "But—er—I take it that one thing and the other may happen to young people. They can't help that, for that's the way our Lord made 'em. But—er—hm—Matty she says as Stina has five hundred dollars in the savings bank, and quite a lot of good things of wool and linen in her chest—and—of course her father had a farm in his days, and it was no fault of his that there were no sons so that the Squire had to lease the farm to his brother-in-law! Now that fellow has taken to drink, and things go badly with him."

"But how has Per Larsen got acquainted with Stina?" asked the widow. "It seems to me that Per Larsen ought to think the matter over. Isn't Per Larsen a widower for the second time? That is what I thought. So Per Larsen has lost two wives. Marriage is a serious thing, Per Larsen."

"It sure is," said the farmer with a sigh, "one can't say that it's all fun."

"Indeed not! Well, of course, Stina is faithful and hard working, but she is very taciturn—she hardly ever says a word."

Per Larsen's small eyes grew lively, and his speech took a slightly quicker tempo.

"Sure, and that's just it. The Missus is quite right in saying that I have been married twice. The Lord help us! One woman gabbled, and the other twaddled, there was no difference. For ten years it was like as if there was a mill whizzing in the room all the time. And my mother, she's still living, she gabbled and twaddled with the wives, and I didn't even have peace when we were eating. But now my old mother never says a word since she had the stroke, and she won't last long, I don't think. And—er—some time after the harvest I rode five miles with Stina, and upon my word, she didn't hardly answer me when I spoke to her, and that pleased me right well. And she even offered me sandwiches, but the two of us didn't make no conversation while we were eating. And the Missus may believe me, when a person has heard so much prating from women in his life, it'll be a relief to get somebody who can keep her mouth shut tight. And one has to have a woman on a farm like mine, or all the inside work goes to the dogs."

"Has Stina given her consent? Has Per Larsen spoken to her?" asked Mrs. Aaby.

"No-o-o. But sure she can't have nothing against it, for it will mean for her to be the housewife on a farm, and there ain't no step-children for her to take care of, and I guess the Lord'll take my mother before Easter. And if *I* don't mind that she got into trouble in her young days—"

"Sure, Missus, what more could she want?" said Matty with an assurance which showed that she was well informed in the matter.

Mrs. Aaby called Stina, who was supposed to be in the kitchen. Nobody answered. She opened the door. The kitchen was empty. The girl had chosen to take to her heels, finding it too embarrassing to overhear the proceedings. When her mistress expressed her displeasure at Stina's absence, Per Larsen said with an approving nod and smile, "That's the way *I* want it! No talking and fooling. Then things'll come out all right."

After Mayday Per Larsen and Stina were married, and the dean's widow poured coffee at the wedding.

HOLGER DRACHMANN

A SHIP IN CHURCH

HOLGER DRACHMANN (1846–1908) was an extremely prolific writer. Three-score volumes reflect the experiences,
the mental and emotional crises, of a life as varied and
eventful as that of his contemporary, J. P. Jacobsen, was
quiet and austere. The son of a navy physician, he
decided to be a marine painter. It was in this capacity
that he learned to know the sailors and fishermen who
figure in his books. On his travels as a "journeyman
artist" he visited England, where the misery of workers
in the sweated trades fired his passion for social justice,
and became the means of driving him into the radical
camp of his own country.

With his distinguished appearance, his personal charm
and fascination, and whatever prestige attached to having been born in the best Copenhagen society, Drachmann was an asset to the young radical movement. But
he was essentially a lyrist and as such a misfit among
the Realists, to whom, nevertheless, he was drawn by
other fibers in his rich, complex nature—not least by
his lust for rebellion. His whole life became a swinging
back and forth between the mutually hostile intellectual
camps of Denmark, just as, temperamentally, he vibrated
between inherited bourgeois standards and his own bo-
hemian tastes.

In the big Copenhagen novel, *Signed Away*, Drachmann personified the two sides of his own nature as two
friends, one a vagabond poet, the other a hard-working
artist-journalist. As a novel the book is chaotic, but it
contains many beautiful passages. In the drama *Wey-
land the Smith*, with a motif from *The Poetic Edda*, he
expressed the discrepancy between the artist's will and
his power. His charming fairy tale play *Once Upon a
Time* is very popular on the Danish stage. It is, however, by virtue of his lyrics that Drachmann holds his
place as one of the great names in Danish literature.

Holger Drachmann

A Ship in Church

THERE they sat, the three of them, old Ole Bertelsen and his two sons, Karl and Kristian, talking together in subdued voices. From time to time they glanced over toward Sören, the third brother, who sat delicately fashioning tiny parts for "the ship" with his huge fingers.

They were all so proud of this ship and so impressed with it that they scarcely dared raise their voices above a whisper when they spoke of it. But if any one had asked them about it, they would undoubtedly have answered quite casually, as if the ship were the most insignificant thing in the world.

Sören sat holding his wooden leg at a right angle from his real leg. The position was somewhat uncomfortable, to be sure, but it could not be otherwise; and sitting thus—with his "jurymast" stuck out to one side; his emaciated, bearded face, with its chiselled furrows of pain, bent carefully between the yardarms and backstays of the topmast; his great gnarled hands moving about in the rigging and on the deck with the sensitive fingers of a doll seamstress—he worked quietly, while his large, calm eyes concealed in their depths a happiness which they would never betray by a single glance.

"She's coming along purty well now, ain't she?" asked old Bertelsen in low respectful tones.

Sören might be pardoned for not answering. He sat with the ends of two halyards between his teeth, his fingers held a tiny little three-cornered block, and in the fast fading dusk of a December afternoon he was trying to pierce the sheave-holes through which the thin tackle had to be passed.

Then he dropped the threads from his teeth, and answered another question which had been asked some minutes before.

"I've found just one worm hole in her bottom. I think that's pretty good for a voyage of twenty years."

"That it is," said Karl with conviction.

"Yes," Kristian agreed, "but remember, Sören, you used a whole big bottle of oil and turpentine in her bottom when you made her."

"And now we'll use one more," said Sören. "And when she's hauled up on dry dock in another twenty years, and others get hold of her—for by that time we may all be worm-eaten ourselves —then they can see that we have been good to her."

"Oh," said old Ole, "who can tell, we may

all be alive then. It runs in the family, you know." Ole was well over seventy, and his sons were along in the forties.

It was about twenty years ago that they had come to an agreement with their neighbors in the village about this matter of a ship. All the other hamlets along the coast had their ships hanging up in their parish churches; why should Vangaa alone lag behind?

It was just at this time that Sören came home after a long trip, and he had one leg of wood instead of the leg of flesh and bone with which he had gone away. He had suffered intensely, alone in the strange hospital and, staunch sailor though he was, he had about given up hope. Proselytizing flourished around the wards of the hospital; the "missionaries" of the different denominations fought over the patients, and Sören had fallen a victim to a rabid zealot with short cropped hair and hard, tightly closed lips. Fire, sulphur, and brimstone rained down upon the poor helpless cripple and when Sören finally departed from the hospital, he left behind him not only one of his legs but his natural good spirits and light-heartedness.

He who had always been clean-living from his youth up now went about repentant for his own sins and for the sins of all the rest of the world as well. With the incessant pain in his leg, and the constant fear of being a burden upon others through the best years of his life, he now suffered besides from moral scruples which had their birth in his painful hospital experiences; and laboring as he did under the heavy burden of a deep-rooted sense of guilt, he embraced with enthusiasm the opportunity to work on "the ship"—the opportunity to do penance for something of that great load of sin which he knew he had accumulated during the long years.

The others scraped the money together for the materials; Sören took the lion's share of the work. After half a year's tireless labor, the boat was finished and christened "The Sailors' Remembrance." It measured full seven feet from stem to stern when it was completed.

With great solemnity it was carried to the church and hung up there. The old minister consecrated it with a sermon that had at least the virtue of length, and Sören blew his nose almost continuously in his cotton handkerchief with the picture of the fall of Sebastopol on it. While the others all went to the tavern after the ceremonies, he trudged the two long miles back home, with his crutch and his cane, and all the way back he struggled with the old devil in him; with thoughts that accused each other and snarled at each other. Had he not looked up at the lovely ship too often during the church services, fearful that it might

begin to swing from side to side on its axis? And
had he not in his anxiety and restlessness neglected
to give that attention to the old minister which
was due to a preacher of the gospel, even though
his speech was concerned merely with a ship?

Then the miserable story about the old minister
all came out, and Sören's thoughts hardly grew
brighter. When a civil official is guilty of embez-
zlement, that is a bad enough example to those
under him, but when a minister of the gospel
scandalizes his congregation, that is much worse.
It is all very well to say that most of the inhabitants of the parish are thick-skinned, but there
are always sensitive souls, like Sören, who suffer
keenly from their inability to disentangle the eternal verities from weak human passions. Day
by day, Sören became more melancholy, and he
was not able, like his brothers, to go and bury his
thoughts with the fishing-nets deep down in the
sea and draw them up again in the form of shining fish.

Then it was that a chance remark of his
father's showed Sören an opportunity for use-
fulness. "S'long as a body has one good leg and
two fists on his arms, he shouldn't just sit and
philosophize, and live on other people," his father
said. Sören felt ashamed of himself, and went
to work with a will. It was the ship that both
gave him the idea and showed him the way to

carry it out. After he had finished that for the church, he rigged out a new one which he placed on exhibition, and no less a personage than an admiral bought it for his model cabinet. After that Sören launched many other ships; some came to harbor in churches and others in toy shops; some sailed the seas of piety and others those of pleasure. And Sören's thoughts went with them all. They no longer tarried at home and ate into his soul and wasted away his strength. They showed him the whole world in all its variety and beauty, and behind it all one great broad humanity. Sören changed from a narrow pietist to a philosopher, and when the first strangeness of the transition had worn off, he knew that he was happier for the change.

So twenty years had slipped by. Each of the three brothers had taken a wife unto himself, and had long ago added several little ones for good measure. Sören had made himself a new "leg," much better than the old English one, even though that had cost him seven pounds sterling. He philosophized, he fitted out ships, he helped his brothers, and he laid a little money aside, and now he was perhaps the most highly respected man in the fishing-hamlet. And that is a great deal for a man who does not fish.

Since the days of the "old" minister, there had been a whole series of clergymen in the parish to which the fishing-hamlet belonged. Indeed, it was something of a training-school for young ministers. The last one had been there two years already. The clergy are always on the carpet nowadays; they are either lauded as shining spiritual lights, or they are denounced as hypocrites. Now this young minister was neither. He was, indeed, but a child, both in his faith and in his actions. The weak son of a man of learning, he had retained from his school-boy days one overwhelming passion. That passion was the sea. He had always wanted to be a sailor, but his health would not permit it, and so he became a theologian instead. He was a typical idealist, absent-minded, other-worldly, and impractical; and he was rather effeminate both in face and figure. His faith was a simple one, and he was not perplexed by any modern heretical notions. He did not know life, and he did not want to know it; had he chanced to meet it face to face one day, he would have stepped politely aside and let it pass, while he hurried home to his study. There, on top of his bookcase, stood a toy ship which he had kept from his school days. Besides his ship he had an unobtrusive little wife and a little boy. In the field just back of the parsonage lay a peat bog with clear water, and here the minister was accustomed to spend many happy hours, playing with his son and his sailboat. It would have been difficult to determine which of the two, father or son, was enjoying himself more. Indeed there were those who thought that the minister took the son along only that he might not be surprised at play alone with his toy.

Every day he walked the two miles down to the fishing beach. There he stood, looking dreamily out over the water, and staring curiously at the fishermen and their boats. One day he was on the point of taking his sailboat with him, so that he might watch it sail on "real" water. At the last moment his courage failed him, and he left it at home, but he never ceased to regret this. He knew the whole theory of sailing and of ship-building and rigging. He had read extensively on the subject, and he had an uncle, an old seaman, who used to amuse himself by teaching him marine terminology. But when it came to talking with the fishermen, he was embarrassed and mute. He had stood aside to let life pass him by, and now life stood aside for him.

Not very many of the fisherfolk were to be seen up in the little white church on Sundays. It was not, indeed, that Vangaa was especially irreligious, but it had somehow become an established custom that one went to church only on the greatest and most solemn church holidays. Those few fisherfolk who had formerly been in the habit of coming more regularly had gradually drifted away.

They couldn't understand the new minister. It was not that they found any fault with him. On the contrary, it was generally conceded that, within his limited means, he was very generous, in fact almost too ready to believe any hard luck story, so that he was often imposed upon by the unworthy. But to church they did not come.

He couldn't quite understand it. He prepared his sermons with the greatest conscientiousness; he had been brought up by his learned father to do everything thoroughly. Sometimes, after his eyes had sought in vain for fisherfolk among the congregation, they would fasten themselves upon the ship that hung there before him, attached by a chain to the loft. He took such a childish delight in the ship that frequently he became distracted in his exposition of the Scriptures, and then he would be forced to pull himself together in order not to lose entirely the thread of his sermon. That ship was altogether too lovely!

But a few months ago he had discovered certain infirmities in its masts and spars and rigging. He talked about it to the schoolmaster and to the church warden, and to several others up in the little village, but they couldn't help him. Indeed, they were scarcely aware of the existence of the ship, though it had hung there these many years in full view of the whole congregation, a good seven feet in length, with dusty little sailors

[183]

clinging to the rigging, with a flag under the
monkey gaff and a pennant waving aloft.

Then one day, around harvest time, a delegation from Vangaa was announced to the pastor.
Sören, the spokesman of the group, shuffled in
across the threshold of the pastor's study, with his
cane and his crutch. His brother Karl and another fisherman followed close behind.

The pastor was embarrassed, and he blushed
and stammered as he asked the reason for this unexpected visit. When Sören felt the minister's
embarrassment, he too became embarrassed, and
stammered and stuttered. Karl tried to explain
for him, but Sören waved him back. Then, finally,
it all came out. The Sunday before Christmas
it would be just twenty years since the ship was
hung up in the church, and now they wanted to
use these few months to take her down and over-
haul every part of her carefully, and then, on the
twentieth anniversary, they wanted to hoist her
up again. Would the pastor give his blessing to
all this, and hold a short dedication ceremony
after the regular church service?

"For you see, pastor," concluded Sören, "ships
are just like human beings; they get slack in the
rigging and crooked in the spars, and dusty in the
corners, even in a few years, let alone twenty.
We fisherfolk don't know how to polish off a
man, inside and out, but it's another matter with

[184]

a ship that all of us helped to build, and that I, Sören Olsen, without praising myself, rigged out."

The young minister blushed again, looked at Sören and said, "To be sure, I have noticed myself that the ship needed overhauling pretty badly. The horn of the foretopmast crosstrees on the port side is broken, and . . . well . . . there is a good deal out of order."

Sören looked at the minister in astonishment; then he turned to his two friends as if to say, "Did you hear that? Foretopmast crosstrees!"

And in truth it sounded just as queer to the ears of these simple fishermen as it would have sounded to those of the minister had they suddenly begun to talk Hebrew.

But Sören merely cleared his throat, and continued, "Well, then, if the pastor will be so good—"

The pastor nodded. "You do your part, and I'll promise to do mine," he assured them.

Three huge paws were thrust out, one after another, and three times the little hand of the minister disappeared for an instant in one of them, and all three fishermen said, "Thank you, pastor."

Then the delegation left. But at the door Sören turned around and pointed to the sailboat on the bookcase. "Excuse my boldness, pastor, but I noticed her there right away. I think she might stand a bit of overhauling, too, and if the pastor would allow me, I'd be so pleased . . . Sometime during the holidays, perhaps."

The minister beamed his pleasure. "Will you really?" he said. "You are a good man, Sören."

"Oh, no, I am only three-fourths of a man, you know. And there is only One who is really good."

"That was spoken like a Christian, Sören."

The Sunday before Christmas had come. It did not begin to get light until almost nine o'clock, but Sören sat and looked at his work in the gray light of the morning. There stood the frigate on a work-bench where bars might be placed under it when the men came to carry it away. The white sails were furled, and the twelve metal cannon glistened on the deck, and tiny sailors in blue coats stood around in the rigging, and a handsome captain with gold braid on his cap stood aft on the quarter-deck, and over him a flag waved from the gaff, and from the masthead fluttered a white pennant with the name clearly written, "The Sailors' Remembrance." Outside the house stood all the boys and girls of the fishing-hamlet and pressed their noses flat against the window panes. Even then they couldn't see very much.

At last eleven o'clock came, and the men carried the ship out of the room and up the road to

the church as carefully as if it were made of glass.
The whole fishing population was there, in high
hats and low-crowned hats; and a band with a
bugle, two clarinets, and a harmonica led the way.
The wives and daughters brought up the rear,
while all the youngsters ran in front and shouted
"Hurrah!" at the top of their voices—and then
hurried back to take another look at the ship.

Finally the church service proper came to an
end, but the congregation kept their seats, and
others came streaming in all the time from round
about the country-side. The church was decorated with branches of young firs and other ever-
greens up around the pulpit, and the Christmas
spirit pervaded the place. Then the solemn pro-
cession marched in and up the aisle with the beautiful ship. The chain from the ceiling was lowered
all the way down, so that Sören and his father
could fasten it midships to a lug that was screwed
in the deck.

"It should really have been an iron bar," Sören
whispered to the old man.

"Sure there ain't a twist in the chain?" asked
Ole anxiously.

"No, I don't think so, but what if she should
swing away?"

"Well, I s'pose she'd stop after a while," said
Ole philosophically.

There hung the ship. Now every one could

see the new copper plating on the bottom, and the gilded figurehead, and the frowning cannon that stuck their mouths belligerently out of the port-holes; and not an eye in the whole church failed to take all of this in.

The minister stood in the pulpit. He was quite pale, for he had sat up most of the night working over this talk, but now that he stood here he had forgotten completely everything that he had thought over with such learning and thoroughness during the night. There hung the ship; he scarcely dared look at it for fear he should be distracted by its loveliness. And there, below, all these new faces stared up at him—all the fish-ermen with their wives and their children. Never before had the church been so well filled, and at the thought of talking to all these people who were here for the first—and probably for the last—time, the little minister became so nervous that he was almost dizzy.

Then the sweet pungent smell of the ever-greens came to him; it was the familiar Christmas smell, and it always gave him peace and self-assurance. He folded his hands, looked down in front of him, looked up again, and began.

He spoke of grace—of grace from above, of the church sacraments, of universal sin, of the government and of the king who guided the helm of the ship of State and of a greater King who held the helm of the ship of Life. But when he tried to connect this helm with the ship above him, he lost the thread of his thought and had to begin all over again with grace.

A slight but noticeable restlessness was apparent in the congregation. The minister looked down, and then he looked up again at the ship which was swinging very slowly. It came to a stop, and began to swing back; while the minister stopped a moment to use his handkerchief. Then he got hold of another thread of thought.

He spoke of the significance of the nave or "ship" in church architecture. Scholars, to be sure, were unable to agree on the term, which was derived from the Greek. And he began to be very erudite indeed, while the ship began to swing once more on its chain.

Then the minister completely lost the thread of his discourse, and the restlessness became greater and greater.

Suddenly he saw a great light; perhaps it was a Christmas light. For look—there sat all these humble fisherfolk and stared up at him with a puzzled questioning in their eyes. They hadn't come to hear about the church sacraments, or their own sinfulness, or Greek words and phrases. They were all poor and simple folk who labored incessantly on the sea and on shore; they were children, all of them—old and young, and they

[189]

had come to him with their childish offering, the ship. It symbolized their very life, their life on battleship or merchant vessel or fishing smack, up and down the high seas, day and night in fair or foul weather. Out of the fullness of their simple, childish hearts they had given this symbolic ship to the church. How was the church to express its appreciation, if not by inculcating her golden rule, teaching them to love one another, to aid one another in the fierce struggle for existence, and to trust in an inscrutable but all-seeing Providence?

It was such words that now fell unpremeditated from the pastor's lips. All the learned discourse, all the fine-spun argument he had committed to memory, was forgotten. For the first time in his life the minister improvised, and, while he spoke thus from the fullness of his heart, he used such words as tide and anchorage, and he concluded with the phrase, "When the Great Captain calls, 'All hands on deck!'" Then he said "Amen," and when he looked down in front of him he saw that all eyes were moist; and when he looked up, there hung the ship as proud and motionless as if there never had been any twist in her chain. . . .

Outside the church Sören stood waiting for the minister. "Thank you, pastor," he said simply.

"Are you satisfied?" the minister asked humbly.

"Yes, after you finally caught the wind. It went a little slowly at first—but so it does for the rest of us too. Now we understand you."

On Christmas Day all the fisherfolk were in church again. They said, of course, that they came just to get another look at the ship, but fisherfolk are a sly tribe.

The day after Christmas Sören took the minister's sailboat home for repairs.

HERMAN BANG

IRENE HOLM

IN ROSENBORG PARK

HERMAN BANG (1857–1912) came of an old patrician family which showed symptoms of degeneracy. His father, who at the time of the author's birth was a clergyman at Als near the Prussian border, was morbidly nervous, and at last died insane. As a child of seven Herman Bang experienced the flight before the victorious Prussians which he described in *Tine,* one of his best novels. His mother figures both in this book and in a later novel, *The White House.*

Herman Bang wished to be an actor. Failing that, he became a journalist, and soon attracted attention by his masterly literary critiques dealing especially with the French Realists. His first important novel was *Hopeless Generations,* which is in part autobiographical, and interesting as typical of the age. In *Stucco* he satirized the pretentions and excrescences that followed Copenhagen's transition from a small town to a metropolis.

The most nearly classic part of Bang's production consists of the stories that have been designated "tragic idyls," quiet, uneventful tales of everyday life, such as the short novel, *By the Wayside,* and the three stories in the volume *Under the Yoke* from which *Irene Holm* is taken. Two novels of artists, *Mikaël* and *Denied a Country,* the first with a French painter, the second with an internationally famous violinist as hero, are somewhat strained and not so well grounded in their milieu as the stories of Danish life.

In his later years Bang was to some extent compensated for his early failure as an actor by his success in reading his own works from the stage. It was on such a reading tour in the United States that he met his death, very suddenly. He was found dead in his berth in the Pullman, near Ogden, Utah.

Herman Bang

IRENE HOLM

IT was announced by the sheriff's son from the church steps after the services one Sunday that Miss Irene Holm, danseuse at the Royal Theater, would begin her courses in etiquette, dancing, and gesture, in the inn, on the first of November, for children as well as for those more advanced—ladies and gentlemen—provided a sufficent number of applications be made. Price, five crowns for each child; reduction for several from the same family.

Seven applied, Jens Larsen furnishing the three at the reduced rate. Miss Irene Holm considered the number sufficient. She arrived at the inn one evening toward the end of October, her baggage an old champagne basket tied with a rope. She was small and worn, with a forty-year-old baby face under her fur cap, and old handkerchiefs tied about her wrists as a protection against rheumatism. She enunciated very distinctly, and said, "Thank you so much—but I can do it myself," whenever any one offered to do

anything for her, and she looked quite helpless.
She would have nothing but a cup of tea, and then
crept into her bed in the little chamber behind the
public room, her teeth chattering whenever she
thought of the possibility of ghosts.

The next day she appeared with her hair curled,
and wearing a close-fitting coat edged with fur
on which the tooth of time had left a visible im-
press. She had to pay visits to her honored
patrons, the parents of her pupils, she said. And
might she ask the way? Mrs. Hendriksen went
to the doorway and pointed over the flat fields.
Miss Holm curtsied her thanks to the three door-
steps.

"Poor old thing," said Mrs. Hendriksen. She
remained standing in the doorway and looked
after Miss Holm, who was taking a roundabout
way to Jens Larsen's house on the dike, to spare
her footgear. Miss Holm wore kid shoes and
ribbed stockings.

When she had visited the parents—Jens Larsen
paid nine crowns for his three—Miss Holm
looked about for a room. She got a little white-
washed chamber at the smith's, looking out upon
the flat fields, and furnished with a bureau, a bed,
and a chair. In the corner, between the bureau
and the window, the champagne basket was set
down. Miss Holm moved in. The morning
was spent in making applications of curling pins,

cold tea, and warm slate pencils. When the curls were in order, she tidied the room, and in the afternoon she crocheted. She sat on the champagne basket in the corner and took advantage of the last vestige of daylight. The smith's wife came in and sat down on the wooden chair and talked, while Miss Holm listened, smiling graciously and nodding her curled head.

The woman spun out the story in the dark for an hour, until it was time for supper, but Miss Holm scarcely knew what she had said. Outside of dancing and gesture, and calculations as to her daily bread—a tedious, eternal calculation—the things of this world had much difficulty in forcing their way into Miss Holm's consciousness. She sat still on her basket with her hands in her lap and only looked fixedly at the line of light under the smith's door. She never went out, for she became homesick as soon as she saw the desolate flat fields, and she was afraid of bulls and of runaway horses. Later in the evening she would boil water on the tiled stove and eat supper. Then she would put up her curls in papers, and when she had undressed as far as her petticoats, she would practise her steps at the bedpost, moving her legs until it made her perspire.

The smith and his wife did not budge from the keyhole. They had a rear view of the leaps of the ballet; the curling-papers stood out from her head like quills upon the fretful porcupine. Miss Holm was so engrossed that she began to hum aloud as she moved up, down, up, down, in her exercises. The smith and his wife and the children were glued to the keyhole.

When Miss Holm had practised the prescribed number of minutes, she crept into bed. After practising she always thought of the time "when she was a student at the ballet-school," and suddenly she would laugh aloud, a carefree laugh, just as she lay there. She fell asleep, still thinking of the time—the happy time—the rehearsals, when they stuck each other's legs with pins . . . and screamed . . . the evenings in the dressing-rooms . . . what a bustle, all the voices . . . and the director's bell. . . . Miss Holm would still wake up at night, if she dreamt of having missed an entrance.

"Now—one—two—" Miss Holm raised her skirt and put out her foot . . . "toes out—one—two—three."

The seven had their toes turned inward—with their fingers in their mouths as they hopped about.

"Little Jens—toes out—one—two—three—make a bow—one—two—three—once more. . . ."

Jens Larsen's three children made the bow with their tongues sticking rigidly out of their mouths.

"Little Marie to the right—one—two—

three—" Marie went to the left. . . . "Do it over—one—two—three—"

Miss Holm frisked like a lamb, so that a goodly portion of her stockings was visible. The course was in full progress. They danced three times a week in the inn-room with two lamps that hung from the beams. The ancient dust rose in the old room under their stamping. The seven were as completely at sea as a school of fish. Miss Holm straightened their backs and curved their arms.

"One—two—three—clap hands."

"One—two—three—clap hands." The seven staggered as they did so and nearly lost their balance.

Miss Holm got dust in her throat from shouting. They were to dance a waltz, two by two, and held each other at arm's length, awkwardly and nervously, as though turning in their sleep. Miss Holm talked and swung them around.

"Good—turn—four—five—good—turn—little Jette."

Miss Holm followed up Jens Larsen's middle child and little Jette and swung them around like a top.

"Good—good—little Jette."

Her eyes smarted with the dust. The seven continued hopping in the middle of the floor in the twilight.

When Miss Holm came home after the dancing lessons, she would tie a handkerchief around her curly head. She went about with a perpetual cold, and in unoccupied hours she sat with her nose over a bowl of boiling water to relieve it.

They had music for their lessons: Mr. Brodersen's violin. Miss Holm got two new pupils, advanced ones. They all kept moving to Tailor Brodersen's instrument, and the dust rose in clouds, and the tiled stove danced on its lion's claws. The number of visitors also increased; from the manse came the pastor's daughter and the young curate.

Miss Holm demonstrated under the two oil-lamps with her chest thrown out and her foot extended—"Move your legs, little children, move your legs, that's it. . . ."

Miss Holm moved her legs and raised her skirt a little, for there were spectators.

Every week Miss Holm would send her crocheting to Copenhagen. The mail was delivered to the schoolmaster. Invariably she had either sealed or addressed improperly, and the schoolmaster had to do it over, while she stood by and looked on with the humility of a sixteen-year-old.

The newspapers which the mail had brought lay ready for distribution on one of the school desks, and one day she begged to be permitted to look at *Berlingske*. She had looked at the pile

for a week before she had picked up the courage
to ask. After that she came every day in the
noon period—the teacher knew her soft knock
with one knuckle. "Come in, Miss; it is open,"
he would say.

She went into the schoolroom and took *Berlingske* from the pile. She read the announce-
ments of the theaters, the repertoire and the criti-
cisms, of which she understood nothing, but it was
about the people "down there." It took her a
long time to get through a column, while her index
finger followed gracefully along the lines. When
she had finished reading, she crossed the passage
and knocked as before.

"Well," said the teacher, "anything new in
town?"

"At least it's about the people down there," she
said. "The old conditions, you know."

"The poor little thing," said the teacher, looking out of the window after her. Miss Holm
went home to her crocheting.

"The poor little thing, she's crazy about her
dancing-master," he said.

A ballet by a new ballet-master was to be per-
formed at the theater. Miss Holm knew the list
of characters by heart and also the names of all
the solo dancers. "You see, we were at school
together," she said, "all of us."

On the evening of the ballet she was feverish,

as if it were she that was to dance. She lighted
the two candles, gray with age, that stood on
the dresser, one on each side of the plaster cast
of Thorvaldsen's Christ, and she sat on her
champagne basket and looked into the flame.
But she could not bear being alone. All the old
unrest of the theater came over her. She went
into the smith's rooms, where they were at supper,
and sat down on a chair by the side of the huge old
clock. She talked more in those few hours than
all the rest of the year. It was all about theaters
and premières, the great soloists, and the master-
steps. She hummed and swayed with the upper
part of her body as she sat. The smith enjoyed
it so much that he began to growl out an ancient
cavalry ditty, and he said—

"Mother, we'll drink a punch on that—a real
arrack!"

The punch was brewed, and the two candles
from the bureau were put on the table, and they
drank and talked away, but in the midst of the
merriment Miss Holm suddenly grew still, great
tears came into her eyes, and she rose and went
to her room. In there she settled down on her
basket, burst into tears, and sat for a long time
before she undressed and went to bed. She went
through no "steps" that night.

She was thinking of one thing: He had been

at school with her. She lay still in her bed.
Now and then she sighed in the dark, and her
head moved uneasily on the pillow. In her ears
sounded the voice of the ballet-master at school,
angry and derisive. "Holm has no go. Holm
has no go." He shouted it, and it echoed
through the hall. How clearly she heard it—
how clearly she saw the hall! The figurantes
practised in long rows, one step at a time.
Tired, she leaned against the wall a moment, and
again the sharp voice of the ballet-master—
"Holm, haven't you any ambition at all?"

She saw their room at home, her mother sitting
in the armchair complaining, and her sister working the busy sewing-machine near the lamp, and
she heard her mother say in her asthmatic voice,
"Did Anna Stein dance the solo?"

"Yes, mother."

"I suppose she had La Grande Napolitaine?"

"Yes, mother."

"And you two entered school at the same time,"
said her mother, looking over at her from behind
the lamp.

"Yes, mother."

And she beheld Anna Stein in the embroidered
skirt—with ribbons fluttering in her tambourine, a
living and rejoicing vision in the radiance of the
footlights, in her great solo. Suddenly she laid

her head down in the pillows and sobbed desperately and ceaselessly in her impotence and despair. It was morning before she fell asleep.

The ballet had been a success. Miss Holm read the criticism at the school. While she was reading, a few small old woman's tears fell on the copy of *Berlingske*.

From her sister came letters. Letters of notes due and telling of sore distress. On those days Miss Holm forgot about her crocheting and would sit pressing her temples, the open letter in her lap. Finally she would make the rounds of "her" parents, and blushing and paling would beg half her pay in advance, and what she got she would send home.

The days passed. Miss Irene Holm went to her lessons and returned. She obtained new pupils, half a dozen young farmhands who had united for the purpose of dancing three evenings a week in Peter Madsen's big room near the woods. Miss Holm walked two miles through the winter darkness, frightened as a hare, pursued by all the old ghost stories that had been current at the ballet school. She had to pass a pond surrounded by willows stretching their great arms up in the darkness. She felt her heart as a cold stone in her breast.

They danced for three hours, and she gave the commands, swung them about, and danced with the gentlemen pupils until her cheeks were a hectic red. When she had to go home, Peter Madsen's gate was locked, and the farmhand went out with her, carrying a light to open the gate. He held the lantern high in his hand for a moment as she walked out into the darkness, hearing his "good-night" behind her, and the gate as it scraped over the stones and was locked. The first part of the way there were hedges with bushes that waved and nodded.

Spring was coming, and Miss Irene Holm's course was drawing to a close. The party at Peter Madsen's wanted to have a final dance at the inn.

The affair was very fine with "Welcome" in transparencies over the door, and cold supper at two crowns per cover, and the curate and the pastor's daughter to grace the table. Miss Holm was dressed in barége with trimmings, and Roman ribbons about her hair. Her fingers were covered with rings exchanged with her friends at the school. Between the dances she sprayed lavender water on the floor and threatened the ladies with the bottle. Miss Holm looked quite young again.

First they danced a quadrille. The parents and the old folks stood along the walls and in the doorways, each one looking after his own off-spring, with an appearance of great awe. The young people whirled around in the quadrille with faces like masks, as cautious in their steps as if they were dancing on eggs. Miss Holm was all encouraging smiles, and French endearments under her breath. The band consisted of Mr. Brodersen and his son. Mr. Brodersen, junior, was working the piano which the pastor had lent for the occasion.

When the round dance began, the tone of those present became less constrained. The men applied themselves to the punch in the middle room, and the gentlemen pupils asked Miss Holm to dance. She moved with her head on one side, raising herself on her toes with her belated sixteen-year-old gracefulness. The other couples stopped dancing, and Miss Holm and her partner held the floor alone. The men came into the doorway of the little room, and all were plunged in profound admiration of Miss Holm, who advanced her feet farther beyond her petticoat and swayed with her hips. The pastor's daughter was so amused that she pinched the curate in the arm. After a mazurka, the schoolmaster shouted "Bravo!" and all clapped their hands. Miss Holm made the ballet bow with two fingers on her heart. It was time for supper, and she arranged a polonaise. All were in it; the women nudged each other with embarrassment and delight; the men said: "Well, old woman, I guess we'll try."

A couple began singing "Our Soldiers Brave" and beating time to accompany the song. Miss Irene Holm sat with the schoolmaster under the bust of His Majesty the King. The general tone once more became solemn after they had seated themselves, and only Miss Holm continued speaking in the parlor manner as the players do in a Scribe comedy. Gradually things became more gay. The men began to drink each other's health and to clink glasses across the table.

There was boisterous merriment at the table occupied by the young people, and it was some time before it was quiet enough for the schoolmaster to speak. He spoke of Miss Holm and of the nine muses. He spoke at length, while all along the table the others sat and looked down into their plates. Their faces assumed a solemn and tense expression, as when the parish clerk appeared in the choir-door at church, and they played with little pieces of bread. The speaker was approaching the subject of Freya and her two cats, and proposed a toast for "The Priestess of Art, Miss Irene Holm." Nine long hurrahs were shouted, and every one wanted to drink with Miss Holm.

Miss Holm had not understood the speech, but was much flattered. She rose and saluted with her glass, held aloft by her curved arm. The festive powder had all disappeared in the heat and the exertion, and she had dark red spots in her cheeks.

There was a great hullabaloo: the young people sang, the older folks drank to each other in private and rose from their places, slapped each other on the back and poked each other in the stomach, out on the floor. The women were becoming anxious lest their better halves should take too much. In the midst of the merry-making, Miss Holm, who had become very cheerful, could be heard laughing carelessly, as she had laughed thirty years before at the dancing school.

Then the schoolmaster said, "Miss Holm really ought to dance." But she *had* danced!

"Yes, but for them all—a solo—that was the thing!"

Miss Holm had understood at once, and a bold wish flamed up within her: they would let her *dance*. But she began to laugh and said to Peter Madsen's wife, "The organist wants me to dance" —as if that were the most ridiculous thing in the world.

Those standing near heard it, and there was a general cry—"Yes—you must dance!"

Miss Holm was flushed up to her hair, and said that "the festive atmosphere was almost too exalted."

And besides there was no music.

And you couldn't dance in long skirts.

A man shouted across the hall, "They can be raised!" and all laughed aloud and went on begging her.

"Yes, if the pastor's young lady will play a tarantella."

The pastor's young lady was surrounded. She was willing and would try. The schoolmaster rose and struck his glass. "Ladies and gentlemen," he said, "Miss Holm will honor us by dancing." They cried "Hurrah!" and began to get up from the tables. The curate was black and blue, so hard had the pastor's daughter pinched him.

Miss Holm and the latter went in to try the music. Miss Holm was feverish and went back and forth, stretching her limbs. She pointed to the board floor, with its hills and valleys, and said, "But one is not accustomed to dance in a circus!"

At last she said, "All right. The show can begin." She was quite hoarse with emotion. "I shall come in after the first ten beats," she said. "I'll give a signal." She went into the side-room to wait.

Her public entered and stood around in a semicircle, whispering and curious. The schoolmaster took the candles from the table and set them up on the window-casement, as if for an illumination. Then a knock came at the side-room door.

The pastor's daughter began to play, and all

looked toward the door. After the tenth beat it opened, and all clapped their hands. Miss Holm was dancing with her skirt tied up in a Roman scarf. It was "La Grande Napolitaine." She walked on her toes and made turns. The spectators looked at her feet and marveled, for their motion was as that of two drumsticks, and when she stood on one leg, the people clapped again.

She said "Faster!"—and began to whirl around. She smiled and beckoned and fanned and fanned. The upper part of her body, her arms, seemed to have more to do every moment; it became rather a mimic performance than a dance. She looked closely into the faces of the onlookers—her mouth opened—smiled—showed all its teeth (some were awful)—she beckoned, acted—she knew and felt nothing but her "solo." At last she was having her solo! This was no longer "La Napolitaine." It was Fenella, the kneeling Fenella, the beseeching Fenella, the tragic Fenella.

She knew not how she had got up nor how she had got out. She had only heard the music stop suddenly—and the *laughter*—laughter, while she suddenly noticed all the faces. She rose, extended her arms once more, through force of habit—and made her curtsy, while they shouted. Within, in the side-room, she stood at the table a moment; it was dark to her, absolutely void.

Then slowly and with very stiff hands she loosened the sash, smoothed out the skirt, and went
in quietly to where the clapping was still going on.

She curtsied, standing close to the piano, but
did not raise her eyes from the floor.   They were
in a hurry to begin dancing.   Miss Holm went
around quietly saying "Good-bye," and the pupils
pressed the money, wrapped in paper, into her
hands.   Peter Madsen's wife helped her on with
her things, and at the last moment the pastor's
daughter and the curate came and asked to be allowed to accompany her.

They walked along silently.   The pastor's
daughter was absolutely unhappy and wanted to
make some apology but did not know what to
say, and the little danseuse continued walking
with them, silent and pale.

Finally the curate spoke, tortured by the silence, "You see, Miss, those people have no appreciation of the tragic."

Miss Holm remained silent.   They had arrived at the smith's house, and she curtsied as she
gave them her hand.   The pastor's daughter put
her arms around her and kissed her.   "Good-
night, Miss Holm," she said, and her voice was
unsteady.   The curate and she waited in the road
until they had seen the light in the danseuse's
room.

Miss Holm took off the barége skirt and folded

it up. Then she unwrapped her money and counted it and sewed it up in a little pocket in her petticoat. She managed the needle very awkwardly, as she sat thus by candle-light.

The next morning, her champagne basket was lifted into the mail coach. It was a rainy day, and Miss Holm crept in under a leaky umbrella; she drew up her legs under her, so that she presented a very Turkish appearance on her basket. When they were ready to drive off, with the postman walking by the side of the coach—one passenger being all the poor nag could draw—the pastor's daughter came down from the parsonage, bareheaded. She brought a white chip basket with her, saying, "You can't go off without provisions!"

She bent down under the umbrella and, taking Miss Holm's head in her hands, she kissed her twice. The old danseuse burst into tears, caught the girl's hand and kissed it. The pastor's daughter remained standing in the road and looked after the old umbrella as long as she could see it.

Miss Irene Holm had announced a spring course in "Modern Society Dancing" in a neighboring town. Six pupils had applied. Thither she went—to continue what human beings dare to call Life.

In Rosenborg Park

EVERY morning in spring, as I went to work, I met a young man and a young woman. Every morning they were walking under the young trees in the King's Park.

They came at the same time every day, and I formed the habit of looking for them. The morning seemed to grow brighter at their coming.

By the inclination of their heads, if by nothing else, you could see that they loved each other, his bending down to hers. But at the bandstand they always stopped a moment, and as they exchanged a smile, they caught a strain passing through the air.

The lilacs were in blossom, and the many bushes were fragrant.

Then it happened that I left town, or at any rate stopped walking through the park.

But the next time I went the accustomed way to my daily work, I saw the same woman walking on ahead of me—alone. I passed her, quickly, so as to make quite sure.

Yes, 'twas she. But her walk was much

slower, and in her eyes there was a look as of a surprised sorrow.

At the band-stand—I was slowly walking after her—she stopped as they had both so often done. And on her face I saw a sudden smile, more painful than any tears could be.

And then she walked away.

But involuntarily I asked myself—

"Through what streets does he go to work now?"

HENRIK PONTOPPIDAN

THE ROYAL GUEST

Henrik Pontoppidan (1857-) was born in Fredericia as the son of a clergyman. He wished to become an engineer, but after passing his examinations, he took a position as teacher of geography and surveying in the folk high school of which his brother was the head. While there, he married the daughter of a peasant proprietor.

Pontoppidan's first stories, in the collections *Village Pictures* and *From the Cottages,* are naturalistic tales of peasant life shorn of all illusion and romance. In the novel cycle, *The Promised Land,* he again describes the peasants, but on this much broader canvas he has room for a greater variety of types. The folk high school is dealt with in a somewhat critical spirit, while the simple peasant family from which the clergyman idealist, Emanuel Hansted, chooses his bride is sympathetically drawn.

Pontoppidan's second novel cycle, ironically called *Lucky-Per,* describes the radical movement in Copenhagen in the seventies and eighties, and introduces many well-known figures, among them Georg Brandes as Dr. Nathan. The hero, Per Sidenius, the son of a clergyman, breaks away from his home, and sets out to conquer the world, but finds that his sluggish blood and inherited traditions paralyze his power of action.

The third great novel cycle, *The Kingdom of the Dead,* is a pessimistic picture of Denmark at the turn of the century, when Liberalism had won its signal victory—a victory which Pontoppidan regards as quite hollow. The author's latest work is the novel *Man's Will* in which he satirizes Danish policies during the World War.

In 1917 Pontoppidan shared with Karl Gjellerup the Nobel prize for literature.

Henrik Pontoppidan

THE ROYAL GUEST

WHEN PEOPLE who are surrounded by
the noise and bustle of a large city try to
imagine life in the country, they usually picture
it as an existence in which the days drag themselves sluggishly on, while every one of the sixty
minutes in the hour passes with the solemn de-
liberateness of a grandfather's clock ticking out
eternity in the quiet room of an old woman. The
truth, however, is that, by very reason of its
monotony, there is no place where time passes
more swiftly and the days seem shorter than in
the country. A week, a month, a lifetime slips
away almost before we know it.

Whenever the young physician, Arnold Höjer,
and his pretty little wife happened to think that
they had been married and living in Sönderböl
for five years, they were struck with amazement.
But then it would be hard to find a more remote
place than Sönderböl. It was inhabited exclu-
sively by peasants, and as far as the eye could
reach over the sparsely cultivated heath sur-

rounding it, there were only a few isolated cottages. Not even a clergyman lived there.

Yet the doctor and his wife did not feel lonely. Inside the fence which surrounded their house with its yard and vegetable garden and gave shelter from the rough winds, they had founded their little Eden, where a little Cain and a little Abel were already romping in the grass, while various useful and prolific animals quacked, clucked, and grunted in the outhouses. Now and then they received visits from relatives and friends, and they had the daily mail and the weekly circulating library—there was enough to occupy them, and they felt quite contented.

It happened that some of Mrs. Höjer's relatives from Copenhagen announced their visit at Shrovetide, and not until the whole house had been prepared to receive them did a telegram cancel their plans. At the last moment there had arisen difficulties, and they had been obliged to postpone their visit to a more opportune time.

Of course the young people were greatly disappointed, but chiefly because of their extensive preparations, the abundance of good food that had been provided, and the necessary trouble of shifting the furniture. Their regret at missing the visit of their relatives did not loom so large.

Henrik Pontoppidan

To tell the truth, after the first annoyance had vanished, they were rather glad to be left to themselves in their little nest.

"Do you know," said Mrs. Emmy frankly when, after having restored the old order throughout the house, they were sitting as usual in her husband's den waiting for the mail, "perhaps after all it would have been a bore to have had that invasion come in upon us. These last few days I have felt almost like a stranger in my own house."

Arnold Höjer looked smilingly at his pretty little wife. If the distance between their chairs had not been so great, and if he had not just seated himself after filling his pipe, he would have given her a kiss for these words which expressed his own thoughts.

They fell to talking about several domestic affairs which they felt had been neglected during the commotion of the last few days. They discussed the health of their children, weighed the timeliness of giving their oldest boy a dose of castor oil the next morning, commented upon the condition of their poultry, and so forth.

Owing to a blizzard, the mail had been delayed, but finally arrived. The hanging-lamp over the table was lighted, and husband and wife had just settled down to reading the newspapers,

[219]

when the sound of sleigh-bells made them lift their heads, while a sleigh swung into the yard and stopped in front of the door.

A moment later the maid rushed in, and with great excitement told them that a strange gentleman was asking for Dr. and Mrs. Höjer.

"Didn't he give his name?" asked Arnold.

"No, but I knew the driver. It's the rector's coachman from Österböl."

"Then I suppose it is the rector's brother-in-law, the surveyor."

"Mercy, no! It's no one from these parts. I'm sure it's a fine gentleman," she added in a whisper. "He's wearing a big brown fur coat."

Mrs. Emmy was embarrassed. As was often the case, she had not found time to dress, but was still wearing her morning gown, which was rather unfit to be seen by strangers. The doctor looked down at himself with a worried frown. When evening came, he was in the habit of indulging in a dressing-gown and embroidered slippers. However, there was nothing to be done in his case. He could not keep the stranger waiting.

"Show the gentleman in," he said to the maid when his wife had gone into the bedroom. He had hardly time to rise before the door opened, and a portly man of moderate height, dressed like an artist, entered and in a melodious voice bade

[220]

him good evening. To judge from his bald temples and bristling grayish-brown curls, the stranger might be about fifty, but his smoothly shaven face was made youthful by full red lips and sparkling brown eyes.

"Have I the honor of speaking to Dr. Höjer?" he asked.

"I am Dr. Höjer."

"Permit me to begin by asking a favor which may surprise you: kindly excuse me from telling you my name—let me come before you as nothing more than a nameless wayfarer. I see that I am startling you. I admit that my request, and indeed my very presence here as an uninvited guest, call for an explanation. But—shall we sit down?"

"By all means."

"Thank you.—To cut matters short: I arrived in Österböl, your neighboring town, this afternoon, to pay a visit to the rector, who is an old friend of mine. I have not seen him for many years, and I have long had the desire to surprise him in his rustic retreat. But as luck would have it, he had just gone away with his family—there was nobody in the house but a hired man and two maids. You will understand my disappointment when I tell you that for the sake of this visit I had taken a long journey, and that during the ride I had become more and more intent on celebrating a merry Shrovetide with my old friend, who in his younger days—maybe this will seem a little strange to you—was a jolly chap and altogether a fine fellow. And here I find only empty and cold rooms, filled with religious tracts and instructive pamphlets on chicken-raising and child-training, which does not happen to be my favorite literature. Then I had the bold idea to go foraging in the neighborhood, throwing myself on the pity of some fellow-creature. The servants at the rectory told me that there was a charming doctor's family living about four miles away, and as my horses were exhausted, I had the rector's coachman harness his—and here I am, most humbly asking your permission to spend a few hours under your hospitable roof, and have a cozy informal chat with you."

"Why, of course—you are heartily welcome. My wife and I shall be delighted if we can give you some compensation for the loss of your friend's company. But permit me, Mr.—"

"I understand. You are thinking that, after all, this does not explain why you should trust me enough to allow me to withhold my name. But you must admit, dear doctor, that even if I introduced myself as Mr. Petersen, wholesale dealer from Aarhus, or Mr. Hansen, architect from Copenhagen, you would not know me a bit better, and all we should accomplish by this would be to limit our conversation, to press it into a corner, thus depriving our fancies of the charm which they may acquire by their untrammeled flight between heaven and earth. Am I not right? Besides, this is Shrovetide, which in a way justifies wearing a mask and scorning the usual conventionalities. Call it a whim, a silly notion, an obsession if you will, only understand that, however seriously embarrassed I am by my intrusion, I shall feel much more natural toward you when in disguise."

The young doctor had to laugh. There was something irresistibly contagious in the merry mood of the stranger.

"Why, certainly—if you wish it. But," he added a little uneasily, hearing his wife light the lamp in the living-room, "we have to call you something. How shall I introduce you to my wife, for instance?"

"Well, you might call me—why, yes—call me Prince Carnival."

Arnold Höjer had to laugh once more, this time quite loudly, but also somewhat more uneasily than before.

"This is indeed the first time we have entertained a royal guest," he said.

"Bravo!" exclaimed the stranger approvingly, "I see that you are one of ours, doctor."

At this moment, Mrs. Emmy appeared in the door to the living-room. She wore her usual peat-brown afternoon dress, which she had adorned with a black bow. The stranger rose and bowed ceremoniously.

Her husband said laughingly, "May I introduce a celebrated guest, Prince Carnival!"

Mrs. Emmy, who had already been astonished by the noisy merriment of the men, looked from one to the other, and finally regarded her husband with an offended glance.

"What does all this mean?" she asked.

"It means, my dear lady, that it is Shrovetide, and that I really claim the right to be this royal person. Of course you know my illustrious family. I am the son of the honorable Mr. Howleglass. My brother's name is Tom Fool, and Harlequin is my cousin. My country is called Lubberland, and I am a travelling salesman for the famous roast pigeons which fly into the mouths of people who desire them."

This time Mrs. Emmy looked severely at her husband, who had become embarrassed, although he was polite enough to continue laughing. He took up the conversation and repeated at great length the stranger's explanation which, however, did not appease his wife. Indicating with an almost imperceptible bow that, if her husband had received him, she, of course, knew her duty, she retired into the living-room. The men followed her soon after.

The young doctor looked ill at ease. He was waiting impatiently for the moment when the stranger should forget his joke and do the correct thing. But the jolly "prince" pretended to ignore the sudden change in the promising Shrovetide mood, and was valiantly striving to keep the conversation going. Finally he sat down to the piano unasked, opened it, and let his fingers run appraisingly up and down the keys a few times.

"It seems to be a long time since anybody has played here," he said. To this Arnold Höjer answered briefly that his wife had no longer time to cultivate her music.

"Time!" exclaimed the stranger, suddenly striking a loud chord. Then he began to play. Mrs. Emmy lifted her head and opened her eyes wide. Before he had played many measures, she realized that he was a master.

"Do you know this?" he asked her.

"No—how beautiful it is!" she answered impulsively.

"That was only the introduction. Should you like to hear the rest? It is a festal march."

She withdrew a little.

"If you care to play it," she said.

"Very well, I shall go ahead. But—" with a

[225]

look at some sconces in which there were still a few dusty candles left from the last christening party—"you must allow me to make these stars sparkle. This music calls for festive illumination. Kindly help me, doctor, will you?"

Arnold Höjer looked doubtfully at his wife, who shrugged her shoulders as an indication that there was nothing to do but to let the man have his way.

The stranger did not stop at the sconces. In spite of Emmy's attempted protest, he also lighted the eight candles in the chandelier.

"Please, Mrs. Höjer! Wonderful what a difference a dozen poor old candles can make! Look here, I have an idea! Don't these stars seem to demand that we also dress in festive attire on this holy evening? Fortunately I brought my valise. And you, dear lady? I am sure you have some charming heaven-blue or hell-red or Himalaya-colored silk gown from olden times hanging in the sepulchral darkness of your closet, where only the moths enjoy it.—Now you are looking severely at me, and glancing at your husband as if to ask him whether the time has not come to throw me out. But you are not going to do it. I take after my glorious great-uncle, His Satanic Majesty, about whom it is written that no one can give him an inch without—Luke, VII, 8."

Arnold Höjer had again burst out into a loud
laugh, whereas Emmy's pretty little face alter-
nated between perplexed anger and amused smiles.

"What in the world is the meaning of all
this?" she exclaimed. "I really think you want
to turn this house upside down!"

"I should like to do just that. I told you who
I am. I want to celebrate the redemption of all
the things which have most ungratefully been
shoved into the corners, buried in the darkness,
abandoned to the mercy of moths and cobwebs.
Do let me have my way! Afterwards, dear lady,
I will play for you—I will open the heavens for
you with my music. Is that a bargain? In
twenty minutes we shall meet here again, each in
his best attire. Doctor, please show me the way
to the spare-room. No, wait—I know where it
is; the maid put my valise there. Au revoir, my
lord and my lady!"

The door had hardly closed behind him when
Emmy rushed over to her husband.

"What are we going to do with that crazy
man? You ought not to have let him in, Arnold."

"I believe he has scared you," he said with a
laugh, instinctively drawing her nearer to him.
It was long since he had seen on her face this
childishly frightened expression which he knew so
well of old.

[227]

"Who can he be?"

"I don't know. But since he is a childhood friend of the rector, I could not very well turn him out. After all, his name does not matter."

"But what are we to do?"

"Well, now that we have begun, I suppose we have to see the comedy through. He is really rather amusing, crazy as he is. And it is Shrovetide."

"But do you think—do you really mean that we should dress as he said?"

"No, of course not. If we put a bottle of wine on the supper table, we have certainly done our full duty by the rector and the season."

"Well, if you should like it—I mean if it would give you pleasure—I have not worn my light silk dress since our wedding."

She had begun to twist his vest-button.

"I do believe you are coaxing . . ."

"Why, no—not at all. I think it's altogether foolish and crazy. But if we *have* to walk around here play-acting—and as you say, it *is* Shrovetide."

"So it is, and anyway it is impossible to carry on a sensible conversation with that fellow. So let us play fools for once."

"But it's perfectly silly—it's crazy!" Emmy repeated, while her husband, boyishly merry and still embarrassed, drew her toward the bedroom.

Henrik Pontoppidan

When, shortly after, the maid opened the door to the living-room to announce that supper was served, she found nobody there but the stranger, who was in evening dress and busy moving some plants from the window-sill into the room.

"Mercy me!" she exclaimed, looking at the brilliant lights. "What's going on?"

"Don't you know that, old sweetheart? We are expecting illustrious company to-night."

"Who's coming?" she asked, chuckling, and approaching in her bedroom slippers, highly flattered at the familiar address.

"One who can not be seen by human eyes nor heard by human ears, you little heart-thief. But now come and help me. We must fix up the rooms."

Meanwhile the master of the house, in shirtsleeves and carrying a candle, was hurrying along the corridor to the attic where his dress suit was hanging in some corner. When he returned to the bedroom, his wife had just put on her evening dress. She was standing before the looking-glass, holding her breath so as to be able to hook her belt.

"Great!" he burst out admiringly, stretching his arms toward her.

"Don't touch me!—Do I really still look nice in it?"

She could hardly hook the dress for nervousness. She had been mortally afraid that he would laugh at her—her heart had begun to pound violently when she heard him return through the corridor.

"You are magnificent, Emmy. I hardly recognize you! Do you know, after all it was a clever idea!"

"Do you think I should put on this too?" She opened a red box on the dressing-table and took out a diadem made of two big leaves of silver filigree. "Do you remember it?"

"Do I? Let's have a look—put it on!" He was standing behind her, looking over her shoulder into the mirror, while she blushingly put the radiant ornament into her hair. "It is grand! Perfectly splendid! You are beautiful, Emmy!"

In a sudden impulsive outburst of half-forgotten happiness, she threw herself against him, clasping her hands round his neck and looking into his eyes. "Do you really think so, Arnold?"

At this moment a vigorous chord was struck on the piano in the living-room. The march sent its tones to them like a turbulent, victorious fanfare. They were motionless. As if spellbound by the music, her hands remained round his neck. Closing her eyes, she pressed his lips down on hers again and again.

Arm in arm they went into the other room.

Now that their minds were attuned to the festive surroundings, they no longer felt embarrassment.

Meanwhile the stranger had decorated the dining-room to the best of his ability. All that the house contained of old silver and fine china had been pressed into service, and in the center of the table stood a bowl with some big yellow roses which he had brought with him. Even the old servant girl, who as a rule could not be persuaded to give up her kitchen dress or her bedroom slippers, had submitted to his magic and appeared in holiday dress with a white apron.

They sat down at the table. The bounteous excellent food intended for the expected relatives had been brought in now. But after all it was neither the food nor the wine that kept up the festive spirit, although the first long-necked bottle was speedily followed by a second. This in its turn was succeeded by a small stout fellow covered with cobwebs and containing fine old Madeira which the young couple had hoarded in the cellar for some special occasion, and now sacrificed.

While still at the table, the stranger began to display other unexpected talents. His valise had also contained a small mandolin, and now he sang a series of gay love songs which aroused great merriment from Emmy not less than from her husband, although the words were often rather bold. He was certainly irresistible, sitting there, jovial and smiling, with his instrument on his knee and his wreath of grayish-brown curls standing out around his bald crown.

His last song was about Romance sallying forth in disguise with an invisible train of tiny followers——mischievous elves and cloven-footed gnomes, coaxed forth from dark attics and cellars to which man in his blindness had banished them. He lifted his glass and brought out a toast for these small ghost-like heart-thieves and brain-robbers and sleep-disturbers who, like certain germs in the wine, kept the drink of life fresh and effervescent.

Arnold Höjer laughingly seized his glass to touch that of his guest. But at the same moment he happened to glance at his wife, who had also taken her glass and, with glowing cheeks, was lifting it toward the stranger in an enthusiasm that was evidently not unaffected by the latter's person. The young husband's laughter was suddenly arrested, and he silently sipped his wine. Emmy saw nothing. The stranger, on the other hand, quickly perceived what had happened, and knew that it was time for him to leave. He lifted his glass once more, thanked them for their hospitality, and said good-bye.

Politely the doctor saw him to his sleigh, while Emmy waved her good-bye from the door. On her way back to the living-room she was singing, and in her enthusiasm was about to throw herself round her husband's neck as soon as he re-entered. But he looked at her coldly, and told her not to bother him.

Emmy thought he was joking, and began to laugh. But when he went to their bedroom and returned wearing his old dressing-gown, she understood that he was in earnest.

"What is the matter?" she asked, seeing him sit down at his desk in his den.

"I have to write some letters. It may take a long time."

Now she began to understand. "Why Arnold—" she said, and went toward him to give him a good scolding. But he turned round to her, looking so pale and angry that she was thoroughly frightened.

"*Please* let me alone. I should think you had had excitement enough for to-night. What you need is to quiet down."

For a moment she looked sadly at him. Then she lifted her head defiantly. "For shame!" she said, and left the room. While undressing, she nevertheless listened at the door from time to time, hoping to hear him rise, and she fought a hard fight with herself to keep away from him.

[233]

After several hours of alternating hope and disappointment, she cried herself to sleep.

The next morning did not bring a reconciliation. Arnold Höjer was called to a patient living at some distance from the village, and was gone the greater part of the day. Not until he was coming home in the twilight and saw the hall lamp shine like a guiding star over the desolate heath did his heart begin to soften. Emmy was sitting at the window in the living-room when he entered. He noticed immediately that, contrary to their custom, she had dressed for dinner and was even wearing a silver brooch which he had given her at the time of their engagement.

He bent over her saying, "Shall we make up, Emmy?" Without answering she turned her brimming eyes toward him like a child who has been wronged. But as soon as she saw the familiar smile on his face, she gave up all resistance and threw her arms round his neck.

However, the fact remained that the serpent had entered their little paradise.

The next evening, when the doctor returned from a professional call in the village and was entering the hall, he heard his wife playing the piano in the living-room. This was such an unusual occurrence that he instinctively stopped and listened. He recognized in the music a part of the melody of the stranger's processional march, which she seemed trying to play from memory.

She stopped at once when he entered. Apparently he had taken her by surprise. She gave him a searching look which confirmed him in the suspicion that her thoughts had been going astray. When he returned from the bedroom after having changed his clothes, she asked him a little nervously if he wanted the lamp. Although the mail had just arrived, he answered No.

"What were you playing?" he asked after a few minutes, interrupting the silence of the darkened room. "It seemed to me that I knew it."

"I don't think so. It was only some exercises."

She could not think of any other reply. She hardly dared confess to herself the silent dreams of her heart—nor is there a name for this surplus of feeling which a man never understands, for this secret hovering around the unknown and forbidden, for this grain of depravity which keeps a woman's love fresh and gives it charm.

When late in the night the doctor sought his lonely bed, he found his pillow crowned with yellow rose-leaves.

It remains to be told that no one in the rectory knew about a strange visitor who had had the misfortune not to find the rector at home. What is more, the family had not been away at all during Shrovetide. It must have been a hallucination on the part of the doctor's maid to have taken the mysterious stranger's driver for the rector's coachman. Furthermore, the rector denied most solemnly any association with that kind of early friends.

However this may be, the visit of the stranger had a decisive influence upon the life of the young couple. The spirit of romance had entered their home and left behind the restlessness and insecurity which is the heartbeat of life, nay, life itself. The paradisaic monotony of their existence had vanished. The serpent had been there with his promise of distant and strange glory. The little smug, self-satisfied happiness of domesticity had been turned out of doors, and had at least for a while given way to the great sad yearning which opens the mind and turns it toward the infinite.

The next summer saw yellow and red roses in magnificent clusters climbing up the walls of the doctor's little home. During the long and stormy evenings of the following winter, music and song sounded more and more frequently from within, and the joyous tones were carried by the wind toward the dark and dreary heath above which a fleet of heavy clouds were sailing forth unceasingly as a symbol of the restlessness of eternity.

GUSTAV WIED

CHILDREN OF MEN

Gustav Wied (1858–1914) has been called by an American critic an "unmelancholy Dane," but though his humor is on the surface, it often covers a cynical and pessimistic view of life. This is true of the two vigorous but gloomy novels, *The Family* and *The Fathers Eat Grapes*. The author is most original in his plays, among which may be mentioned *Four Satyric Dramas* and *The Weaker Sex*. His work is a mixture of apparently contradictory elements. In some respects he belongs with the naturalists, but his love of fantastic caricature is the foe of realism. His love of the idyllic, which appears in the story *Children of Men* is counteracted by his cynical satire.

Gustav Wied

CHILDREN OF MEN

THEY were sitting high up under the bluff, in the mild summer evening, half sheltered by overhanging sweetbriers and blackberry bushes heavy with fruit. Behind their backs was a flat, smooth stone, rising to the height of a man straight up from the yellow clay, while a sun-bleached, weather-beaten board, probably an old wagon seat, served them as a bench. Yet they could look out over the thick, leafy green copse of low-stemmed beech and ash, down to the sea, rolling blue and vast and sending its murmuring ripples in over the pebbles on the strand.

The spot was lonely and quiet, far from the noise and labor of the day. They had come upon it while wandering along the shore, and there they were sitting while he spoke.

"Yes, up here is the place for the house! It must be shining white as the driven snow, and the roof shall be thatched, and roses and wild ivy will twine around the doors and windows."

"Yes," she said, "and the windows must have

old, old tiny green panes, and over the door we will put the antlers of the largest deer in the forest, and the swallows will build under the eaves, and the stork have its nest on top of the barn-roof every summer."

"But there are no meadows or marshes in the neighborhood," he demurred; "there's no food for the stork."

"It must live here anyway," she said decidedly. "I want to see it come flying home every evening, and I want to laugh at the young ones when they dance on top of the roof with their long, lanky legs and flap their wings and look as if they were going to tumble on their noses into the yard every minute."

"Very well, then we take the stork," he said, and kissed her little white hand, "but no children—they cost too much. We will just have a big green parrot, which will sit on its perch in a cage in the dining-room and say, 'Good morning, old citizens,' when we come in to drink our coffee."

"A parrot by all means," she nodded, "but we must have one tiny little baby too!"

"It would certainly have to be a very small one," he replied, smiling and stroking her hair.

"Ye-es," she said, "just a wee little thing—like this," and she showed the size with her fingers.

He kissed her, and went on, "In the dining-

room there must be a green painted panelling, a
high green panelling, and above that a shelf holding queer old crocks and dishes; and the chairs
shall be green and have stiff backs with scrolls
and with red flowers and rushes painted on them,
and there shall be an old copper tea set on a
green table in the corner."

"And a big old green clock with urns on," she
added.

"A clock with urns, yes, and an old square, fat-
bellied iron stove with Adam and Eve and the
Fall, and Pharaoh drowning in the Red Sea."

"And now the sitting-room?" she asked.

"The sitting-room?—It must have three windows with a view over the tree-tops to the sea."

"But then we'd get all the forenoon sun!"

"They must be bay-windows, filled with flowers
and fragrant herbs—deep bay-windows, so the
sun can't come into the room but only throw a
few long, golden stripes over the floor and furniture. In the middle of the room there shall
be an oval table inlaid with ebony, with great
carved claw-feet, and we must have low, upholstered chairs, and an upright grand piano in
the corner near the hall. On the center-table
there shall be an enormous broad-leaved palm set
on a high dish of dark red terra-cotta."

"Where shall we put my sewing-table?"

"Your sewing-table? In the middle bay-window, which is to have leaded panes and be painted like the old solemn church windows with pictures of saints and inscriptions in deep blue and bright red and chrome yellow. Ferns and ivy will grow in the sill, and there shall be yellow fleur-de-lis and white water lilies in long, slender vases, and a cut-glass bowl with darting gold-fish eating bread out of your hand. And we must have doves!—snow white and sea blue and rust brown doves, circling around your head as you stand on the steps of the veranda under the roses and ivy; they will perch on your head and on your arms and on your shoulders, and peck grain from your hand and from your lips; and you will stand there dressed in white, with short slashed sleeves and pale blue stockings and shoes, and with a string of red corals twined around your neck."

She threw her arms around his neck and laid her head on his breast, smiling happily.

"And now the cabinet?" she asked—"and your study?"

"The cabinet must turn to the east," he continued, "with a huge chestnut outside of the window, a tree with a crown as big as a thousand-year-old cedar of Lebanon; and at the foot of the tree there shall be turf of the softest, brightest grass, with tables and chairs of bent flecked boughs, and hammocks, and croquet and tennis

for our guests—and a telescope two feet long
and turning on a pivot, so we can follow the ships
on their course over the sea."

"But the furniture in the cabinet?"

"You can decide on that," he replied; "it is
to be your room."

"No," she said, "you do it better."

"White," he nodded, "yes, white, with spindle-
legs and delicate tracings of gold, upholstered in
silk with large flowers on a pale blue ground,
fastened with round-headed nails of dull gold.
The walls shall be covered with leather-paper,
embossed in pale gold, and the curtains and por-
tières must be of the same color and texture as
the stuff on the furniture. The center-table shall
be oblong with a carved, gilt-edged top, and
above it shall hang a chandelier of glass with
prisms and tears, and stars nebulous and pale like
blue frozen milk."

"And the fire-place?"

"There isn't going to be any fire-place; for
spring and summer will be warm and radiant
with light and sun, and in the autumn and winter
we shall live in our apartment in Copenhagen."

"Now there is only your study left," she said,
—"and the bedroom."

"My den shall be in the gable-end toward the
west, where I can look miles and miles into the
country over hills and valleys and woods and

lakes blushing in the glow of the evening sun. It will have only one large Gothic window with a full, heavy curtain. The rugs shall be skins of wolf and bear, and the furniture of oak, austere and dignified. The tapestries shall be woven with pictures of knights in shining mail and ladies in sendal and ermine, and the walls hung with armor and swords and shields. And there must be a secret door that glides open when you press a rusty nail behind the bookcase."

"Oh," she breathed, shuddering, "and where does it lead?"

"Down into a dark underground passage, where the former lord of the manor has been walled in for a hundred years—or, no, it leads to the round tower-room, where you are lying in the great, wide, oak four-poster. You lie waiting and listening and looking out into the dark room, which is lit only by the small lamp on the marble table at your head. You have been reading, but now the book is resting on the white sheet in front of you, and you are lying with your arms behind your neck, and your dark hair forms a frame around your face. You are longing and listening and looking out before you with great, dreamy eyes. Then you hear the secret door slide open, and you smile and half raise yourself on your elbow, and listen again. You hear steps, soft, stealthy steps, coming nearer and nearer. Quickly you put the book down on the table, throw yourself back on the pillow and close your eyes. A door is carefully opened, a face bends down over yours, and, with a scream that sounds like a cry of joy, you put your arms around my neck and press your lips to mine. . . ."

So they babbled, these two, as they sat in the mild summer evening under the sheltering roof of the fragrant blackberries and sweetbriers and looked out over the green cupolas of the trees, to the sea that rolled its murmuring waves in toward the foot of the bluff.

When the sun had disappeared behind the western hills, and the dew began to fall, he rose from the bench, saying, "I am afraid it is time to go home; your mother must be waiting for us with the tea."

Silent, and with minds that felt strangely tired and vapid, they walked slowly down through the forest to the railway station.

Suddenly she spoke. "How I wish we could eat supper out here!"

He twisted his head nervously. "But, dearest, you know very well that—"

"Yes, yes," she answered hurriedly, pressing her cheek against his arm, "it was nothing but a stupid notion of mine. We have certainly spent enough money to-day."

Again they walked on without speaking.

[245]

When they stood at the ticket window, he turned his face away, embarrassed, and asked, "I suppose we'll go home third class?"

"Yes, yes," she said eagerly, "yes, of course! There are so few people at this time of day, and we save almost a crown."

KARL LARSEN

PEASANTS

KARL LARSEN (1860–) belongs with the Copenhagen authors, but has not confined himself to his native city. He is a master in depicting types and milieus, whether he deals with the quaint and often disreputable characters of Copenhagen's byways, like his Hans Peter Egeskov and Kresjan Vesterbro, or with the silent, undemonstrative country people in *Peasants*. With a sensitiveness to language, at once philological and artistic, he is an adept in letting his people reveal their exact status by a word or the turn of a phrase. In addition to his short stories, Karl Larsen has written psychological novels, among which *Dr. Ix* is regarded as the most noteworthy.

Karl Larsen has been an indefatigable collector of letters from simple and obscure folk. His visit to the United States resulted in the publication of many revealing letters from Danish-American immigrants. He has also written books of travel in which a keen power of observation is evident.

Karl Larsen

PEASANTS

OUT IN the little wood, the farmer Sören Jensen and his cottar were felling a tree, when they saw two blue-coated gendarmes come riding down the road. One of these dismounted and nailed up something bright and red on two of the trees. Then they cantered on in the direction of the town, their uniforms glittering against the white snow in the fields.

As soon as the blue-coats were well out of sight, the two peasants hurried over to see what it was they had posted. It was a placard.

Sören Jensen read.

"It's about Hans Peersen," he said. "He's escaped from jail, and now they're offering us a hundred crowns reward if we catch him."

The cottar looked about as if Hans Peersen might be concealed somewhere near them. "What's that?" he asked.

"Well, read it for yourself!"

But the cottar didn't seem to care particularly about that. They went back to their tree, and continued to discuss Hans Peersen and the posters while they worked.

"I wouldn't care to earn that hundred crowns," Sören Jensen vowed. The cottar agreed to that readily enough, for there was no doubt that the fugitive could take care of himself.

"Well, I don't know about that. This cold weather has been enough to take the fight pretty well out of him in two days. Still, it would be an ugly way to earn money—for he was a fine young fellow, Hans was, when he worked for me."

"Well, some one will have to catch him," said Jens.

"That's so. He can't hold out much longer in this weather," the other agreed. And they spoke no more about it.

When the farmer came home, he told his wife what he had read on the placards out in the woods.

"Lord save us!" she cried, and jumped up in alarm.

"He won't hurt *us* any," said Sören Jensen.

"I'm not so sure. He's most likely got bad since he's been in prison."

"Hans Peersen was a decent lad when he worked for us," said the farmer, "but every one treated him like a dog. And that Swedish guard whose throat he cut tormented him early and late. For he could get plumb crazy about a woman."

The goodwife was alarmed all the same, and started to leave the room.

"Don't say a word about this to those silly girls, or to the men either. I told Jens to keep his mouth shut."

The wife said no more, but all day long she was ill at ease.

Toward evening the dog in the yard suddenly began to bark, but a voice spoke to it in the darkness, and the uproar ceased at once.

The farmer's wife started up.

"It's terrible how nervous you are," Sören said, as he took a lantern and went out.

In the middle of the yard stood a man with the dog beside him.

"Good-evening, master," he said, and you could hear from the quaver in his voice how he shook with cold.

It was Hans Peersen. Sören started and almost dropped the lantern when he saw how miserable the lad looked. "Lord, is that you, Hans!" he said.

"I won't hurt *you,* master."

"No—but I guess it'll be best if I don't seem to know you at all, Hans," said the farmer.

"I can't get food any more," the other said simply.

Sören Jensen made a quick decision. He turned and went back into the living-room, where his wife stood, almost out of her senses.

"Now don't you say a word about all this, Bertha, do you understand?" he said sharply, when he saw that she was ready to scream with fright. "It's nobody's business, and there's nothing to be afraid of."

He went out, and the wife saw his lantern move toward the empty wing of the house where the help ate during harvest time. Then it disappeared entirely.

In a short time the farmer returned and rummaged around alone in the kitchen; then she saw the lantern move toward the wing again, and disappear once more.

Inside the deserted room sat the two men. The gleam from the lantern cast a fitful light over a part of the table.

Hans Peersen was greedily eating dry bread and salt meat without a word.

"Why don't you put a little lard on the bread?" Sören asked.

But Hans just ate.

A long time passed while neither spoke, but when Hans was draining the last drop from the brandy bottle, Sören said, "Your health."

"Thanks for that, master," the fugitive responded. "And thanks for everything else, too."

"We got along well together, didn't we, Hans?"

"It was the only place I did get along, master."

"I suppose it was."

They were silent a moment. "Now you must crawl up into the straw, Hans, and in the morning get away through the hatch before it begins to get light. . . . Good-night."

Hans looked up quickly. "I'd like to talk with you for a minute," he said.

"What about?"

The prisoner looked the farmer in the face. "I can't manage any longer," he said.

"No, I don't suppose you can."

"They've been down in Ellerup, the police. I saw them nail a placard on a tree, and I wasn't any farther away from them than I am from you right now."

"Yes, they've been nailing up those placards around here too."

"Has the master seen them, then?"

Sören Jensen nodded slowly.

"About all the money they offer for me?"

"Yes, Hans, I have."

"That's a lot of money."

Sören said nothing.

"It would be easy enough to earn it," the other continued.

[253]

"Yes, Hans, it would, if you don't give yourself up."

There was a short pause. "Wouldn't master like to earn that money?" Hans asked at last.

The farmer looked at the lad for a long time.

"It would be such an easy matter," Hans repeated.

Sören Jensen stood up abruptly. "Get up in the straw now, Hans. And see to it that you get away early—before it gets light, so that I don't get into trouble. I might easily, you know."

"Yes—but doesn't master want to earn that money?"

"No, I don't want to," the farmer said shortly.

"I remember—I heard master talking about a little carriage, one like Anders Jensen's. A hundred crowns would come in handy, you know. And then . . . it might be kind of—kind of a little remembrance of me, as you might say—Because they're going to catch me anyway, you know," he added, and continued to look hard at the farmer.

"Well, then it'll go hard with you, Hans."

"I know that, master—if nothing happens. . . . But I thought—master has always been so good to me . . ."

Sören Jensen was silent.

"Won't master drive me in to-morrow, then?"

"All right, Hans, if it must be, then I'll drive you in."

.   .   .   .

Next morning every one on the farm knew that Sören Jensen had captured the murderer, Hans Peersen, just out on the road. He had been so weakened by hunger and cold that he couldn't defend himself at all.

The cart was hitched up. "But I don't want any staring or gaping when we drive off," Sören Jensen had announced. "I don't want to see so much as a cat in the yard."

Sören himself brought breakfast over to the prisoner in the empty wing where he had slept during the night. Everybody watched them from within the rooms, though keeping away from the windows; they saw how the farmer and the prisoner came out together, got into the cart, and drove off. Hans Peersen was wearing Sören Jensen's own sheepskin coat. Sören had borrowed another from a neighbor.

Neither of them spoke as they drove along the snow-covered country road.

Only once Sören said, "It's a dark and toilsome road I'm driving you, Hans."

And Hans answered simply, "Let's not talk about it, master. . . ."

Finally they came to the market town and

drove up to the court house. A pair of indifferent eyes stared out at them from behind a window pane.

Just then a young man with gold braid on his cap and a portfolio of papers under his arm came hurrying down the steps of the house across the way. The farmer and his prisoner climbed down from the cart, and Sören tipped his hat to the young man.

"If you please," he said, "I brought Hans Peersen."

"Hans Peersen? . . . Hans Peersen!!"

In a twinkling the young man leaped up the stone steps of the court house and cried, "We've caught him—the murderer. The murderer!"

A door was flung hastily open, and two officials came out into the hall.

"He's nothing but a young whipper-snapper," said Sören Jensen to Hans.

Hans said nothing.

But the young man with the gold-braided cap was dumfounded when he saw the farmer shake hands with the murderer.

"Good-bye, master—and thanks," said Hans.

"Thanks yourself, Hans," said the other.

Hans Peersen mounted the stone steps to the court house. Sören Jensen watched him disappear within.

JOHAN SKJOLDBORG

PER HYWER'S SUMMER DAY

JOHAN SKJOLDBORG (1861-) was one of the pioneers and is still one of the most distinguished of the "Jutlanders," who broke with the literary traditions of the capital. Whereas Drachmann, Schandorph, and Pontoppidan wrote of peasants and fishermen from the standpoint of more or less sympathetic observers, Skjoldborg and the other Jutlanders wrote, not only about the plain people, but from those people's own point of view—though with a subtle and conscious literary artistry fully equal to that of the older school.

Skjoldborg was the son of a crofter in Thy, the very region where the story which represents him in this volume is localized, and it requires no stretch of imagination to surmise that Per Hywer's experiences as a herdsboy were once his own. He was led naturally by early impressions to become the champion of those who till the soil and get only a small share of its rewards. His novel *A Fighter* is the epic of a poor crofter who carves a living out of the sand-blown shores of West Jutland. *Gyldholm,* which was published in 1902 and first attracted attention to the author, depicts the misery and degradation of the laborers on one of Denmark's large private estates. It is a dark picture, but presented in a quiet, objective manner without comment. In the end a ray of light from the social revolution that has been going on in the outside world penetrates the darkness.

In the last decade Skjoldborg has published a series of books in which he pleads for a fuller human development, against those who think only of material reforms. Among these books may be mentioned *New Men, Jens Jakob's Sons,* and *The Parson at Lögum.*

Johan Skjoldborg

PER HYWER'S SUMMER DAY

THE DAWN was misty.

But the blue waters of the Limfjord a little way out reflected the first faint gleam of day; the mist vanished like the vapor on a window pane one has breathed upon, and the village houses that nestled alongside the fjord, like a flock of sleeping cattle in a damp meadow bottom, stood out more and more clearly. The light fog lifted very slowly, rose in the air almost imperceptibly and yet so that it was possible to follow it with the eye until the white-washed wings and gables of the village houses stood revealed in the morning sun.

The first person who came out from the village was a little boy. He was in his shirt sleeves, and his bare legs and knees stuck out below his rolled-up pants. He had tied his lunch box to his back with a piece of string; it was out of his way there. Under his left arm he carried a jacket in case it should rain later in the day, and in his right hand he held a whip.

It was little Per Hywer, the first one of all the village folk to be up and about.

He tramps through the heavy dust of the road on his short legs with a sturdy, even, heavy step. He is out here because he has to be, because it is his duty. Every step he takes is a determined one, an expression of will power, and for this reason there is something plodding about his gait; it is not the light, playful walk of a child.

His little body would rather be asleep.

But the law is over Per Hywer, the law that none can evade, the inevitable, all-powerful law. His quiet trudging shows that he knows he is under the control of forces which it is useless to contend with. There is nothing to be done about it.

Per Hywer is just eight years old.

He marches along confidently at the same steady determined pace until he reaches the last house on the eastern outskirts of the village, "Morten's House," standing by itself among the first ranges of sand dunes. Here Per stops and looks back at the village. His skin is so dark, so tanned by sun and wind, that his eyes look quite white as he turns them quickly from one side to the other. He eases his lunch box over to a more comfortable position, and examines his whip to see if it is in good condition and if there is "crack" enough in it.

Johan Skjoldborg

He is ready. It is four o'clock, and Per Hy-wer's working day is about to begin.

A woman comes down the road leading a cow at the end of a rope. She stops at the sand drifts where Per is waiting. Just behind her comes another woman with two cows, and within a few minutes the road is swarming with no less than forty of them, besides Lars Flyholm's big gray bull.

It is Per's task to lead these cows from the homes and farms around the village to the common, which lies some three miles east by the Bygholm Ford, and to pasture them there during the day.

The women and the few decrepit old men who have come to this gathering place stand with the ropes in their hands, gossiping, until every one is assembled. Then Morten's Hannah screams in her shrill, piercing voice,

"Well, boy, are you ready?"

It is a signal! All ropes are loosened from the horns of the cows, and the women give the creatures a push so that they can get under way properly. Per rushes around, whip in air, first to one side and then to the other, in order to keep the herd together and prevent the cows from getting into the few cornfields that lie along the road between the town and the heath beyond.

He runs so hard that the dust forms a cloud around him and covers the legs of the cows. Now Per is wide awake. Now everything depends upon him. And he is so anxious that people shall say he is a clever boy—especially for the sake of his father and mother. They are poor, and have more than their share of troubles and worries anyhow.

The women stand around a while watching him drive the cows down the road. A little off to one side stand two grizzled old men, resting on their sticks.

"He is a little fellow to take care of all those big cows," one of them says sympathetically, and scratches the back of his neck with his forefinger.

"That he is, but he's a smart little chap," replies the other, and nods his gray shaggy head as he speaks.

Per feels the eye of the public resting upon him. He is conscious that he is an object of observation and comment. His eyes are everywhere, and he hops around like a frolicsome lamb; things seem to be going pretty well this morning. He swings his long whip and cracks it loudly over the heads of his cows so that every one can hear that he is not afraid. But his heart is in his mouth at the thought of the heavy responsibility that rests upon him.

"Don't go to sleep now, boy," Bold-Stine yells after him in her strident voice.

"See that they get fat by to-night," Lars's Marie says heavily. She is so fat herself that she puffs when she walks.

Trine Krag stands with her hands folded under her apron, as magisterial as a judge, in the center of the group; her husband is the wealthiest man in town. "Don't let them stand in the water too long," she says. "Don't forget, now, young one!"

And Andreas's wife stands with her arms akimbo and screams, "Now just you try to drive my cows out in the marsh to-day, and I'll box your ears for you; I haven't forgotten the last time, you good-for-nothing brat!" She lifts her arm threateningly, and Per can see her standing on the sand bank, her lips going like scissors.

The jabber of the women follows Per down the quiet road like the notes of screeching birds.

They can say anything they like to him, as long as they speak kindly. He is so sensitive, little Per. It seems to him that most grown folks have such hard voices. . . .

Per gets his motley herd safely out of town and drives it down the road to the Ford. He looks so tiny alongside all those large animals, and when he runs over to drive back those who try to separate from the herd, he gets quite lost in a deep ditch or behind a knoll, like a little man-ikin.

He yells at the cows, berates them, uses bad words, in order to bolster up his own courage.

But his voice is on the verge of tears.

He knows what is at stake. He realizes what it means to be alone with the herd all day long. He is going out into the great loneliness. Every step carries him farther from his home, from his village, where people work and talk together, and where other children go to school and play with each other. . . . And he has another long, terribly lonely day before him.

He runs back and forth, cracks his whip lustily, and shouts; he is determined to strangle the fear that surges up in his heart.

Per wants to be a plucky boy.

Halfway out a little heath-creek cuts across the road. The low water gurgles merrily over brown and gray and red and blue stones, and Per thinks that these vari-colored pebbles lying on the bottom of the stream are the loveliest things he has ever seen. . . . But they have to be seen through the clear running water, for as soon as he lifts them out they lose their luster and look just like ordinary stones.

The cows drink their fill of the cool water in the stream, sticking their muzzles into the

water so that they form circles on its surface.
And when they have slaked their thirst, they stand
awhile, complacent, as if they had thoroughly enjoyed their morning drink, the water dripping
from their mouths.

Per lies down on his belly and drinks until
his stomach is distended. It is important to
drink enough now, for it is impossible to get any
fresh water over in the bog; it is rotten and
stagnant in the swampy ditches over there.

He fills a medicine bottle, too, and places it
carefully in his lunch box, for the people that
gave him his food to-day—his employers take
turns—belong to the stingy ones who give him
neither milk nor beer.

This brook is like a tavern, a baiting place on
the way.

At last Per reaches his destination, Green Hill,
with the boggy common below, stretching out
to a shallow bay that cuts in from the Limfjord.

The cows, with the empty stomachs of morning, rush out to the wet marsh grass that grows
in tussocks between sweet gale and creeping wil-
low. They stretch forth their thirsty muzzles
and sniff the salty marsh air that is wafted to
their nostrils.

While the cows attack the long grass, Per sits
down on top of Green Hill to catch his breath.

He is hot. From this hillock he can watch the whole herd. He counts twice to make sure that they are all there.

Satisfied, he opens his lunch box. He is curious to see what they have given him to-day. Perhaps there is something especially good. He expects nothing, but he cannot help looking anyway. He lifts the cover off and finds five thick pieces of black bread with lard and salt, and a cheese crust to munch. But down at the very bottom of the box there is a pancake. Per smiles happily to himself, for he considers this a rare delicacy, and he eats it up at once. Then that is over with. He takes a little drink out of the medicine bottle, holding it out in front of him after each sip to see how much is left, just as he has seen his elders do with the brandy bottle. Hmmm!

Then he sits still, quite still, and lets the sun beat down on him till the warmth quickens every pore in his skin. He lets the vapor from the damp heath pour in over him. He listens to the distant bird-calls from the bay and to the insects buzzing around his head. He lets the soft summer breezes caress his cheeks. Not a limb is moving, not a thought stirring in him. He himself is like a sound or a wind breathed away in the sun.

After a time he awakens to his surroundings

again and finds himself sitting on top of Green Hill.

He wonders how this knoll came to be so nice and round, and how it is always able to stay so green, a fine verdant green out here in the heather! It is most pleasant to rest on. Per turns and looks back at the village. All the houses seem so small. He can see the ridge and part of the gable on his own house. Yes, indeed, it is far away. He sighs. It is such a long time till evening. He lies on his stomach and stares out toward the village.

But it can't be otherwise.

Yet he likes Green Hill. No matter which direction the wind is from, he can always find shelter here. And on one side is a foxes' den where he has dug himself a seat, and even when it rains he can pull his jacket over his head and sit there and be quite comfortable. Per stays on Green Hill as much of the time as he can. It is his summer home.

Meanwhile the cattle are spreading out. A few of them have wandered away to the north, dangerously near Mads Bold's farm. Can the animals perhaps smell the corn behind the fences? Per jumps up and runs over toward them. Mads Bold is a hot-tempered fellow. He has been to sea, and folks say that he has killed people and taken their money—that is how he got so rich.

If the cows should ever break into his field, he might keep them until the damage was paid for, and that would cost as much as Per could earn all summer long. . . . He increases his speed. His father would have to work a long time to pay the fines, and all because Per had been a bad boy and not tended to his business. Per is running so fast now that he stumbles among the knolls and hillocks, and falls down. He jumps up quickly and hurries on. The thorns tear long scratches in his bare legs.

"Hey, hey," he shouts at the cows, and cracks his long whip. "Turn around, there." But as soon as he has one of them turned, another has gone back. They must smell the corn, all right. "Hey, hey," Per beats them with his whip, but they don't budge. Each one sets its course stubbornly toward the cornfield; they are determined to get in there, and Per is kept running from one to the other so that the perspiration pours from him. When he is in a position to strike a blow, he grits his teeth and lets go for all he is worth. These animals are full of spite and meanness, they just want to plague him, and they are stupid beasts, besides . . . "Hey, hey," Per rushes wildly from one to the other. "You darn bone-bags," he cries. And he beats and beats them till the air hums. "Hey, hey." If the cattle ever get in there and get a taste of the corn, he will never be able to drive them out again. Never. Perhaps even the others might come up and join them, all forty of them. They could eat up all Mads Bold's corn in no time at all, every single stalk. And that man is without pity.

Ah, how much there is at stake!

Per Hywer feels that his whole future hangs on the outcome of this struggle, that this will decide whether he is to be a happy or an unhappy man. His breath is singing in his throat now, and his eyes are twice their normal size. He shouts and screams and swears, and bounces around like a rubber ball. He is straining every muscle; he is fighting for life. . . .

And he wins.

For he is tireless in his tenacity, and he literally wears the cattle out, discourages them, and drives them back to the main herd to the accompaniment of all the blows that can be rained on their stubborn hides.

While this conflict between Per and the cows has been under way, the Tovdal girls' cow has begun to browse serenely homeward. The three unmarried sisters have inherited their house and their cow from their parents. They are very kind, pleasant old maids, but they fondle and indulge this cow so much that it is quite spoiled.

Now it is trotting off by itself along the shore toward home. It is up by Green Hill already. . . .

So Per has to be off again. It would be humiliating if the cows went home on him. He throws off his coat—he is wringing wet from perspiration—cuts diagonally across the heath, and gets in front of the refractory animal so that it has to turn around. Then it gets a real run, for Per drives it right back into the midst of the herd.

Per drops wearily on a little knoll; he is so breathless that he can scarcely stand up. He has scratched the skin off his shins and torn one of the knees of his pants. It is worst about the pants. . . .

His blood is pounding in his temples. He is burning hot, and has to wipe his face on his shirt sleeve every minute. But it is not long before his racing heart slows down, and the fires within him are quenched. Everything within him becomes still, in harmony with his surroundings. A great peace settles on him, and his eyelids droop. . . .

He jumps up quickly. He is afraid of falling asleep at his post. After all, everything depends on him. He looks over at the browsing herd that is entrusted to his care. Lars Flyholm's gray bull towers high above all the others like the king that he is. He is the largest animal Per has ever seen. He is something to look up at—almost like a house. An elephant is probably not nearly so large. In fact he should like to know if that bull were not the biggest animal in the world.

It is not long before Per sits down again; he is so tired, and it is so pleasant to rest out here. He can feel how sweet it is in all his limbs. His head feels so heavy, he props it up with his hand.

In that moment Per Hywer's eyes close, and he is asleep.

But he is awake again in no time, frightened. He runs up to a high knoll near by and counts all his cattle, three times over to make sure. He knows he is responsible for them.

Now he dares not sit down again right away; he wanders in along the bay toward Green Hill. A lapwing is terribly excited; it circles, screaming, around him. Per thinks it is a beautiful bird, with its snow-white breast, coal-black wings, and glistening dark green back. But he doesn't like its shrill caw; there is something grating in those hoarse notes. And then it flies right at one, like a dog that is going to bite. He teases it a little; when he comes close to its nest, it becomes frantic, flaps its wings furiously, and flies right at Per's head. That is great sport. But when the lapwing really gets near enough to graze Per's ear with a wing, he retreats headlong, leaving the victorious bird circling around and screaming imprecations after him.

Up here on Green Hill everything is so quiet. Per can look far, far out. East of the fording place, in Kjettrup, lives the doctor, the little bearded man he saw last spring rattling through the village in a high leather-covered lorry. There, too, is the apothecary's where all the rare herbs and curious medicines in the world are to be had. It would be fun to get over there some day. And there is Skærpinggaard, the prison with all its cells. What might they be like? Per shudders to think of them. And a little to the north, behind Kjettrup, Hingelbjerg hills lift their round domes up into the sky. It couldn't be very far from there to the ocean. . . . Over toward the west lies Fæggesund mill, at the very southern tip of Hannæs, way out in the fjord. He would like to get out to that point; from there one could shout over to Morsö. And to the south you can see the islands of Fur and Linö swimming out in the bay, while behind them Himmerland's steep cliffs are anchored immovably in the water. And across the water he can catch a glimpse of Lögstör's red tiled roofs, glistening in the sunlight. All those red houses are a market town. He would like to get over there some time too.

All of this is Per's world; it stretches out before him every day, and in the center of it all is Green Hill. And there he will stay; he is fastened as by a tether-peg. But one day, when he is grown up and there is no one to boss him any more, he will go out into this world and see it all for himself, both on this and on the other side of the Limfjord. He will take a big ship and go as far as it can sail.

But now here he sits, alone—every day alone. He can't even go over to see Kren Tamsen, who stands over there on the heath and digs peat. He doesn't dare, for Kren Tamsen always scolds him roundly and chases him back and tells him to take care of his cows and mind his business. He could run over to him so easily, too, and it would be such fun to be with him for just a few minutes, just to hear somebody talk. But he must not.

And Karen Tovsgaard who stands up on Lyngbjærg and cuts the heather with her sickle —she is too far away altogether. . . .

He finds his own home among the houses of the village. The sun glistens on the bit of tiled roof that he can see. If his arm were long enough, he could reach out now and pat his house

[273]

on the roof, just as one pats a dog one is fond of.

If only he had a dog . . . He wanted one so badly, but his father said that a dog ate too much.

Per Hywer looks wistfully over to the village houses. He bites his lower lip while a single tear trickles down his cheek.

Two men are going toward the ford. He wonders who they are; it's not easy to make them out in the shimmering sunshine. No doubt they are going over to the east side. One of them is probably Morten, who ferries people across in his flat-bottomed boat, and the other is some one who has to get the doctor, or perhaps he has to report something important at Skær-pinggaard.

Per doesn't lose sight of the two men all the way, and he wonders idly who might be sick, or dead—whether it might be an invitation to a funeral. Or perhaps it was a burglary they were going to report. Per amuses himself by guessing at a number of things. But when Morten and his companion come abreast of Green Hill he can hear that the stranger speaks the Thy dialect, and he deduces that it must be a man from Thy who wants to go over to the wise old woman in Himmerland.

It was wonderful what people said that woman could do. She must be a witch. And the sheriff couldn't arrest her, because, whenever his carriage came near her house, it would turn over, or the wheels wouldn't go around any more—

Per is lost in thought.

He is awakened by the sun burning his bare skin; the heat stings him, and the tops of his ears smart where the skin is peeling off.

A quick glance at the cattle shows him that the herd is restless. He rushes away at full speed across the heath. Not an animal in the whole herd is quiet. They switch their tails, stamp and kick, toss their heads, and jostle each other. They are fidgety, nervous, irritated by the heat of the sun, maddened by gadflies and buzzing swarms of insects that rise in clouds from the long rushes.

From one end of the herd to the other there is unrest. Per is active wherever the danger seems greatest. But the restlessness increases every moment. It cannot continue in this way, something is bound to happen soon. The cattle have a strange look in their eyes that makes Per afraid. They look sick, as if they were suffering agonies, vicious as if they would gore him, wild as if they had suddenly gone crazy. . . .

Then little Per Hywer becomes terribly frightened. What if the herd became mad? They could toss him high in the air on the points of their sharp horns, or trample him with their

[275]

heavy hoofs deep down in the soft earth. They could run, bellowing, in all directions, sweeping over and destroying everything in their path.

His head seemed to swim, and his heart almost stopped beating, as these thoughts swept through his mind, and he realized how helpless he was. . . . And then he began to hit out wildly with his whip, to shout and scream as if he were crazed with fear.

At the same moment Morten's cow tosses her head in the air and gallops away down to the water. And in a few minutes all the other cows are bolting behind her, running like mad, and stopping only when they are standing up to their bellies in the water.

Thank God! So that was it.

Then there is peace. Per knows that they will stand there quite motionless for hours.

It is not nearly noon yet. The sun hasn't even reached Livö.

Per likes the damp sea smell down here on the strand. It is shallow here, and the surface of the water is studded with bunches of ferns. Per splashes around in the low water—it is quite warm. Then he walks in toward the firm damp strand where he can see the imprint of his bare feet, and where he can write and trace figures with the handle of his whip in the mud. Just a few feet in there is a low ridge of washed-up, sun-dried pebbles. He gathers the prettiest of them and fills his pockets with them and with snail shells. And all the time he listens to the sea gulls and the sandpipers whose caressing, complaining notes linger long on the salt air of the lonely strand.

But after a while this, too, becomes monotonous. Per hurries back to Green Hill, eats a couple of slices of his black bread, and, drawing his coat over his face, composes himself for a little nap. He can do this safely enough as long as the cows are standing there in the water.

And when he wakes, there they all are, in the self-same place; all forty of them and the big gray bull. The sun has traveled a little farther toward the west now, and the light falls slantwise on the spotted hides of the cows as their images are reflected in the clear water.

In whatever direction Per looks, the world seems to have gone to sleep; even the ships out on the fjord are motionless. It is so quiet, so lonely, so far from any human being.

The larks are circling over Green Hill, singing. It is easy enough for them to be happy— they can fly anywhere they please; they can fly way over to Öslös town if they want to.

Ah, how slowly the time passes! And the silence rests so heavily over the desolate heath, the earth is weighed down with it.

Per feels utterly forlorn.

And he dare not even go over to Kren Tamsen.

But just let them wait until he is grown up. Then he will show them. He will go out into the great world, and when he comes back he will be a rich man. That will teach them all something!— Andreas's wife, who always scolds him, and Kren Tamsen and all the others in Öslös town.

Per springs up energetically.

He sights something way out in the ford; he cannot tell whether it is man or animal yet. In any event it is moving toward him. It is not a carriage, it looks more like a horseman, but he can see several heads and many feet, so it is hard to tell what it all is.

A long time passes. And Per has no thought for anything else than what he can see out there in the low water. What can it be?

Ah, it is a string of horses, he can see that when they land on the shore—a long string of them, each one tied to another's tail.

They are coming from the market, of course.

There are some brown and some black, a gray and a roan, but the one Per likes best of all is a chestnut with white fetlocks. It is a colt. Per can tell by its bright yellow hoofs that it has never been shod.

A young fellow is riding on the first horse, and he has a real saddle to sit on. When he comes abreast of Green Hill he turns around, stands in his stirrups, and shouts back at some of the more restless animals near the end of the line.

That is a sight now, Per thinks. Such a voice the fellow has, and he's not afraid. . . .

Now Per knows what he wants to be when he grows up—a horse dealer. He will get a blue duffel greatcoat like the one Anders Vabbesgaard has, and then he will travel around the country buying horses by the hundred, and take them from one market to another. And he will have a pocket-book, like Johannes Hamburg's with paper money in it. Yes, that's what he will do, and then when he has made all the money he cares for he will come back home and buy Söndergaard, cash down, and he will get a spring-cart and a couple of Norwegian ponies just like Görup's. Then you bet Kren Tamsen and all the other stiff-necked fellows in town will bow and scrape to him!

Per Hywer sits on top of Green Hill, the throne of his childish dream kingdom, and follows the string of horses with his eyes until it disappears in the horizon over toward Lyngbjærg.

Meanwhile the cows have begun to wade in toward land and to pasture in the tall grass. And when Per looks more closely, he discovers that the Tovdal girls' cow is on its way home again. Devil take the beast! Per hardens his heart against it. He sneaks along behind a knoll until he is in front of it, jumps out and seizes it by the tail. Then he beats it. He drives it down to the bog, right out into the water, where it sinks down in the soft mud to its belly. Then it gets the rest of its well-earned punishment.

When Per's anger has spent itself, the cow heaves a deep sigh, as if everything were lost; it lowers its great head and looks at Per with two large sorrowful eyes.

At once Per knows that he has been a bad boy. The Tovdal girls always give him the best food of all; there is always one boiled egg and sometimes two, that he can sit and look forward to during the day. They are so good to him. And now he is mistreating their cow. . . . They always give him a bottle of good sweet milk, too, milk from their own cow, and now it is standing out there in the water and groaning under his whip. Oh, little bossy-cow! Per runs over to it and strokes its nose and caresses it.

What if it were unable to get out of the quagmire? What if it couldn't get back on land again? Per's whole body burns at the thought. It would be a terrible loss!—the Tovdal girls are so poor, and this is their only cow. . . . He will never be happy again.

Per bursts into tears, he walks around the pond

wailing. He is desolate and inconsolable; it is all his fault.

All his other woes are nothing compared to this.

How will he ever be able to look people in the face again? And how will he dare to go home to his father and mother?

He prays to God up in His high heaven to help him this time—just this one time, then he will always be a good boy.

He tries every conceivable method to bring the cow out. At last, after half an hour, his efforts are rewarded. He leads the trembling beast over to the clean water, pulls a tuft of grass and washes the mud from its feet, so that no one shall see what has happened. He pets and caresses it, and brings it some of his own food.

Ah, yes! Per remembers a hymn he has learned:

None knows the day till the sun has set.

He has suddenly become quiet and humble in spirit; he walks slowly toward the heath north of Green Hill, picking crowberries as he goes.

He looks up to the sun; it is setting toward the horizon. He stands and measures the exact point on the heath that his shadow reaches. Then he

[281]

steps off the distance. . . . It is as many hours
after noon as there are steps in his shadow.

All this time he keeps an attentive eye on the
cattle. They are hurrying to eat all they can before evening. The herd down in the pond really
looks its best along in the afternoon, about this
time—all the motley-colored hides look so clear,
the grass is such a rich green, and everything over
toward the east seems so clean and distinct.

A deep peace has settled down over the cattle
busily pasturing there in the shadow, enjoying the
cool evening air. It is a sight worth seeing.

All the same, Per would like the time to pass a
little faster. He holds the palm of his hand
straight out between the sun and the ground.
. . . There are as many hours before sunset as
there are widths of his palm.

Per munches the berries he has gathered on the
heath until he is quite black around the mouth.
At last there is only one short hour left, and he
can begin gradually to round up the cattle and
start toward home.

Rounding up the herd is not without its difficulties, for some of the cows are lazy and lag behind; others are nimble enough, and still others
bolt away because they want to be milked; the
milk is dripping from their teats.

Per wants to come back to town with his herd
nicely assembled and in good order.

Johan Skjoldborg

His little legs move along so willingly and nimbly, now they are going homeward.

He can already see a few figures up by Morten's house, standing high in the sand dunes, a few that are waiting to take over their cows.

Per smiles to himself; he dances along the road. Now he will hear people talk again.

Even if they scold him. . . .

MARTIN ANDERSEN NEXÖ

BIRDS OF PASSAGE

MARTIN ANDERSEN NEXÖ (1869–) says of his hero, Pelle, "All his joys and sorrows have sounded in myself from the time I could crawl—in my mind, in my stomach, and on my back." His parents were originally country people; they lived in Copenhagen at the time the author was born, but after a few years moved back to the father's old home, the island of Bornholm. They were very poor, and the boy had to make himself useful. Like Pelle, he was apprenticed to a shoemaker, but, disliking the indoor life, he became a bricklayer's helper. Through the kindness of friends he was enabled to spend some time at Askov Folk High School, where he had his longing for books satisfied in some measure. He was nearly thirty years old before he began to write.

Nexö took his name from one of the towns on the island of Bornholm. His first stories dealt with the laborers and fishermen of that region where he had spent his childhood, and he uses this background also in the first volume of his novel cycle, *Pelle the Conqueror*. With this story of a proletarian boy, Nexö at once won international fame. It was followed by the story of a proletarian girl, another novel cycle entitled *Ditte: Daughter of Man*.

Always impassioned for social reform, Nexö after the World War has looked to Soviet Russia for inspiration. His book *Toward Dawn* is an enthusiastic account of his visit to that country.

Martin Andersen Nexö

BIRDS OF PASSAGE

PETER NIKOLAI FERDINAND BAL-
TASAR RASMUSSEN KJÖNG, whose
name—following inviolable phonetic laws not to
be explained here—in the course of time took the
form of Nebuchadnezzar, was a man who had
seen the world and knew the human race.

By trade he was a shoemaker; by nature, a
wandering journeyman. He was one of those
people in whose blood the rotation of the earth
has become an urge, and who therefore feel
themselves compelled to rotate around our globe
like so many satellites. The desire to set out for
the unknown was the moving power of his life;
and he knew nothing finer than to break away, no
matter from what. Thus he broke away from
happiness several times, and felt all the happier
for it.

He had wandered through the greater part of
the civilized world, clearly and firmly defining
civilization as synonymous with the wearing of
leather shoes. He knew all the ins and outs of

the German hostelries and the French highways, had walked across the Pyrenees and Alps more than once, and had stood with one foot in Switzerland and the other in France, spitting far down the Italian slopes. He had been in Sicily, at Gibraltar, in Asia Minor.

On his travels he had become acquainted with all the mysteries of modern traffic. He knew where it was possible to hang between the wheels of a freight car, and where it was more advisable to pretend having lost a ticket or to appeal to the generosity of the conductor. He slipped to Sicily from Gibraltar, by hiding in the cable-hold of a big steamer. After a while his hunger drove him to the deck, where he received a sound thrashing and countless threats of being thrown overboard to the sharks. But, after all, he reached his destination.

From Sicily he was to go as a stoker on another steamer, thereby earning his passage to Greece. But as it was soon discovered that he knew nothing about stoking, he was put ashore in Brindisi. Here he rubbed his feet with tallow, and walked north through the country, around the Adriatic, and down on the other side. It took him months, but this time also he gained his end. And what better use could he make of his time? King Nebuchadnezzar possessed some of the patience of a planet; he wandered for the sake of wandering, without any other purpose and without seeking other distractions. In the Balkans he had the pleasure of being captured by brigands who, however, rejected him with the greatest contempt after discovering the condition of his clothes. Afterwards he used to say, with a magnificent gesture, "A mouse saved the king of the animals, but a louse saved King Nebuchadnezzar."

He took a short trip to California to have a look at the gold; but there he quickly came to the conclusion that gold was too heavy an article for a wandering journeyman, and he hurried back to New York, hanging between the axles of a coal car. On this occasion he made the discovery that the Americans really were practical people. In Germany the railroad employees would go peering under the trains with lanterns in search of tramps, who were then pulled out and dragged to the police court. There they were questioned, and often solemnly expelled from the district because of their criminal use of the benefits of society. But in America a man would run back and forth with a hose, and simply squirt cold water under the train. That made one's clothes freeze when the train put on its hellish speed, and for the rest of his life a fellow would have rheumatism in his left shoulder.

In New York he tried to get a job, first as chief cook and then as deck hand, in order to earn his passage back to Copenhagen. As both plans failed, he had a stroke and fell over in the street. All he then had to do was to open his eyes a little at the right moment and whisper, "Dane." He was taken to the Danish consulate, and from there transported back to Denmark.

He had indeed seen life and mankind! His trade had carried him over half the earth. He had worked in all big cities, as short a time as possible in each so as to get around and see them all. He had, as it were in passing, wheedled every secret out of his trade. He did not spend much time working, but what he produced was masterly. His work stood out among that of thousands of others as long as there was one whit left of it.

He thought with a smile of the greasy little shop where he had learned his trade. Now he was going to make things hum. It was his plan to settle down in Denmark and profit by his experience in the great world, following the maxim that a man owes his best to his own country. He hung around for about a month, so as to accustom his digestive organs to home cooking, whereupon he went to work in a shoemaker's shop.

But King Nebuchadnezzar was used to moving in big spaces, according to great simple laws. On his wanderings he had learned to eliminate and discard. Life had taught him thoroughly that most of the accessories which were burdening the shops were unnecessary baggage—at least to him who had the unique talent of simplification. The big apparatus set in motion by a Danish shoe-maker before beginning his work could not but seem comical to a man who more than once had turned out first-class products, sitting by the way-side and only equipped with an awl, a knife, a small amount of shoemaker's thread, and the broken leg of a chair for the final polishing.

The result was that he did not hesitate to sell the superfluous tools wherever he went. But al-though this did not impair his work, his bosses did not like it, and deducted the cost from his wages. They even fired him and threatened to turn him over to the police.

He began to work in his lodging, and extended his economy from tools to material. Moreover, he knew the value of cardboard, and thus was able to save a surprisingly big part of the leather de-livered by the bosses according to exact measure-ment. He sold this, and used the money to stretch his Blue Monday to Wednesday evening.

His comrades considered him a genius, by which they meant a person who could turn out a marvelously neat piece of work with the speed of lightning and out of almost nothing, and who loved idleness and hunger and little drams above anything else in this world.

Doubtless King Nebuchadnezzar was a genius. When he worked, he worked—nobody could say that his fingers acted like thumbs. A howling blue flame—zip! Two pair of ladies' shoes done before five. Then he would drink up his double wages, sleep off his debauch on a pile of paving-stones or behind a fence, and at a pinch be ready to resume work next morning.

But he did not like to do this. He preferred to hustle three pair together in one day, instead of working two days in succession.

While at work, he was lost to the world. But when he would straighten his back to go on a spree, he would sometimes find that he had to go alone. Time after time the most ridiculous of all phenomena spoiled his plans: people had no time. The Lord help us, no time to carouse! He could not understand it, but it was a fact.

It was comical beyond words. It took him some time to have his laugh and finally discover that he was a lonely man. His comrades had simply gone back on him and his firm convictions, and had—perhaps a little sheepishly—continued their drudgery so as not to fall behind. They had become useful citizens, petty respectable members of society with stomachs and earnest political consciences. They jogged to work at seven in the morning and went home at six in the evening—he could have set his watch by them if he had had one. In the evening they went to political meetings. They even married and shuffled to the circus with wives and children on Sunday afternoons. They called that enjoying life—phew!

Those that went on sprees were no longer men of his kind who felt the need of hammering out the dents given them by drudgery. More and more the magnificent debauches passed into the hands of professional toughs. King Nebuchadnezzar was not a tough. He was simply a free man who happened to have moved around and seen the world while his colleagues continued being slaves.

Well, that was their own funeral—if they were willing to be drummed together in factories and big workshops at the stroke of the clock, all right! King Nebuchadnezzar went on working in his lodging, refusing to work in the shops. He was his own boss. He was not going to have a foreman standing around watching all his doings. And as to being a member of the Union and having to obey all its orders down to the very air one breathed—the devil, no!

King Nebuchadnezzar was quite able to look after his own affairs. He wanted the right to do three days' work in one and spend the next two days enjoying life. No need to worry about the prices. One day he learned that the Union had succeeded in prohibiting all home work. He was unspeakably scornful. "They can't touch *me*," he said, and continued working in his own way. Thanks to his efficiency, the bosses employed him whenever they needed an especially good man.

However, they could only employ him secretly, and ordinarily they preferred to follow the rules laid down by the Union. One never knew what to expect from King Nebuchadnezzar: right in the middle of a piece of pressing work ordered by some prominent person he might suddenly become possessed by the devil. Nor could he live on air while the few notabilities Denmark could boast were wearing the shoe leather that came from his hand.

Like all geniuses, he finally came to the conclusion that conditions in Denmark were too narrow. He would have to turn his back on his miserable country once more. He had kept the great world in mind, and always thought of it with gratitude and joy. Once more he broke away.

But he had lost the exhilaration of former days when his bones, like those of the birds, had been filled with air, and he felt that he must flit from one place to the other. The centrifugal force had left him; only gravity remained and bound him to the earth. He could not understand it; still it was so. It was an effort for him to set out

[294]

on his flight, whereas it had formerly been an effort to remain quiet.

One no longer flew out at random—one sat down soberly and thought the matter over. The rotation of the earth no longer whirled mountains and rivers and unending white roads through one's brain. Now the question was whether or not one could stand the wear and tear. Certain things were required, especially strong feet; and it was advantageous to have a stomach that could crush stones. In the course of time he had lost these two assets. Then there was the general feeling of heaviness as if one were glued to the earth. The great world with its eternal restlessness and tension no longer tempted him. He had become afraid of it. A bit of a home with soft boiled food, warm clothes, a room with a clean bed, was all he aspired to now.

He tried to realize his wishes and keep the wolf from the door by allowing himself to be supported by a feeble-minded woman who lived on what the day might bring. They were always squabbling except when they were drunk. But a year or two of this life cured him thoroughly of all desire for a home and family. Let others enjoy domesticity as much as they wanted to; he knew now what it meant!

He tried to take up his trade again, but the

door was irrevocably closed to a vagrant like him. Finally he resolved to accept what great men in antiquity had accepted before him: meals at the cost of the community. To this end he sought and received admittance to the prytaneum situated on Aaboulevard between Örstedsvej and Svineryggen—sometimes referred to as the public Workhouse.

.   .   .   .

He was at once given awl and waxed end, and shown his seat among the shoemakers. But he had not entered the place in order to create any unfair competition with the outer world. Neither had he revolted against fixed working hours and workshop rules in order to sit as a slave with cropped hair in the workroom of the inmates and be granted one hour's liberty in the yard, dressed in the uniform of the institution and walking at the regulation pace. He loved liberty still more than his art, and, thanks to the rheumatism in his shoulder and his sadly trembling hands which were utterly unable to hold the point of the knife away from the vamps, he was declared impossible as an artisan.

The officials then tried him on the light brigade which every day swarms over the bridges and markets of Copenhagen, armed with brooms and shovels. He would saunter along and pass his broom indolently over the pavement, while the sparrows fluttered wildly in the sweepings, and life around him pulsated in a restless, feverish chase. He would watch the passionate hurry with a mild, sedate smile like one who knows the stakes but is safely out of the game. He had lived as deeply and fully as any of the rest, therefore it tempted him no longer. But when he saw a street-worker stride over piles of stone or gravel to his coat and take a clear, little bottle out of his pocket, he would feel a faint pang and a longing to lift it caressingly to his mouth. But otherwise he was quite satisfied and envied nobody—not a mother's soul!

One afternoon as he was sweeping Höjbroplads, lost in quiet, happy content, he saw something which robbed his philosophical heart of its calm and made it pound and flutter.

A woman came shuffling from Köbmagergade, crossed Höjbroplads, and walked toward the Bourse. She wore a black, shiny straw hat, the brim of which had become detached from the crown and was jolting on the bridge of her nose so that she was peering over it as through a vizor. Besides this, she wore the remains of an old French shawl, a thin, scant skirt, and prunella shoes. Her cheeks and nose were protruding like three red pippins. She leaned forward and wriggled her hips coquettishly, not lifting her feet, but sliding them over the pavement. His expert eye saw at once that she did this so as not to lose her shoes: both vamps were split.

His wildly pounding heart told him that the woman was Malvina, his lady, his last and only great—but also unhappy—love, the woman who had shared her bed and her liquor with him, whom he had beaten and who had returned his blows, according to their relative states of drunkenness—the lady whom he had bidden a heart-rending farewell the day when they had knocked at the door of the workhouse, and had been admitted respectively to the female and male departments.

Evidently she had a free afternoon and was going out on a jaunt—Malvina who from the time of her confirmation to her eighteenth year had been the mistress of a decrepit count!—Malvina who with all her hoarseness could lisp so genteelly, who smacked a bit of all strata, from court to gutter!—the only being he had ever met who, like him, had some of the rotation of the universe in her blood.

And now she was going on a jaunt!

An irrepressible impulse to go along once more, to have just one more fling, awakened in him. He was on the point of throwing his broom aside and calling to her to wait and take him with her. But a remnant of his old presence of mind shot up in him. He dropped the broom, became quite pale,

[298]

and staggered over to the overseer, Petersen, whom he asked for permission to steal away quietly as he felt sick to his stomach.

Overseer Petersen knew that King Nebuchadnezzar had no greater wish than to spend the rest of his days in the workhouse. He looked doubtfully first at his watch, then at the policeman under "the Clock," and finally at the patient. Really the man looked alarmingly ill.

"Do you think you can manage to get home by yourself?" he asked.

"Oh yes! But, of course, if I had ten öre I could ride right to the door."

"Well, see that you catch that bus!"

But King Nebuchadnezzar did not catch the bus, he was too feeble to hurry. He staggered over to Thorvaldsen's Museum where the street car was standing, but it started before he reached it, whereupon he followed it at an anxious trot, beckoning sadly to the conductor.

Overseer Petersen shook his head with misgivings. Nebuchadnezzar must be sick indeed if he thought he could catch up with an electric car. Oh well, there would be another in a minute, there were enough of them.

When King Nebuchadnezzar's calculation told him that there were houses between him and the overseer, he slackened his pace and turned from the Stormbridge into the Palace yard. It was important not to be suspected and caught on account of his uniform. Behind the Bourse he bought a huge yellow envelope for three öre and a newspaper for two öre. The remaining money was spent for a quid of tobacco. He never chewed tobacco, but simply felt uncomfortable with money in his pocket. It occurred to him that he could give the quid to his comrades. Later he realized that he might have spent the money for a milk toddy, but he was not the man to deplore his actions. He stuffed the newspaper into the envelope, put it carefully under his arm, and left the Palace yard walking as straight as an orderly on a confidential mission. The policemen on Knippelsbro looked askance at him, but he went ahead with the assurance born of an easy conscience.

He sauntered around in the bystreets behind Christianshavn market until he caught sight of Malvina, who disappeared through the door of a many-windowed house in Dronningensgade. He knew her errand at once, and went straight up to the third floor where many one-room apartments opened into a long, pitch-dark corridor.

Upon hearing Malvina's clothes rustle in the dark, he said solemnly, "Good day, Lady," and took hold of both her ears and kissed her.

"Mercy, how you scared me, little Nezzar! It

might have been a strange fellow for all one can see here," she said coquettishly.

"Are you looking for the Prince, dear Lady? I shouldn't wonder if he had been ditched."

"No, I heard him cry a minute ago. But there is no key in the door."

King Nebuchadnezzar examined the lock with expert fingers and peered through the keyhole. "That is as simple as they make 'em," he said in an undertone, "if one only had a bit of wire." He thought for a moment. Then he tiptoed a few steps down the corridor to a door behind which a woman was scolding and some children were yelling. He picked the key out of the door and returned. The key fitted exactly.

"You are a great fellow, Nezzar," Malvina simpered.

"No, the landlord is a stingy louse who has had one kind of key made for the whole shooting-match," he answered modestly, and put the key back as noiselessly as he had taken it. "That's what he is."

"Oh, you," said Malvina, rapping his fingers with small, genteel blows, faintly suggestive of aristocracy. "You always want to joke about nasty things. In our department we change every week, I want you to know."

King Nebuchadnezzar did not understand her.

When she was acting the countess, the meaning of her words was sometimes hazy to him. But he knew that the origin of her refinement was genuine enough.

"Lady—" he said, and solemnly held the door open for her.

They entered a small room with one and a half narrow windows. The other half of the second window belonged to the kitchen, which measured six feet each way, and was separated from the room by a partition. Through this arrangement an alcove was formed in a corner of the room, just big enough to hold an old wooden bed, which was covered with rags. The space under it was filled with bottles. Half a table stood on its two legs leaning against the opposite wall, and in a dirty wicker cradle under the window slept a six-months-old baby sucking a pacifier made of an old curtain. The curtain had been tied into many pacifiers, which had been sucked and discarded in their turn, and were now dragging on the floor. The baby slowly pulled its present pacifier in and out while sleeping. Each time the whole heavy row was lifted and lowered; it looked like a ball fringe. The unused end of the curtain was thrown over a nail.

On the only chair in the room sat a boy of two or three years. He was tied to the chair and was evidently supposed to be looking out of the near-by window. On the window-sill before him lay the gnawed-off crusts of some lard sandwiches. The boy was asleep, his heavy head hanging down inertly to one side. His feeble breathing sounded like soft whistling. He opened two big eyes and stared at them.

"My stars, Sonny, Sonny!" cried King Nebuchadnezzar in a delighted falsetto, and stretched out his hands with a stage gesture, "don't you know your own father, eh?"

Between them they untied him, and Malvina placed him on her knees and began to clean him a little. Meanwhile the happy father strode around, giving vent to his delight in short exclamations—"You look fine that way, girl! You look mighty fine being good to him! If you could only see for yourself how fine you look with him on your lap!"

The child let them fuss with him without showing any noticeable interest. He seemed strangely dull and apathetic, breathed heavily and audibly, and evidently was not in the least impressed by the course of events. It was as if he had once for all made the resolution to walk through life unaffected by its ups and downs. There was a certain drowsiness over him. He did not by any movement help Malvina in her work, but went on breathing with a heavy, snoring sound which might well be interpreted as a purring of content.

"He makes himself heavy," said Malvina, "he just wants to be petted. And do see how plump he is, Nezzar!"

"He doesn't jabber any too much, does he?" said Nebuchadnezzar musingly. "I wonder if he can talk at all? How old did you say he was?"

"Three years, Nezzar—three years and then some. Mercy, that you could forget that!"

"Why—a man has so many more important things to think of."

Three years—oh, well, then there was time enough for him to have his say, even if he should turn out to be a Rigsdag deputy.

"He may still learn to talk the leg off an iron pot. By the way, have you ever thought of what profession he is going to take up?"

"Lord, no," said Malvina in a frightened voice.

"Still that is as important as anything I know of! There are all kinds of possibilities in such a little body. He is a human seed, to express it nicely. Who knows, maybe some day he will sit astraddle of the whole cake!—It would be grand to see that day."

"Well, I think he is going to be a confectioner," said Malvina, in response to the word cake. Besides, she was fond of sweets.

King Nebuchadnezzar made a grimace of despair.

Martin Andersen Nexö

"I don't mean any offense, Lady, but you
women have no imagination. No—the time of
handicraft is over. Or did you ever know a finer
craftsman than King Nebuchadnezzar? And
what did he get for it? Nowadays you've got
to have *head*—brains are what tell in our day,
see? And his head is big enough, Lord knows!
—The little brat!"

King Nebuchadnezzar had taken the child's
head between his big hands. "Is the yeast working in there? Is it, Sonny?" he said, laughing
through tears. The thought of the boy's great
future stirred him and made his hands tremble.
"He doesn't say a word, he doesn't even blink.
I tell you, there is backbone in him. And do you
know, Malvina, I can feel the workings up here
in his blessed little dome. His mind is busy even
now. He'll be a good one, I tell you! Just see
how calm and cool he is! Small as he is, he acts
like our Lord himself, knowing the ins and outs
of the whole thing. I guess nothing will hang too
high for *him!*"

King Nebuchadnezzar began to whistle softly,
gazing into the unknown. With his thoughts in
the far future he did not hear Malvina ask him
for his handkerchief. Anyway, he could not have
given her any. Out there in the future his own
existence was being repeated in a bigger and more
successful way. He himself had beaten the

record, but only in a matter which already was doomed. He had won the race hundreds of times, but he did not feel victorious. But when Sonny grew up, things were going to hum. He could sense the turmoil and bustle, and had taken part in enough of it to feel dizzy for Sonny.

His thoughts were gradually released from the future, and with a sigh he came back to earth and discovered that his throat was dry. He took a few turns around the room and sent his restless eyes investigating in all corners. "I wonder how the wine cellar is getting on?" he said, pulling out the bottles from under the bed and holding them to the light. "Bone dry all along the line! Fine state of affairs! See here, don't you think your sister has an account somewhere around here?"

Malvina shook her head. She was busy cleaning the boy's nose with a corner of her handkerchief.

"But, my goodness, they live in style! Here she is supporting the family, and he has his sixteen crowns a week and can spend every öre of it! And you think they would have no account where one could charge a drop of liquor?" Such nonsense was incomprehensible. "Sonny, can you say 'Daddy'? My, now you look pretty! The Lord help us, I think he takes after both of us, Lady. That is what comes from agreeing in everything!"

He took a turn into the kitchen, which was the size of an ordinary table.

"They can afford running water, the spendthrifts!—Ah!"

He came back to Malvina and the child.

"Sonny, can you say 'Daddy'? Well, give me a smack, girl! You look fine with a little one on your knees! If you could only see yourself!"

But Malvina was pouting.

"You always find fault with my relatives. And yet they are grand to Sonny, keeping him here for nothing."

"Oh yes, they are good enough according to their lights," said King Nebuchadnezzar appeasingly. "Don't get on your hind legs, Mally!— Sonny!" He fumbled in his vest pocket for some gift for the boy and got hold of the tobacco quid. The deuce take it! Here he might have spent that darned five öre on something for the boy— cream, for instance. Cream was not a bit too grand for such a prince. He sauntered back to the kitchen and began to look over the plate rack, driven by some desperate hope.

Suddenly he gave a little surprised whistle: he had found a ten-öre piece under one of the cups.

He came back to Malvina with joyful, dancing steps.

"See here, Malvina, girl of my heart! run down and get five öre's worth of cream for the Prince, and brandy with the rest of the money. Tell them it is for a sick person, and they will give you better measure."

Nobody on earth, least of all Malvina herself, could help buying brandy with all the money. For one thing, the cream was sour at this time of day, also there was none to be had, and finally one could not buy brandy with less than ten öre. King Nebuchadnezzar was not the person to utter reproaches after hearing these altogether satisfactory reasons; and Sonny was already man enough to feel sufficiently compensated by a few drops of brandy on a crust of bread.

But after the drink it was as if the coziness of home life had vanished. King Nebuchadnezzar no longer felt the quiet satisfaction of dwelling in the bosom of his assembled family. Every now and then he went to the window and looked out. Some of his old flourish had returned. He was still buoyant, and felt the need of some personal outlet—the need of one more bout with the world, to say it nicely.

It was an unusually beautiful day, one of the few days when the sun triumphantly pierces the veil of smoke generally hanging over the city, and pours a flood of light over the streets. The sky, a marvelous blue between the trees on the old rampart, seemed to be nothing but limitless, im-

material space, resting in lucidity and peace. It
was like looking into limpid infinity.

King Nebuchadnezzar shook himself.

"Such a day ought to be celebrated," he said,
"and not be spent sitting here moping. Besides,
Sonny is sleepy. I think I'll go out and get a
breath of air.—If one could only have raised a
few coins."

He sighed and cast a searching glance at the
bare room.

"You can't show yourself publicly in that out-
fit!" said Malvina.

"No, of course, it would be better to be in
plain clothes, but there are clothes enough in the
wardrobe—any amount of them."

They examined the contents of the bed, and
unanimously chose the least ragged pair of trousers and the remnants of a brown overcoat. King
Nebuchadnezzar donned the finery, and contemp-
tuously threw the tell-tale garb of the workhouse
inmate on the bed.

"Now when I take a stitch here and there, you
will look fine," said Malvina, and stroked him
caressingly.

"Yes, that isn't half bad," he said delighted,
"but they'll nab me anyhow when they see my
socks."

"You'll have to let down the pants, Nezzar."

"That won't be enough! But never mind, it'll be all right to go barefoot in wooden shoes this time of year."

"I shall certainly not go with you if you are barefoot. There are plenty of others I can go with!"

"Did you think I meant it?" he said hurriedly. "We are not that far gone yet." He spoke swaggeringly, yet remained irresolute.

"You might try the attic," suggested Malvina.

"That was just what I was thinking of," he answered calmly, anxious to maintain as much as possible of his superiority over his lady. He went out quickly, and returned soon after, carrying a shabby high silk hat and a pair of worn-out boots with side inserts of elastic. "Look at the mud boats," he said, showing them triumphantly. "Of course it's a bum piece of work—still they are always better than wooden shoes. I hate wooden shoes more than anything. They ruin the profession. And think of the club-footed walk they give!"

The clothes looked like crumpled paper that had been unfolded. But the couple only heeded the actual holes, and Malvina searched in vain for needle and thread. The baby in the cradle now began to move and cry, and they realized that Malvina's sister would soon come back. With much petting, they again placed Sonny on the chair near the window, and tied him so that he would not tumble out.

"It's fine for Sonny to sit there and look at the sky," said King Nebuchadnezzar, patting him gently on his thin hair. But Sonny preferred to sleep. His head dropped heavily down to one side, and he began once more to whistle softly.

The baby was angry. She had lost her pacifier, and was crying furiously, raising her naked stomach till her little body formed a bridge resting on her head and feet.

"She is hungry, poor thing," said King Nebuchadnezzar and looked around for an inspiration, "look how she humps her stomach. Would you like something poured into your little tummy, eh?"

He shyly patted her tense little drum. Then he took the empty bottle and held it to the light for inspection, but not the least particle was left. The last drop had been poured on Sonny's crust.

"It does seem a shame," said Malvina, "of course, she's not ours, still it does seem a shame."

She found a few morsels of bread which she held under the faucet, to moisten them before tying the lump into the curtain above the other knots. The baby stopped crying and began to doze, moving the whole machinery up and down with her small pumping apparatus, without realizing that she had now one more ball to keep going.

For a while King Nebuchadnezzar stood and looked at her patient drudgery. "She goes at it like a regular steam engine," he said musingly. "She'll be great when she grows up! Whew—I should hate to be the man that crosses her way. But shan't we cut all that old stuff off? It's a pity for her to lie there working at the whole mess."

"No, we better not; perhaps Sister wants to use the curtain," answered Malvina.

They sauntered aimlessly down the street. Malvina took her Nezzar's arm and walked along mincingly. "You'll take us to a nice place, won't you? Not to anything low-down? There are good places enough where *you* can get in." She spoke with such conviction that King Nebuchadnezzar felt extremely poor and powerless.

She left all details about the choice of a place entirely to him. Now and then she threw a rapt glance at him, but otherwise kept her eye modestly to the ground. It was so long since she had gone out with a man that she felt as if it were the first time. She felt as bashful as a young girl, and that was a lovely sensation. This, however, did not prevent her from stealthily watching the stores from which people turned their heads to look after the couple. King Nebuchadnezzar looked fine in a silk hat, and she knew that they created admiration of all by their appearance.

"I know where you are going to take us," she said gaily and hung heavily on his arm. But she did not know, and did not care to know. She only said it to express her blind faith in him. She wanted most of all to hang on his arm and with closed eyes walk straight into the light. Then, when they were in the full illumination, she would open her eyes quickly, and let herself be hurt and dazzled by the sudden radiance which would make her cry out.

How beautiful life could be!

King Nebuchadnezzar felt a little uneasy. When they reached the bridge leading to the heart of the city, he turned, and a minute later he turned again. Certainly, there were places enough. The whole city, brimful of splendors, was offering itself. The difficulty was to be sure of choosing the right place, so as not to sit there and be sorry afterwards. He himself would have preferred to begin at one end and "do" the whole town lengthwise and crosswise. But that was out of the question if one had a lady along. He was just waiting for an idea which might save the day, a "darned good little hunch," such as he had had hundreds of time before. Meanwhile one simply had to keep going, and King Nebuchadnezzar varied his manœuvres like a skipper who tries to kill time while tacking in wait for the pilot.

Malvina began to take notice. "It seems to me we are going in a circle," she said surprised.

"But really, the first thing is to get needle and thread," mumbled King Nebuchadnezzar offended. "A gentleman——"

Malvina hugged his arm and looked innocently up to him, astonished at his angry tone. And Nebuchadnezzar felt with a pang his responsibility toward this woman who walked by his side looking forward to a merry evening. She knew perfectly well that he had not a red öre, but she simply believed in him. And under normal conditions this would have been the right thing to do, for King Nebuchadnezzar was ordinarily not without resources when planning for a good time. But to-day his genius didn't seem to be at home. He did not feel a trace of that play of intelligence which in ways numerous and varied had supplied him with cash when he had needed it.

"We might go and dance in 'The Decanter,' " he said crestfallen, "only they won't let us in." He had the sad sensation that he was failing in the main issue. Sure, the world was chock full of excitement and fun, but what was the good if one no longer knew how to nab them? He had never quite realized the value of money, but now it began to dawn on him. Money was all right after all, when one was worn out and could think of nothing else.

Rather downcast, they sauntered up on the old rampart and sat down on a bench. The sun was setting. The dying day enveloped the city in a purple mist, which was wafted in and out among the trees on the rampart like voluptuous exhalations from a glowing, joy-sated world.

A short distance away some children were singing and dancing rounds under the trees, and at the end of the street the tower of Our Savior's Church shone in its golden luster. It was impossible to be sad, and gradually they forgot their grudge against life and began to chat innocently about nothing and everything. The evening filled them with well-being and gentleness. With a tinge of melancholy they watched the sun take its leave, unhindered, as something too great to have its right disputed. Before it disappeared, it kissed their vapid faces and made them blush once more in giddy anticipation. Their eyes had perhaps never before shone so beautifully; far away over the city hovered the festive glow that was kindled again in them. For a short while ineffable joy—happiness unknown to the world—flowed into them and inflated their shrivelled hearts.

Malvina had persuaded a little girl to go home for needle and thread. Eagerly she mended her big beautiful man here and there, surrounded by a crowd of open-mouthed children. King Nebuchadnezzar had to lie down on the bench to make the work go more quickly, and was told to turn round so as to be mended on all sides. He lay tossing about like a frolicsome puppy, overdoing everything, and making monstrous puns in order to amuse the children. In spite of the dying light, Malvina used her needle deftly and completed her work in the twinkling of an eye.

"There, Nezzar," she said, looking into his eyes elated. The last obstacle was overcome.

He gave her a humble and impotent look in return. Alas, the obstacles were overcome; there was no longer any hiding-place. Behind this careful mending, a secret hope had been lying in wait for him—for why make one's self so smart? Surely, there must be a reason! Now this hope failed before their very eyes, and revealed man's miserable poverty when deserted by his intelligence.

All his life King Nebuchadnezzar had kept his faith in himself. It had been present as a gigantic ruin in his dream of this very day, and had lured him into the attempt to revive his youth for one evening, to make a journey round the world on a small scale. That ought to be a mere trifle for a man who had tramped comfortably and easily through three continents without having a red öre in his pocket, and had partaken of all that life had to offer. And now the miserable end of

it all was that he was sitting here, in the most self-
evident place in the world, and had to admit his
inability to pay fifty öre for admission to a dance-
hall!

Of course one could always do something or
other without money. Even the poorest bum
must have connections enough to get a glad evening out of them without spending any money.
Malvina hinted as much—after all, the women
expected to hang on and get a good time out of
the men. But King Nebuchadnezzar was not of
the kind that sponged on his acquaintances. He
much preferred to play the returned American.
He had not gone out to-day to nibble a crumb
here and there, but to visit once more the happy
hunting grounds of his youth. If he found himself pushed out of the game—well, then he could
call it square and return to the Institution if need
be. But sit and lick the plates after the banquet
—no, he couldn't do that. Leave that to those
who had never been at the festive board themselves. "One has obligations toward the other
fellows in the Institution," he argued aloud, thinking that even a woman would understand that.
"One represents them all, so to say. But you go
ahead, Lady! You will always find some guy—
you with your face!"

But Malvina only clung still tighter to him and
declared that she cared for nobody else in this

[317]

world and wanted to stay with him. She could always find somebody else some day when he was not along.

"I expected as much of you," said King Nebuchadnezzar with emotion. "You answered as I should have done in your place."

Malvina accepted his praise with a brave smile, but suddenly burst out crying. She let herself go like a young girl, as if this were the first time her world had broken down around her. King Nebuchadnezzar did not try to console her with words, but put his arm gently round her. With her head on his shoulder she sobbed herself to sleep.

The evening had set in. Darkness was gathering under the trees of the rampart, and in the streets the lamps were lighted one by one, twinkling in the dusk. King Nebuchadnezzar's eyes had assumed a strange, far-away expression.

He was gazing into the distance, farther than any one could see. He had not the heart to stir and possibly awake Malvina, and he felt frightfully lonesome—so lonesome that he had to let things take their course and confess to himself that it was all over. He was absolutely good for nothing. He had grown old. It was a relief to acknowledge this at last, instead of trying to prop up the impossible by putting a tired shoulder to it. Well, now it was over. Life could no longer be snatched in passing. It lurched by so swiftly that, if he tried to jump on board, he only split his skull against the pavement.

But he had had his day. He had been no common trash. Gosh almighty, how he had made things hum! What precious memories he had! He could not restrain himself any longer, but felt that he must have a partaker in his reminiscences. When Malvina awoke, however, and looked at him, his whole glory faded before the disillusion in her eyes. Perhaps she had dreamed that she was in the midst of splendor.

They sat huddled close together, neither feeling the need of words. King Nebuchadnezzar wondered that Malvina did not scold him. A while ago he would have wished her to do so. It would have led to a brawl, and he could have withdrawn from it with the air of a man who would have redeemed everything if, woman-like, she had not spoiled the game by her squabble. But now he had surrendered to decrepitude, and was grateful to her for not throwing it up to him.

There were thickets growing on the slopes of the rampart, in which children and tramps had made little paths. The darkness put a soft shroud over the foliage, and here and there through the bushes the glimmering of ripples and the rustling of reeds told of the near-by water in the moat.

Something about all this went softly to King

Nebuchadnezzar's heart, like a greeting from his great and good days. Here he could still in his present poor condition taste the sweetness of our great earth. A night in the open was something which he could still afford, and at the same time the gist of the whole thing. All he had attained in his life, nay, Life itself was founded on the furtive thrill he had felt when sleeping under the stars and awaking drenched by the morning dew, in the center of the whole universe. Surely, he was yet equal to as much as that!

But Malvina jumped up offended. She wasn't going to make her bed in the open air like she wouldn't say what kind of a woman. They were not used to that in her department. "We have decent beds, with all comforts—but I can certainly take myself away if you are going to be vulgar."

King Nebuchadnezzar gave her a despairing look while she carried on. She needn't have put on her aristocratic airs for his sake. He had felt the pain and loneliness of old age, and was not going to quarrel with anybody.

"You are acting so Spanish this evening," he said with a bitter smile. "One might think that one of the overseers had begun to make eyes at you."

"Why, Nezzar, for shame!" she exclaimed, offended, "you know very well that I am no scab."

Well, why not?—If that would lead to one or

two small concessions. He, too, began to realize the importance of concessions, and was already slowly adapting himself to his new and humbler existence. This called to his mind the hayloft of Jensen, the livery man. He was now tired and longed for a rest, and such a hayloft could be perfectly splendid—the best thing next to a haystack in the open air.

He made his suggestion meekly, and to his surprise Malvina did not object, but rose silently. For a short time they walked southward on the rampart, then descended and crossed an empty lot where there was quite an accumulation of old boilers, rusty iron plates, and heavy, half corroded cables. Through an opening in the fence they entered a yard surrounded on three sides by low buildings and wooden barns. A black, factory-like building stood on the fourth side. King Nebuchadnezzar had taken Malvina's hand and was pulling her with him. They walked in the shadow of wagons and lumber piles, and were steering toward a low building from which was heard the steady sound of champing horses.

King Nebuchadnezzar stuck his head through the open upper half of the door and whistled softly. A youthful tension had come over his movements. He stood there straining every sense, ready to light out or change his tactics at the faintest sound. After all, this tasted mag-

nificently of old times and the outer world. He
turned and signaled to Malvina with his eyes
while he stealthily unhooked the door. Then he
entered the stable on tiptoe, and Malvina shuffled
after him.

"Here is the hotel," he whispered, and looked
around in delight. "Look, Malvina! Horses,
and beautiful hay. No ordinary draught-horses
either—just notice the manure; you smell the difference at once. The stable boy has gone out—
fine fellow! Well, get up in the hay, Lady!"

He climbed up the ladder to the hayloft, and
Malvina followed him. It was hard for her, and
she held her dress together with unnecessary
tightness in order to show her disapproval of
Nezzar's vulgar exclamations.

That night King Nebuchadnezzar dreamed of
the big plains and the starry skies: He had prepared for next day's hike by rubbing his feet with
tallow and lacing his stomach firmly. Now he
was resting in the finest haystack, gazing toward
the distant mountains, and quietly anticipating
what was to be found on the other side of them.
Overhead the universe was moving to its eternal
music. He sensed the unending melody of the
vast night, and knew from this that he was alone.
But it did not make him sad.

Malvina, dreaming too, was in "The Decanter"
and was dancing the old dance called "The

Crested Hen." She daintily lifted her dress far up on one side, for her leg was covered in its whole length with yellow silk.

.   .   .   .

Overseer Petersen had returned with his light brigade, and learned to his surprise that King Nebuchadnezzar had not yet arrived. It happened now and then that one or another of the inmates made themselves scarce for a couple of days, but they generally returned of their own accord. Even if not, they were always easy to trace, so the event did not arouse much concern.

Yet the authorities began to take a few leisurely steps to find Nezzar, and at a certain point his trail converged with Malvina's. She, too, was missed, and as their former relations were known, the matter began to look a bit more serious. Their connection with the family on Christianshavn was also known, and the investigations were started in Dronningensgade.

Here the man had come back and found the inmate's uniform in his bed. He saw at once how matters stood, and, knowing that they would be bothered by the police, he preferred to report his find at once to the station.

This double alarm stirred the police to action. Search was made, and all trails led to the Christianshavn rampart. But there they ended.

In some way or other the eloping of the indigent

[323]

couple gradually changed its aspect and appeared romantic instead of comical. The beautiful summer night spun its mystic web around them. Perhaps the air was filled with love that night. Be this as it may, little by little their excursion took the shape of a love drama. The daily papers were notified, and the moat examined as far as possible during the night.

At dawn a policeman who knew all the ins and outs of the haunts of Christianshavn took it upon himself to investigate them one by one. A little later in the morning the sun rose over the distant mountains and tickled King Nebuchadnezzar's nose. He rubbed his eyes and awoke to the most odious of all sights, a red-haired policeman! However, he had by long experience learned to deal cordially with the archfiend, and said yawning—after having extricated himself from Malvina's arms— "Well, are we to beat it?"

The sergeant nodded.

"We would have come anyway by ourselves, but of course it's nicer to be sent for. You have a cab, I suppose?"

"There is one waiting in the square," said the sergeant laughing.

They found it, and all three stepped in. Malvina and King Nebuchadnezzar were equally delighted. They had received permission to have the top down, and were now leaning elegantly

back in their seats. They were driving home
from the banquet, a little dizzy from the splendor.
The light and music were still pulsating through
them and made them exuberant. King Nebuchadnezzar waved his hand condescendingly at
the passers-by, and Malvina threw kisses at them
with her fingers. Then they both laughed, and
the policeman pretended not to notice.

"After all, that was a worthy ending," said
King Nebuchadnezzar, as they swung up before
the gate of the Workhouse.

Malvina said nothing, but graciously put her
finger to her closed lips and bowed slowly. King
Nebuchadnezzar took this as it was meant—it
was the high, aristocratic world's way of saying
"Thanks for buns and chocolate," and he respected her silence. He lifted his old silk hat,
made a deep bow to Madame, and entered his
prison like a high-born guest from Bredgade who
deigns to taste the food of the poor.

It turned out to be their last fling. Malvina
had caught cold in the night and died shortly afterwards, and King Nebuchadnezzar never again had
the courage to compete by himself with the big
world. Scenting future defeats, he preferred to
live in his memories of the glorious days in which
he had held his own so valiantly.

JOHANNES V. JENSEN

ANN AND THE COW
LOST FORESTS

JOHANNES V. JENSEN (1873–) counts among his fore-fathers a long line of Jutland peasants. In his early works, among which *Ejnar Elkær* was the most note-worthy, he wrote in that style of critical self-analysis which became the fashion after Jacobsen's *Niels Lyhne*. He soon turned to more positive themes, however. A trip to the United States was influential in giving him that interest in facts, that admiration for achievement and for material and technical progress, which is charac-teristic of him. At the same time he felt drawn to the solid, old-fashioned, tradition-bound peasants of his na-tive region, and described them in his first collection of *Himmerland Stories,* followed after an interval of years by two more volumes.

In his philosophical travel book, *The Gothic Renais-sance,* Johannes V. Jensen first propounded the racial theory which became the underlying theme of his sub-sequent works. In the Gothic race from which regenera-tion was to come he included the Danish Jutlanders and their kinsmen, the English and American Anglo-Saxons. The Danish historical novel, *The Fall of the King,* deal-ing with the unhappy monarch Christian II, and the two novels of modern American life, *Madame d'Ora* and *The Wheel,* were links in the history of the Gothic race. They preceded the great cycle, *The Long Journey,* which is the author's most monumental work, comprising the independent novels, *The Lost Land, The Glacier, Norn Guest, The Trek of the Cimbri, The Ship,* and *Chris-topher Columbus.*

Jensen's later works include several volumes of poems marked by originality and poetic imagination; some col-lections of pithy essays; five volumes called *Myths* con-taining exquisite nature tales, and a Himmerland novel, *Jörgine.*

Johannes V. Jensen

Ann and the Cow

IN the cattle-pen at Hvalpsund Fair stood an old woman with her cow. She stood off a little to one side with her solitary cow, either because she was modest or because she wanted to attract more attention. She stood there so tranquilly, her head-dress drawn slightly down over her forehead on account of the sun, and knitted on a stocking which was already long enough to be turned back into a thick roll. She was dressed in a quaint, old-fashioned style, with a blue skirt that smelled in a home-like way of the dye-pot, and a brown knitted shawl crossed over her flat chest. The head-dress was faded and wrinkled after its long sojourn in the drawer; the wooden shoes were flat-bottomed, but she had polished them. In addition to the four needles she plied so swiftly with her worn hands, she had an extra one stuck in her gray hair. She stood with one ear toward the music which came from the booths, but she also looked now and again at the people and animals that traded and crowded beside her.

All about her and coming from all directions were noises and confusion: the neighing from the horse-stalls, the bustle of boats on the beach, the crashing of drums and loud cries from the clowns; but she stood there in the sunshine, oh, so calmly, and knitted on her stocking.

By her side with its head near her elbow stood the cow, bored and stiff-legged, chewing its cud. It was an old cow, but a good one, with a healthy-looking coat of hair and a really noble bearing. It was, to be sure, somewhat knobby in the hind-quarters and along the back-bone, but that was the worst that could be said about it; the udder bulged soft and hairy beneath its belly, and there were not too many rings on the pretty black and white horns. It stood with moist eyes, chewing for the second time its cud. The lower jaw moved steadily from left to right and when it had swallowed, it turned its head and looked about, again to stand with motionless jaws while the next ball of cud rose through the gullet and up into its mouth. The insides of it sang vibrantly, like the deep notes of an organ, each time it breathed, and it drooled contentedly at the mouth. It was a sound, healthy cow, which had experienced what can happen to cows, and arrived at years of discretion. It had given birth to calves without even seeing them or getting a chance to lick them, and had then consumed its fodder and given its milk in good faith. And now it chewed its cud here as willingly as anywhere else and swung its tail in stiff spirals at the flies. The tether hung carefully twined about one horn, for the cow did not care to play the vagabond or run loose. The yoke was old and smooth-worn, without either iron over the nose or inturned pegs, for this cow had really no need of such contrivances. It may be noted that it wore its new rope to-day, not the old thin worn one with which it usually grazed. Old Ann wished that she, that is to say the cow, should look her best.

Since it was a good cow and obviously ripe for slaughter, it was not long before a man came over, looked at it, and ran his fingers along the well-groomed hide—a familiarity which the cow resented, but not enough to become vexed about.

"How much for the cow, granny?" asked the man, transferring his stern look from the cow to Ann. Ann kept on knitting.

"It is not for sale," she replied. Then, as if to put a courteous period to the conversation, she dropped the needles out of one hand and with it wiped herself industriously under the nose. The man hesitated, but at length walked away; he seemed to find it difficult to take his eyes off the cow.

Not long thereafter a dapper and smooth-shaven butcher flicks his cane against the cow's horns and lets his plump hand glide quickly over the smooth flesh.

"How much for the cow?"

Old Ann looks first at her cow, now piously regarding the cane, then turns her head and appears to find something interesting to look at far off in the distance.

"It is not for sale."

Done. Our cattle-dealer walks off in his blood-stained duster. But almost immediately afterwards there comes another man desirous of making a purchase. Old Ann shakes her head.

"The cow is not for sale."

When she had in this manner turned away many men, of course she became known; they began to gossip about her. A man who had once before tried to buy the cow and had been refused now returned and made a bid that was more than tempting. Old Ann said "No" in a very firm voice, but she seemed to be worried.

"*Is* it sold, then?" asked the man.

No, it certainly was not sold.

"Yes, but why in all the world do you stand here, then, and parade the cow?"

Old Ann hung her head, but stubbornly kept on knitting.

"What? Why do you stand here with the cow?" asked the man, who now felt himself positively insulted. "Is it your *own* cow?"

[332]

Yes, it certainly was that. It certainly was Ann's cow. She added that, really, she had had it since it was a calf; yes, really she had. If talk could appease the man, thought Ann, it should not be lacking. But he interrupted her.

"Do you stand here and make fun of people?"

Mercy! Ann is silent under this blow. She knits as if she were delirious. She knows not where to *look,* she is so bewildered. And the man, angrily, persists—

"I say, are you come to the Fair to make fun of people?"

It is then that Old Ann stops knitting. And as she loosens the tether from the cow's horn in preparation for the homeward trip, she fastens her wide-open eyes beseechingly on the man.

"It is such a lonely cow," she says, confidingly. "It is *such* a lonely cow! It is the only one I have on my little farm, and it so very seldom gets out among other cattle. And so I thought I'd bring her to the Fair, so that she could mingle with her own kind, and enjoy herself a bit; yes, really, that's what I thought. And I meant well; it couldn't do any harm to any one, and—and so it was that we came here. But we aren't for sale, and so we may as well be on our way. And *I'm sorry,* I should have said. And good-bye. And thank you."

LOST FORESTS

KORRA was the name of a man who tilled the soil. When he had saved some money, he went to town to buy a slave.

The dealer showed him several slaves, but Korra was not satisfied.

"I suppose you want me to drag them all out here," the dealer grumbled. It was noon, and the slaves were all asleep.

"I can always go elsewhere," Korra said simply.

"Well, well!" The dealer pulled the chains, and the slaves filed out sleepily. Korra looked at them all, examining each one very carefully.

"Feel this one, he's a fine husky fellow," said the dealer, and pushed one of the slaves forward. "What do you think of him? Hasn't he a powerful chest? Strike it and see. And look here at his wrists; the tendons are like the strings of a violin. Open your mouth!"

The dealer thrust a finger in the slave's mouth and turned him toward the light. "Now you'll see some teeth," he boasted. He drew the back of a knife across the slave's teeth. "Look! Those teeth are like steel. They can bite a nail in two."

[334]

Johannes V. Jensen

Korra bethought himself yet awhile. He ran his hand over the slave appraisingly, pressing the smooth muscles with the tips of his fingers to see if they were firm. Finally he made up his mind to buy him, paid the price with a scowl, had the slave unmanacled, and took him home.

Before many days had passed, the slave fell sick and began to pine away. Now that he was no longer in the market, but had settled down permanently, he began to long for the forests whence he had come. It was an excellent sign; Korra knew the symptoms. One day he sat down beside the slave, who was lying flat on his back with no interest in life, and began to talk thoughtfully to him.

"You shall get back to your forests, never fear. That I promise you, and you can rely on my promises. You are still young, you know. . . . If you will till my fields for me, willingly and industriously, for five years, I will give you your freedom, even though I have paid for you. Five years. Is it a bargain?"

And the slave worked. He took hold like a demon. It was a joy for Korra to sit in his doorway and watch those muscles knot and quiver under the brown skin, and Korra did this for many hours a day, for there was nothing he would rather do. He began to realize that the body is a beautiful thing and a delight to the eye.

Five years, the slave figured—as many solstices as he had fingers. The sun had to turn ten times. Every evening he watched the sun go down, and he kept track of the number of times with markers of stones and knolls. When the sun had turned the first time, he counted on the thumb of his right hand. After the passage of another solstice—and it seemed an eternity—the index finger was free. These two fingers he loved above the others which still served to mark his bondage.

Thus telling the days and marking the passage of time became the religion of the slave, his inner wealth, his spiritual treasure, which none could take from him or dispute with him.

As the time passed, his calculations expanded, became broader and deeper. The years drove by as great boundless abstractions which he could not grasp; but with every new sunset glow the slave recreated his hope and reconsecrated his faith. Time, which was evanescent in the present, appeared interminable, once it was in the past; and the future seemed infinitely distant.

In such wise the slave's spirit was deepened. As his longing brought infinity into time, so his world became infinite, and his thoughts boundless. Every evening the slave stared thoughtfully into the distant west, and each sunset brought more and more depth into his soul.

When, finally, the five years had ebbed away—
it is so easy to say the words—the slave came to
his master and asked for his freedom. He
wanted to go to his home in the forests.

"You have been a faithful worker," Korra admitted meditatively. "Tell me, where is your
home? Is it in the west? I have often watched
you staring in that direction."

Yes, his home was in the west.

"It is far away then," said Korra.—The slave
nodded—far away.—"And you have no money,
have you?"

The slave was silent, dismayed. No, that was
right, he had no money.

"Look you, you can get nowhere without money.
If you work for me for three more years—no, let
it be two—I will give you enough money for
your travels."

The slave bowed his head, and went into harness again. He worked well, but no longer did
he keep track of the passing days as formerly.
On the contrary, he gave way to day-dreaming,
and Korra heard him wail and babble in his sleep.
After a time he fell sick again.

Then Korra sat down beside him and talked
to him long and earnestly. His speech sounded
prudent, full of wisdom, as if grounded in honest
experience.

"I am an old man," he said. "In my youth,

I, too, longed for the west; the great forests beckoned me. But I never had money enough for the journey. I shall never go there now—never until my spirit goes there when I die. You are young and able, and you work hard, but are you any stronger or abler than I was in my youth? Think about all this, and hearken to the advice of an old man. And see to it that you get well again."

But the slave mended slowly, and when he took hold again, it was not with the old enthusiasm. He gave way easily now, his ambition was gone, and he liked to lie down and sleep between jobs. Then one day Korra whipped him. It did him good, and he wept.

So the two years slipped by.

Then Korra really gave the slave his freedom. He went forth into the west; but months later he came back in a miserable plight. He had not been able to find his forests.

"Do you see?" said Korra. "Didn't I warn you? But no one shall say that I am not good to you. Try again, and this time go eastward. It might be that your forests lie in that direction."

Once more the slave set forth, this time with his face toward the rising sun, and finally, after long wanderings, he came to his own forests. *But he knew them not.* Worn out and defeated, he turned his face to the west, came back to his master, and told him that though he had found woods, great woods and small, they were not his own forests.

"Hmm!" Korra coughed.

"Stay with me," he then said warmly. "While I am alive you shall never lack for a home on this earth. And when I have been gathered to my fathers, my son will see that you are taken care of." So the slave stayed.

Korra aged, but his slave was still in his prime. Korra fed him well that he might live long, kept him clean that he might be in good health, and at reasonable intervals whipped him so that he should be meek and respectful. Nor did he stint with rest; every Sunday the slave was free to sit on top of a knoll and stare out into the west.

Korra's farm yielded in abundance. He purchased woods and cleared them and put them under the plow that his slave might have work, and the slave felled trees with a will. Korra was wealthy now, and one day he brought home a female slave.

The years passed, and in Korra's house there grew up six stalwart slave boys. Like their father, they worked diligently. Only when one is working does the time pass, their father told them. And when the time has passed, weary we are borne into the everlasting forests. Every rest

[339]

day he took his sons with him up on the knoll where they could watch the setting sun, and he taught them longing.

Korra was old and decrepit. He had, indeed, always been old, but now there was nothing of him left but age. His son had never been strong, but they had nothing to fear from any one, for each of the slaves could fell a man with one blow of a club. They were splendid fellows; the flesh was tight on their iron muscles, and their teeth were like a tiger's. But the times were safe enough. The slaves swung their axes and felled trees.

HARRY SÖIBERG

THE OLD BOAT

HARRY SÖIBERG (1880–) is one of the younger of the Jutland writers. His background is precisely that coast strip in West Jutland where the interests of the sea and the land are joined and sometimes clash, as in *The Old Boat*. In his early works he has shown the reverse side of the great and vaunted national undertaking, the reclamation of the heath. *The West Jutland Pioneer* is the story of a farmer who with superhuman effort wrests a farm from the wilderness, hoping to found a home for his family—only to see the heather encroaching on his fields again, when his strength is gone, and his sons have left him to seek more easily tilled soil in America. It is a tale of primitive heroism told with simplicity and dignity.

In his later books Söiberg develops a far more subtle psychology. His chief work is the novel trilogy, *The Land of the Living*, interesting from its varied characterization and the spiritual experiences described. Its hero is a young farmer who thinks himself doomed because of a murder committed by his forefathers. He first seeks aid from the brimstone preacher of a dissenting sect which has gathered adherents among the fishing population. Disappointed there, he turns to an unfrocked clergyman who is considered insane and called "the crazy parson," but who possesses a higher wisdom in his loving kindness to all living creatures.

Söiberg's latest work is *The Sea King*, the first volume of a new novel cycle. The scene is again West Jutland, and the "sea king" is a fishing master who dominates his village.

Harry Söiberg

The Old Boat

ALONG the western coast they use a boat of ancient type. No one knows anything about its origin, which connects with the burial mounds rising above the heaths and uplands back of the coast. It has the shape of an old viking vessel with raking stem. It is clinker-built and flaring in the beam, like a boat meant to face breakers and the open sea. It holds the heart of the coast dweller as no other type, and since time immemorial it has been used for deep-sea fishing, life-saving, and other great deeds done at sea. On its thwarts the men along the coast have grown to manhood, and there they are as much at home as are the dwellers on inland plains upon their horses.

A few miles from the shore an old sea-going boat of that type stood near the home of a peasant-fisherman. Years ago they had carted it along the heavy road leading from the shore across the heath. It was the will of the old man on the farm when he abandoned the sea.

The boat stood along the northern side of the

house, a lot of caufs stored beneath its bilge, and its lofty stem turned westward as if placed in that direction by a loving thought.

When the sea wind came swooping across the bluffs and descended on the open plain where lay the farm, it smote the bow so that one could hear ribs and strakes groan as if the boat had been laboring in a heavy sea. It was a sound that seemed to come from a living thing, and quite different from the wail of the wind around the house gable. Every board quivered, and across its rail flew a spray, not of water, but of sand and straw, which the wind swept in beneath the thwarts.

Inside the house the old man sat on a chair beside the big fireplace, carving rakes and other tools with a knife that trembled in his gnarled hands. His back was bent and his shoulders stooped as if worn out by too much toil on the thwarts.

For weeks the winter storm had raged over the country, filling every room in the place with its brawling.

Through the windows he could see the clouds race past, looking enormous and massive as if the wind had seized every bit of air above the sea to push it inland, across the crouching bluffs and the vast heaths. His glance was alert, and he took notice of every different kind of sound as in the

days of his youth, when he could sit indoors judging the ways of the sea and figuring out the proper
time for fishing.

Now there was hardly a boat to be found along
the shore. . . . Like his own son, who tilled the
farm, every one else in that district had, as far as
he could hear, turned his back on the sea. The
plow was now the favorite. From farther inland
bright new plow bills had been brought to every
farm, and the men were furrowing the heath as if
they expected to find gold where formerly could
be found nothing but food for a few sheep. And
the sea was abandoned.

There he sat very still, but watching everything
that went on around him. His face was utterly
void of all expression, but in his pale blue eyes the
light of the day raised a dreamy reflection as if
living memories were still astir in his soul.

All of a sudden his eyes would cling to the pegs
in the roof-beam. There, winter after winter,
he had stood mending those nets that now rotted
in the barn, useless and worthless.

In such moments he seemed to feel the humiliation of his senile job of carving teeth for rakes
and handles for flails . . . instead of holding the
net over his knee, going over it mesh by mesh, or
giving a helping hand to his son on the latter's
return from the sea.

But the farm throve, he had to admit. There

were eight cows in the byre, while in his own and his father's time they had never had more than two. And the flock of children was increasing, too. Three flaxen-haired lads and a little lassie filled the days with their playful noise and bustle, so that sometimes one did not even have time to think. And one by one they had found their way from the arms of his daughter-in-law to his own knees.

When he had been sitting like that for a while, he would often rise and go outside to stop at the western end of the house, at the selfsame spot where, through the long years, he had been wont to stand watching the shifting of weather and wind at sea. One foot dragged behind through the gravel, and with a trembling hand he leaned heavily on his stick.

Then, while he listened across miles of land for the sound of the breakers, his eyes became filled with the vision of something that was far, far off. And later he staggered around the house corner to the boat, where he always found something to potter with. His hands glided gently along the rails. Then he would put the oars where they belonged, or use his hands to scoop out the sand and straw which the wind had piled into the boat.

On those thwarts he had sat during the years of his youth, until his turn came to take his father's place at the tiller. With such thoughts in his mind, he stood there nodding his head and talking to himself and the old boat.

But inside the house they smiled and said that Grandfather took as much care of his old boat as a woman of her best room.

Once in a while it also happened that he made his way from the house to the barn, where hung the nets and all his tackle . . . just as if he expected that some day those things might be put to their proper use again.

Then the young wife would laugh outright and give her husband a sidewise glance—

"Now Grandfather is longing for the sea again. . . ."

.   .   .   .

But as the flock of children increased, the old boat seemed to come back to life again. One after another the boys, led by the hand of the Grandfather, would make the tour from the house to the place where the boat stood. One by one he had lifted them up to the rail with the same tense expectation as that displayed by a peasant when, for the first time, he places his little son on the back of a horse. And this went on until they became tall enough to crawl into the boat without help.

"Now we'll sail away," he used to say, smiling at them with an expression that seemed eloquent of all sorts of tempting adventures.

By this time the eldest boy was ten . . . a well set up lad, with his shoulders in the right place, with the blue of the sky in his eyes, and the gold of the sun in his hair.

It was a day in early spring. The boy stood in the stern, one hand on the tiller and Grandfather's sou'wester covering his ears. His two younger brothers sat on the foremost thwart. They had put out one of the oars and were moving it back and forth across the sand with tremendous efforts because the breakers were right ahead of them. Their little sister sat in the middle of the boat, all wrapped up like a girl who has come along for the fun of it.

The sun was shining over the open plain, lighting a gleam in every straw and glistening in every window pane. The song of the larks had been heard for a long time above the fields and the heath. The farmer came around the corner to get the harrow which all through the winter had been leaning its rusty teeth against the house wall. The time to seed the soil was drawing near.

Smiling he looked at the children's game.

"We're sailing for England, Father," the boy at the tiller yelled. "Do you want to come along?"

"No, Kresten, I have to get out in the fields."

He looked as if his figure had been pressed together so that it lacked the height it should have

[348]

had. His knees were bent, and his arms hung loosely with a suggestion of weariness. In his earlier years he also had been at sea, until the triumphant advance of the plow across the heath had caught his entire fancy, like that of so many other men in that district. Now he picked up the harrow and walked off.

"Let go the anchor," roared the boy at the tiller. "We have made land."

The smaller boys pulled in the oar, rushed up to the prow, and threw an old grapnel as far overboard as they could.

The spring sun lighted up their faces, and their eyes shone with the joy of actual experience. All around them was spread the vastness of the glimmering sea which the two youngest had not yet seen . . . but which nevertheless was always present in their minds as something toward which they could point.

"This is the place where we get our cargo. . . ." And they swung themselves over the rail in the manner of fishermen who never let go their hold until they have firm ground under their feet. In another minute they were loading the boats with caufs, while their little sister moved aside as one too small for such a wild play. They piled the boat full clear up to the rail.

Then they lifted anchor while the helmsman yelled to them to get out the oars in time to clear

[349]

the breakers . . . and the boys worked as if it had been a question of saving both the boat and their own lives.

At that moment the grandfather came out of the house with his arms full of tackle that was to be dried in the sun. Every spring he did the same thing in order to keep nets and ropes from rotting away. Carefully he spread his things along the fence on the northern side of the house, testing every line and mesh with a sort of tenderness.

The boys called to him as soon as they caught sight of him.

"You must come sailing with us, Grandfather . . . we have a big catch in the boat."

He turned toward them, smiling happily.

"I have grown too old for the sea, children," he said.

But he walked over to the boat just the same.

"Are you not afraid of being blown ashore . . . ?"

"Not at all," Kresten replied. "The sea is quite calm. You can stand it, Grandfather . . . there isn't sea enough to make Sister sick even."

And they held out their hands to him.

"You are a lot of stalwart fellows . . . one like me couldn't get on board even."

But they threw a couple of caufs overboard for him to step on, and then they pulled him in gleefully.

[350]

There he stood, a timid smile flickering over his face. The game of the children seemed to put new life into his eyes.

"You must steer, Grandfather."

"No, no, Kresten . . . you are the master. I'll sit here on the thwart."

It was years since he had sat like that. . . .

"Now we must save the crew on board that ship," he said. "It has been wrecked, you see."

But that made Kresten drop the tiller and come over to him.

"Please, Grandfather, tell us about the time when you got the gold watch."

And the smaller boys came crawling over the caufs to listen. The grandfather stroked their hair and patted their cheeks.

"Of course, I can tell," he said with a laugh, "if you really care to hear."

And he began to tell about that time when he was handling the tiller with which his grandson had just been playing . . . three times they had had to fight their way through the breakers before they succeeded in saving the crew out of the rigging of the wrecked ship. As a reward for this deed, the government of a foreign country had bestowed on him the precious timepiece that for years had been hanging on the wall beside his bed.

The children listened to his tale with eyes and

ears agog.   When he was done at last, they cried,
    "Tell us about the time when the wreck-master's
son and hired man were with you and got
drowned."
    "No, children," he said, "that tale is too grim."
    But he had to tell it after all . . . the story
about the time when the old boat had to cross the
breakers in such weather that their whole catch,
all their tackle, and two men were lost.

.   .   .   .

Then it happened, one summer day, that the
boys strayed along the road leading to the sea,
beyond the rising ground bordering their own
plain on the westward side, into strange heaths
known only to the oldest.   The two younger ones
held each other by the hand, clinging closer to
each other the farther they went.   Kresten made
detours now to this side and now to that, discovering all sorts of things that had to be shown to his
brothers.
    But after they had been on the way a while
he calmed down and joined the others on the road.
They had stopped and were looking back full of
fear.
    Then he took them by the hand, one on each
side.
    "Come on now," he said, "and you'll have a
look at the sea.   As soon as we get over that hill,

we have it right ahead of us . . . and that's
where Grandfather used to sail."

All three of them walked on. Their eyes were
staring straight ahead as if they expected a miracle
to occur at any moment. The sun shone lustily,
and the air about them was full of song and
jubilant sound that bewitched their minds with
the glamour of glorious adventure.

When they reached the crest of the gradually
mounting road, they stopped, still hand in hand,
staring at the blinding light that far away seemed
to rise above the land like a range of glittering
hills.

"That's the sea," Kresten explained, and the
other two gazed at him with frightened eyes . . .
for it seemed to be floating high up in the air.

But he grew more and more excited.

If they only walked a little farther, they would
be right there, he said, pulling them along.

Then their ears caught a rumbling sound as of
something of gigantic bulk that came rolling
toward them across the land. They strained at
his hold on their hands and stood listening like a
couple of scared little animals.

"That's the breakers," he told them.

But their lips began to quiver, and they broke
into tears, crying that they wanted to go home.

"It's nothing to be afraid of . . . it just beats

against the shore . . . and there are a lot of pretty stones that we'll pick and bring home with us."

Step by step he kept urging them on.

The moment they reached the bluffs, he let their hands go and ran forward. There he stood beckoning to them, surrounded by a flood of light so dazzling that it looked as if the sun were pouring all its rays toward that one spot.

"Come on," he cried. "Come and see for yourself . . . there is nothing to be afraid of."

Finally he ran back and pulled them up to the edge of the nearest bluff. And in that moment all their fear vanished. On their faces appeared that wondering smile of the child that is offered an unexpected gift. Then they clapped their hands together as if to hold fast that marvelous sight.

Kresten ran down to the shore and began to search among the rocks.

"Come and see," he cried.

Little by little they ventured to join him, almost crawling across the sand, and soon they were also picking pebbles.

Right under the bluff stood a lighter and a boat. They went over to look at them. Kresten climbed into the boat.

It was full of nets and lines at which they stared eagerly.

"They use it to fish with," Kresten told them.

He seated himself on one of the thwarts, looking across the open sea in front of him . . . and suddenly a serious expression crept into his face. It was as if a will had come to birth in his childish mind.

"As soon as I am confirmed I shall take to the sea as Grandfather used to do," he said.

His very movements seemed to grow more determined. Everything seemed to fall into harmony within him. It was as if some hidden instinct had burst forth and taken full possession of him.

"I don't want to always trudge in the fields as Father does."

His brothers gazed at him with eyes full of admiration.

Hour after hour they tarried on the sands. Kresten ran out to the edge of the surge, but there the other two did not dare to follow him for fear of being caught by the water.

Not until the sun was setting, and they had grown very hungry, did they tear themselves away.

At the farm they had grown anxious when the children were not to be found anywhere.

When the afternoon came, and they had not yet returned, messages were sent to the neighboring farms, but nowhere had they been seen.

The grandfather took the road to the sea in search of them. On the crest where they had stopped he stopped also to study the fading land, while the sky overhead was still aglow with the rays from the rapidly sinking sun. His face was full of prophetic agitation.

Then he saw them coming.

"O my Lord . . . oh, dear children," he cried aloud as he stumbled forward to meet them.

Tired out, he stopped in the road until they joined him.

"Have you quite forgotten your home, boys?" he asked. "You have scared us nearly to death."

Taking the hand of the youngest, he shepherded them homeward.

Kresten walked along with eyes glued to the road, knowing that the responsibility rested on himself. But suddenly he turned his head toward his grandfather and said—

"When I am confirmed, I shall go to sea. . . . I shall get my living out of the sea as you used to do, Grandfather."

The old man looked steadily at him, a sense of joy welling up within him. His lips quivered, and he was eager to encourage the boy. Instead, however, he rejoined—

"The time for that is gone, Kresten. Your father will need both you and the others."

All the home folk were gathered at the western

end of the house when they arrived. The father promptly grabbed Kresten.

"A good licking," he cried, "that's what you'll get for being away all day."

But the grandfather interceded.

"No," he said, "you let them alone. Can't you understand how tempting it must be to run off for a sight of the sea . . . that's what we used to do when we were boys."

And left alone they were.

.   .   .   .

When fall came, Kresten was given a rake and made to work with the others in the fields from morning till night. Until then the fall had always been their best time. Then they tumbled in the haystacks, and the ride home on top of the swaying load was the day's triumphant climax.

Now he had to take his place in the line of grown-up people and work away like a real man. And if for a moment he dropped his rake to run after the other two, he was scolded for thinking of nothing but play.

The father kept the boy close to himself and talked to him of rakes and scythes as if these were the only things that could make a man of anybody.

Throughout the following winter he had to help feed the cattle and clean the byre whenever he was free from school.

[357]

During that time a strange stillness settled on his childish mind. His face acquired an expression of seriousness as if he were outgrowing his playfulness. At the same time the look in his eyes grew distant and dreaming as if his head were full of thoughts he could not share with any one else.

During that period it happened frequently that they found him sitting on the rail of the old boat, his legs dangling outside . . . or they saw him use the respite brought by Sunday to take the road leading to the sea.

There he would walk for miles along the edge of the water, collecting all sorts of strange plants and seaweeds which he knew had come from the great depths where the fish could be found in vast numbers. Or he might sit on the top of a bluff like a dreaming child that has caught a glimpse of fairy lands far beyond the open sea.

One day, when his father had struck at him in anger on account of his carelessness, the grandfather found him lying on the bottom of the old boat, sobbing wildly, with his face buried in his hands. The old man leaned over the rail and touched him.

"No, no, Kresten," he said, "that is not the way to take it."

"I am not going to be a peasant," the boy cried, still sobbing. "I shall go to sea as you used to

[358]

do, Grandfather. If they won't let me, I'll run away from the place."

The old man put out a shaking hand to pat the boy's head.

"May the Lord guide you, my boy," he said. "But one must obey one's father."

At last he got the boy to sit up on the thwart.

"If your mind is so set on it, I think it can be arranged when you grow a little older. In my young days there was nothing finer than to ply the sea. . . . And I can see," he went on, "that you will never cut much of a figure with plow and scythe."

The next summer Kresten attended to his work so that his father was fully satisfied, and so that he received both praise and pay for the diligence he showed.

During the winter he had the usual instruction from the pastor, and in the spring he was confirmed with great solemnity.

When it was all over, the whole family gathered in the living-room, the father on a bench, smoking his pipe, the grandfather in his chair by the fireplace.

It had been a great day. At church Kresten had proved among the best in answering the questions put by the pastor.

He was now sitting at the table, still surrounded by a reflection of past glories.

Then the father took his pipe out of his mouth and looked at the boy.

"Well, Kresten," he said, "now you have grown to be a real man, and that is good, for your work is badly needed on the place. It may be all right at times to serve others, but the best thing after all is to serve oneself."

Kresten changed his seat and looked a little uneasily at his father. Then he rose from the table and walked out on the floor. Everybody was staring at him. His mother, who had just come in from the kitchen, stood in the doorway watching her son with pride in her eyes.

But the boy made a gesture at once regretful and defiant.

"No, Father," he said, and as he spoke he seemed to grow strangely quiet and firm. "I may as well let you know it now. I have no wish to serve . . . there is just one thing I want, and that is to go to sea as Grandfather used to do when he was young."

The farmer rose from the bench.

"What are you talking about, boy? No one cares any more for fishing along this coast. The time for it is long past."

"I know how it is . . . but I shall go to the city and ship on a smack in the way it is now done . . . and if you won't let me, I shall run away from home."

[360]

For a moment it looked as if the father meant to strike him.

But then the grandfather rose from his chair and took up his place beside the boy—

"You had better let the boy alone. . . . When you in your day had your heart set on the plow, I let you go your own way. And I guess that is the only thing that brings happiness. . . . If the boy wants to go to sea, let him go in the name of the Lord. You should be able to get help enough out of the other two."

Kresten's eyes grew dim with tears as he grabbed the old man's hand.

"I want to go at once," he blurted out. . . .

A month later his mother and the old man escorted him to the door. His father had kept out of sight all day.

There the boy stood, his smaller belongings carried in a bundle on his back. His box and his bedclothing had been sent ahead of him, and his grandfather had written a letter to some one who could get him the opening he wanted.

Quietly he shook hands first with one and then with the other.

"May the Lord be with you," said his mother. "And may it bring you happiness."

Then he walked off along the road leading to the train that would take him to the port which served as starting point for the fishing fleet.

[361]

GUNNAR GUNNARSSON

THE DARK MOUNTAINS

GUNNAR GUNNARSSON (1889–) is one of a small group of Icelanders who, writing in Danish, but choosing subjects from their native land, have enriched Danish literature with an exotic element. He is best known for the stories dealing with the fortunes of the Borg family, published in English under the title *Guest the One-Eyed*. It is a tragedy of crime and life-long penance. *The Shore of Life* has for its central figure an Icelandic clergyman; *A Wolf in the Holy Place,* a politician in the capital city Reykjavik—both men who fail from inherent weakness of character.

Blessed Are the Simple (or "Poor in Spirit") is a story from the time, some years ago, when the Spanish Influenza devastated Iceland, the hero being a physician whose life is sacrificed in the epidemic. *The Sworn Brothers* goes back to the discovery and first settlement of Iceland for its theme.

Gunnarsson is also the author of a dramatic poem, *The Beast with the Halo*. His chief medium, however, is fiction.

Gunnarsson's outlook is tragic, his prevailing tone one of gloom. When a spiritual victory is won, it is at terrific cost, but often the end is defeat. The story included in the present volume is characteristic as showing the futility of man and the overpowering might of nature.

Gunnar Gunnarsson

The Dark Mountains

MIDWAY across the desert of rock and stone that men here call the Dark Mountains, there stands a cairn. And under the lee of it, sat Vigfus Glumsson, of Vatni in Hrafnsdal, making preparations for a meal. He had brought food with him for the journey, and was making the most of it. With a pocket knife he shovelled out smears of stale, yellow, rancid butter from a carved box and spread it across the half of a stodgy pot-loaf, hacked off thick strips from a fat leg of mutton to put on top, and finally cut off a good deep slice of the bread thus garnished, which he proceeded to devour with leisurely enjoyment.

He was talking half to himself as he ate, uttering one sentence aloud, and then letting his thoughts run on in silence till his mouthful of food was done.

Certainly it was a grand idea—magnificent. . . .

He could not help conjuring up a vision of his

return. He would greet the others at home with a thoughtful, absent air, quietly, with dignity, so that they could not but remark it and fall silent, waiting for him to speak. They would mark his wrinkled brow. . . . He checked the flow of thought for a moment, and with perfect seriousness put up his hand to feel if the wrinkles could be made sufficiently deep and venerable-looking. . . . They would note his expression of reserve, and look for something out of the common. And then he would ask to speak to his father. Yes, in his father's own room. And there he would stand silent for a while, and then at last he would say—

"Father, I've got an idea. . . ."

Vigfus had some cold, heavily sweetened coffee in a good-sized bottle. This he drank in gulps, carefully shortening as he neared the bottom and saving one mouthful till he had swallowed the last bite of food; leaned his head back and sucked at the bottle-neck like a child with a sugar stick; suddenly remembered he was twenty-two and must behave as such; rose up with a start, uttered a short laugh, and, taking aim with the bottle, flung it at the cairn, where it was smashed to pieces.

Then he glanced round and shivered slightly.

It was abominably cold, there was no denying it. And the gale was blowing now more fiercely from the north, as the day wore to a close. Well, he had a fifteen-mile tramp to warm him before he got home. And in the meantime, something else that was not to be sneezed at.

With a crafty smile he loosened an intricate arrangement of tight leather straps, close-buttoned jackets, and swathings of long woolen comforters, bringing forth at last a flat spirit flask from a well-protected inner pocket.

Ah! That was the stuff! It wouldn't do, of course, to let Ingileif know that he always carried a dram when on a journey—after that brother affair. But there was no denying it; a drop of spirits *was* a good thing on a journey to keep out the cold and keep up one's strength—of course, as long as you didn't take too much.

Vigfus screwed on the zinc cap again, looked to see how much he had left, felt—with the touch of a smile in his eyes—at the pocket before putting the flask back again for the time, and then returned to a pedantic restitution of the complicated system aforementioned.

Hahaha! Leifa—if she only knew that the box with the rings was there in the same pocket with his flask!

The rings were to be his Christmas present to her, and were indeed the secret reason why he had wrested the doubtful privilege of making the Christmas journey to the trading station from Jon of Mel. Jon was always ready for any journey or adventure; but Vigfus had been loth to confide in him of all men the first news of his betrothal to Ingileif.

Buttons and buckles and knots resettled to his satisfaction, he knelt down to stow the contents of his roomy pack. He felt about aimlessly for a little. There were the twisted Christmas candles; there was the yeast for Bagga at Hjaleigu; and there was the silver spoon with the initials, finely engraved with many flourishes, I. T, ready for Leifa's birthday on the third of February. He *must* have one more look, though there was little time now to waste. And all those wrappings round it— He remembered in a flash the goldsmith he had visited the night before—the man's slow smile, his melancholy brow. He had done the work with his own hands, in the quiet of the night.—Would he—*could* he keep from showing Leifa the spoon before her birthday?

A gust of wind caught the loose snow that lay in tiny drifts about the cairn, lifted it fanwise in the air, and flung it into his face as he knelt over the pack. Some of it got into his throat, he coughed and choked, blinked his eyes and shook his head angrily, turned his face aside and swore.

Oh, well—anyhow, he must be getting on, or he would not reach home before bedtime. And they were expecting him—to-morrow would be Christmas Eve. He would have to look in at Hjaleigu this evening, or Bagga would not be able to get her cakes done in time. And there were one or two other places he had to call with the little things he had been asked to get for neighbors there. They would be waiting for the raisins, too, at home.

He found the paper of raisins, which his fingers half unconsciously had been seeking, worked a hole in it, and swiftly shook out a handful of the fruit, which he ate with relish, albeit not without some qualms of conscience.

There were none too many, as it was, for the Christmas cooking—and the little ones would want a handful between them. After all, he was no longer a child.

He felt suddenly distressed; the hole in the paper would tell its own tale.

His mother would smile in that quiet way of hers when she saw it—and think of the rings.

He fastened the pack with a vicious jerk.

They had told him the same thing before, more often than he cared about—that he would never grow up. And after all, he was bigger than his father now. And stronger than any one he had ever put to the test. . . . And now those miserable raisins would betray him. He would take a good big chew of tobacco to get the taste out of his mouth. . . . And then it was really time to get moving.

He rose to his feet, took from his pocket a
brand new tobacco box, bit off an inch of the
plug, snapped down the lid, stuck the box in his
pocket again and—spat out the quid the next moment with a grimace of disgust.

Ugh—of all the beastly stuff—

Then, recollecting himself, he glanced round
anxiously, and smiled with a comfortable feeling
that there was no one to see.

And indeed he *could* chew a quid of tobacco
when he liked. It was only that he thought it
better not to risk feeling bad out here in the
mountains.

But enough of that. What was it he was
thinking? Ah, yes, the house. It would have to
be just about here, on the spot where the cairn
now stood. The house that was to be a refuge,
a place of safety for travelers forced to cross the
mountains in winter. And there were many such.
For this was the only road from the hill settlement, where he lived, to the trading station.
And every year there were some who set out and
never returned. Only last winter four had been
lost that way, and two of them at this very season,
just before Christmas. But now he, Vigfus, had
hit on a plan to alter that. No more of those
death-journeys; it was done with now, once and
for all. Just build a house up here—a couple of

human beings could surely manage to keep themselves alive even here—a house where travelers from the trading station could find rest and shelter when the weather made it dangerous to risk the crossing of Long Ridge. Those going in the opposite direction could always turn back if overtaken by a snowstorm, and most of them would know that side of the mountains well enough to find their way down to one of the homesteads below. But people coming from the trading station and caught in a blizzard half way had no choice but to go on. They would mostly be unacquainted with the eastern slopes, which were, moreover, difficult and dangerous to cross, with their belts of tall rocks. There was no other way for them but to risk the crossing of Long Ridge, the narrow pass a mile in length. And Long Ridge was dangerous in a snowstorm—one needed to keep a good look-out.

He turned his eyes toward it now. A straight, narrow ridge of rock, falling away precipitously on either side to a deep abyss.

Yes, it was here on Long Ridge that most of them perished, that was sure enough. And the two chasms had been given ill-omened names. The Silent Gulf, for that to the north; the Death Gulf, to the southward. Probably because the gale blowing from the north would fling the traveler down in the southward chasm; the other, having listened and guessed its purpose, holding its breath the while.

He peered around him. This was no joke. There was a snowstorm coming up. And if he had not gained the farther side before it came . . .

He carefully refrained from completing the sentence in his mind.

He quickened his pace. Already he was well out along the ridge.

Again he looked around—warily, with sharp turns of the head.

The snow seemed to have turned darker now— it had been gleaming white before.

He noted that the only dark spots were where the rocks rose steeply out of the sea of snow. All else was white; a cruel, merciless white.

A desolate place it was—not a trace of life. No movement but that of the wind—the icy wind. Even the ravens seemed to be staying at home. And how quiet it was! What had become of all the sounds on earth? He would have been grateful for the least little cry to break the monotonous whisper of the wind; even the melancholy cry of a raven.

The snow was so chill and insensible—so hostile to life itself, a thing of death and horror. It was different here in summer, when the earth was warm and living, breathing forth its mystery in every stalk of green, singing forth its joy in the ripple of every gay little stream, with thousands of voices, bird and beast, calling in answer.

But in winter it was a desert. And every winter some met their death here. It was but rarely the bodies were found. The Death Gulf was impassable. There they would lie, well away out of reach. The very thought of it—to lie there rotting in the open like so much carrion—to fall down there among bones and rotting shreds of clothing—and lie forever and ever, where none came but the ravens to pick out one's eyes, and then the foulness of life bred in one's own dead flesh. . . . And suppose there were some truth after all in the popular belief that the gates of Paradise were closed to all whose earthly bodies had not been laid to their last rest in consecrated ground—that those who perished in such wise as this must live on as ghosts, as outlawed spirits, drifting horrors of the dark and lonely places. . . .

But—would they leave him in peace in his house. . . . *His house*.

Vigfus stopped suddenly. A leaden heaviness had seized him; he could hardly breathe.

No, no, it was not that he had meant. Not that—no, never for a moment. To come and live here himself? No, no. . . . With Ingileif,

[373]

with little Leifa perhaps? No, it was not to be thought of. His father had a farmstead down below, and he, Vigfus, was to take it over that spring; the tenant had already been given notice to quit. And, besides, there were plenty of others who could. But move up here himself? With Leifa? No, no, impossible!

But would any one else be willing?

Hardly. But every one would see the need of carrying out the plan. And they would look to him, of course, as the one who had conceived it . . . they would expect *him* to carry it out himself. They might even consider it his duty. That was always the way; he had shown them what to do, and they would not even do it. They would realize the value of his idea, and then selfishly, brutally expect him to . . . they might even have the audacity to demand it. Yes, they would say it was his duty. Come around hypocritically pretending; saying they knew he would regard it as a privilege. Oh, yes, he knew them! Likely as not one or another of them had had the same idea already—several of them, perhaps—and been wise enough to say nothing about it. Just so as to get out of making the sacrifice. It would be just like them. But—no, they shouldn't get *him* that way; he knew better than that! He —he, too, would *say nothing about it*.

The wind had dropped during the last few minutes. But now it broke out again in earnest. A sudden hurricane gust flung Vigfus off his feet.

The change came so unexpectedly that he lost his head for the moment, sprang up, and screamed aloud.

Only the naked storm had reached him as yet. But he could see the snow bank bearing down sullenly from the northward, thick, dark, and impenetrable, across the white waste—surging irrevocably toward him. It rolled on like a mass of breaking waves, rushing and hissing now like some pitiless monster. A minute or so, and he would be swallowed up in the rushing turmoil, lost and blinded. Heaven help him if he had not reached the stone pillar at the farther end of the ridge before it came. He could see it already; that must be it, on ahead, all white with the snow.

His heart was beating violently; it struck him now that he was over-excited; he must try to calm down a little. What had come over him—to cry out like that—and with no one to hear him anyhow—well, thank heaven for that! If only he could be sure *they* hadn't heard him—the Beings down there in the gulf. Likely they would not care to be wakened from their sleep; or, if so, they might feel a wish for company. Some of them had been brutal enough in life, no doubt— no, no, he didn't mean that; they were good fel-

lows all, of course, of course. He—he would
have been glad to stay with them for a while—any
other time. But he was pressed for time just
now—on his way home—to his sweetheart—with
the rings in his pocket—and a silver spoon with
fine engraved initials—a little birthday present—
hehe! But he would be coming that way another
day, no doubt, and would have more time.

What nonsense. What on earth had put such
silly fancies into his head!

He felt he deserved a little smile of indulgence,
and gave it himself—for want of any one else to
do so—with kindly condescension, yet at the same
time tacitly granting that he was a clever fellow
after all, a man who had neatly manœuvred out
of an awkward situation. . . . *Say nothing about
it,* yes, that was the way.

Then all at once the blizzard was upon him, a
vicious darkness that blinded his eyes till he could
not see a hand's breadth ahead. It chilled him,
too, thickly clad as he was; and to fight his way
through was like wading in a roaring torrent. At
every step he risked being flung over the abyss.
But it could not be far now to the landmark; he
would sight it soon—and then he would get out
his flask and take a good nip.

The mountain side from there would be easy
enough; he knew every step of that. And then
once home and safe in bed; sleep and rest—sleep

[376]

and rest. . . . This should be his last journey over the Dark Mountains in winter at least—and alone; he would take good care of that. It was too dangerous. These blizzards were no joke, and to tackle them single-handed!

But—why, there was the stone—the landmark —thank heaven, at last.

He leaped forward in delight—only to feel himself the next moment leaping down a precipitous slope *that should not have been there!*

He felt only astonishment at first, then in a flash he realized that what he had taken for the landmark was only a whirl of snow. He tried to check himself . . . slipped and rolled helplessly . . . faster and faster. . . .

The blizzard drowned his cry of horror and despair— *"God in Heaven . . . Help. . . ."*

XXIII. *America of the Fifties: Letters of Fredrika Bremer*

The journal of an American tour, illustrated with sketches by the author. The translation of Mary Howitt, revised and edited, with an Introduction, by ADOLPH BURNETT BENSON
Price $2.00

XXIV. *Norwegian Fairy Tales*

Translated by HELEN and JOHN GADE, from the collection of Asbjörnsen and Moe. Drawings by Kittelsen and Werenskiold
Price $2.00

XXV. *The Swedes and Their Chieftains, by Verner von Heidenstam*

Stories of Sweden's great men from the coming of the Swedes to the beginning of the present century of peace. Translated from the Swedish by CHARLES WHARTON STORK. Illustrated

XXVI. *Hans Christian Andersen, by Himself; The True Story of My Life*

The autobiography of the world's most beloved story-writer. The original edition in the contemporary translation of Mary Howitt. Illustrated
Price $2.50

XXVII. *Norse Mythology: Legends of Gods and Heroes by Peter Andreas Munch in the Revision of Magnus Olsen*

An authoritative book brought up to date. English version by SIGURD BERNHARD HUSTVEDT
Price $2.50

XXVIII. *Woman Power: A Novel, by Gustaf af Geijerstam*

Translated from the Swedish by ESTHER RAPP   *Price* $2.50

XXIX. *Norway's Best Stories: An Introduction to Modern Norwegian Fiction. Stories by eighteen writers.*

Translations by Anders Orbeck. Introduction and Notes by HANNA ASTRUP LARSEN
Price $2.50

XXX. *Sweden's Best Stories: An Introduction to Swedish Fiction. Stories by Sixteen Authors.*

Translations by CHARLES WHARTON STORK. Introduction and Notes by HANNA ASTRUP LARSEN   *Price* $2.50

XXXI. *Denmark's Best Stories: An Introduction to Danish Fiction. Stories by Fifteen Authors.*

Introduction and Notes by HANNA ASTRUP LARSEN   *Price* $2.50

SCANDINAVIAN MONOGRAPHS

I. *The Voyages of the Norsemen to America*

A complete exposition, with illustrations and maps, by WILLIAM HOVGAARD   *Price* $7.50

II. *Ballad Criticism in Scandinavia and Great Britain During the Eighteenth Century*

A comparative study, by SIGURD BERNHARD HUSTVEDT
    Price $5.00

III. *The King's Mirror*

A famous treatise, translated from the Norwegian of the thirteenth century, with an Historical Introduction, by LAURENCE MARCELLUS LARSON   *Price* $5.00

IV. *The Heroic Legends of Denmark*

Revised and expanded for this edition by the author, the late AXEL OLRIK, in collaboration with the translator, LEE M. HOLLANDER   *Price* $5.00

V. *Scandinavian Art: A Survey of Swedish Art, by Carl G. Laurin; Danish Art in the Nineteenth Century, by Emil Hannover; Modern Norwegian Art, by Jens Thiis; Introduction by Christian Brinton*

The first comprehensive discussion of the artistic production of the three Northern nations; in one volume of 660 pages with 375 illustrations   *Price* $8.00